A PATCHWORK OF DARKNESS

THE DARKNESS SERIES
BOOK ONE

ANDREAS RYK

TREASURES
— OF —
DARKNESS

PROLOGUE

THE HALLWAY WAS ENCASED IN EMBERS, CRACKLING AND POPPING WITH waves of hot light.

A long, windowless corridor stretched before him and gave the appearance of staring into the eyes of a snake and watching its flaming tail unfurl. The walls, mottled with twisted shadow, were covered with peeling tile which flaked away. Fear gripped him. He wanted to run, but his limbs were limp, numb. Slowly, they dragged him forward as the corridor bent up and down, dancing to an invisible wave beneath.

The closer he approached the metal door at the end, the more a deep terror took hold. With sharp breaths, he concentrated on his numb right hand and forced it against a wall. The movement continued. It felt like he had a rope tied to his waist and a force beyond his sight was pulling, dragging, tugging him straight through. In a frenzy, he jammed his fingernails against the wall, but the wet-felt texture transformed into rigid cement—bending his nails backwards and flinging his hand away.

Oh, gods, how he wanted to scream. However, his throat,

his head, his eyes—none of them obeyed, and he was left staring forward into the depths of the door, so close his breath condensed on the metal. This was impossible. He had to stop, he had to. There was no way he was ready to go through. What would his brother think? His sister? He couldn't just leave them.

Fueled by adrenaline, he forced his mouth to creak open. However, in place of a scream air was sucked out by an onslaught of smoke and dire heat. This was it. The door in front of him swung open. The smoke and heat were whipped back, and light enveloped him. It wasn't warm. It was frigid. Constrictive. Wound so tightly the darkness covering his eyes would be the last thing he ever saw.

As he tumbled into a shadow-filled abyss, a feeling emerged he didn't expect: understanding. Not that he understood anything of what was happening; rather, he suddenly felt understood as though he was stuffed under a microscope and everything he was and meant to be were magnified millions of times until each atom of his being was laid bare. Right as the last pinprick of light separated itself and evaporated into the backdrop of darkness, another feeling came upon him. It grasped his throat before jolting to each limb. It was so intense. No matter what he did later, how many drugs he took, how deeply he slept or how much he prayed, the feeling remained as meaningful as the first time he met it.

It was hatred. An unadulterated acrid compress that squeezed him until he felt his being collapse. The sensation was so intense, it woke him up from death itself.

CHAPTER

ONE

"IT WAS A HATRED SO INTENSE THAT IT WOKE HIM UP FROM DEATH itself." Kane closed his brother's hardcover biography and rolled his eyes. Leaning back his chair, he mentally added: *What a diva* before tossing the book across the room. The eight glasses of wine Kane had drunk earlier only worsened his aim, and the book crashed against an adjacent house plant which promptly toppled to the ground. *Shit.*

Muffins, his sister's gray tabby, hissed and scampered away. "What the hell was that?" His sister came running into the room. Without even looking at her, Kane felt an accusing stare begin to form at the sight of soil and plant spread over the carpet.

"What the hell is wrong with you?" She rushed over to assess the damage and shoveled soil back into the pot.

With him? What the hell is wrong with her?

"You're the one who gave me wine and a copy of my arse-hole brother's biography. In parallel." More angry words sat on his tongue, each waiting their turn to lash out. Sue shot him a glance that said, *So help me, I don't care if you're bigger than me, I*

3

will beat you. Kane pushed the harsh words aside, pursed his lips and shrugged.

Or at least, that was his intention. He was already feeling more than a bit buzzed and against his better judgment added, "Who reads this schlock? *It woke him up from death itself.* If he was so good at waking up, why the hell is he so dead now?" At this, Sue's face bunched up in a painful wince.

Fuck. Delightful buzz here or there, Kane recognized how awful his words had been—a sentence so vile and callous, he wouldn't have been surprised if the planter she was cleaning came flying over at his face. Why not? He deserved the sting of his words, not Sue. Why would he try to hurt her like that?

Kane bit his bottom lip, the bitter aftertaste of his words stuck in his mouth. Perhaps he deserved even more. After all, today was the fifth anniversary of their brother's death. Well, his second death, and the first one he had spent with his sister. Begrudgingly.

It wasn't for lack of effort on her part. It had simply been far more appropriate for him to celebrate (if that was the proper term) alone, in silence, dim lights and drowning in at least one bottle of whiskey or, preferably, something stronger. If he was really feeling low, a date with a corner prowler in an hourly motel.

Surprisingly enough, his sister didn't toss the plant at him. Instead, she sank to her knees and rubbed her eyes. Tears? What the hell? He'd expected a fit-filled rage, exploding with foul language. Even a slap across the face. In fact, he may have preferred it. He had heard she'd softened over the past year but hadn't believed it a word of it. Guess the rumors were true. He didn't know what to do with this milder Sue and felt numbness overtake a sudden jealousy.

"Why are you here?" she asked, rubbing her cheeks. Kane thought she intended to sit by him, that her words would be some incantation to open the gates to a compassion and intimacy they'd never known. Instead, she simply leaned against the wall and stared at him with red gleaming eyes.

Truth be told, he had no idea why he was here. Although the look on his sister's face told him he better figure it out.

How odd. The only other times he had seen his sister so distraught was when Mom had died. Her eyes had been completely dry for their father. During both those times, a quick pat on the shoulder and a few mumbled words of comfort were enough to snap her back into her usual, high octane self. This was different, however. Damn, he really had jacked this up.

"I don't know," Kane said, looking away as the shame pierced the wall between his emotions and the flimsy, alcohol-fueled reality he swayed in. "I guess it's that..." he trailed off, looking away from his sister's glare and through the window into the city lights. What a night.

"It just pisses me off when he writes—wrote—junk like that. I mean, who seriously believed him?" A grunt was followed by a ten-mile stare through the same window. "What was it, bored housewives, capricious religious leaders, corrupt politicians? Anyone looking for some dogma so they could control—"

"I believed in him," his sister whispered barely loud enough to hear. Kane nearly fell out of his seat. Sue believed him? "And I know his death has been tougher than you let on." With this, she stood and left the overturned pot and soil where it lay. "You two always had such a stupid competition with each other, always fighting and bickering."

"That's what brothers do," he mumbled weakly, cringing at how trite he sounded.

Sue traipsed to where Kane sat, her gaze listlessly caressing the shadows of long forgotten memories. "And when worse came to worse, and Mom and Dad were coming for blood, somehow the two bickering brothers would band together and make a pact to blame the mischief on me."

Kane smiled as his inebriated mind drifted back to a time when holes in the wall, broken dishes or viruses on the family computer were his or his brother's fault. Of course, for their parents, it would frequently be Sue's fault. Hot headed Sue. She'd taken her revenge, of course, but two were stronger than one.

"I see so much of him in you." She caressed his face. This was too much. The old Sue wouldn't have invaded his bubble so intimately.

Dammit, now he was getting emotional. He nonchalantly rubbed his eyes.

"Of course you do." His head whipped away sharply. "We were twins after all."

"One in flesh, but not in spirit." Sue chuckled, and Kane knew she was remembering how her parents would yell that after catching her brothers fighting.

This brought a pleasant memory for Kane, and welling tears gave way to a light, mischievous smile. "Yeah, definitely not in spirit."

A long, meaningful silence followed with both siblings spun in the threads of their own memories before becoming tangled in a joint nostalgia. Lighting their curtains on fire, making a dogsled with the family lab, stealing the car to drive to a local concert. He and his brother truly were rotten apples dropped from their parents' tree. When had they grown so apart? Kane closed his eyes, exhausted from his stroll down memory lane. His brother was gone, and memories wouldn't bring him back.

Before any more tears could form, he stood and sighed dramatically. "Who the hell tipped that pot over?" he asked with faux desperation. "Muffins?" He shot the cat a scornful glance, although it barely opened its lids upon hearing its name.

"Cat must be an alcoholic," he said, sauntering over to the mess while moving slowly so he didn't tip over himself.

"I'll get the vacuum," his sister said with renewed energy. "And don't let the cat near the wine. He's had enough."

Kane cleaned what he could by hand and placed the pot and dry, dying plant once again on the stand. As Sue had yet to return, he poured himself another glass of wine before taking a large furtive swig from the bottle. Yuck, it was too dry. Why couldn't Sue have bought something sweeter?

After chugging his glass in quick, successive gulps, he paced around the living room. Most of the soil remained scattered across the carpet like a crime scene at a botanical garden. This mess wouldn't get any better without industrial-grade suction. Speaking of that, where the hell was his sister?

Had she forgotten where she'd placed the vacuum? Sue hadn't been one to care for the little details of household work, like keeping things alive, and it was a true shock to see Muffins, her cat of ten years, looking as healthy as it did. Muffin's first year with his sister was riddled with constant reminders for vet visits, water bowl sanitation, and an overflowing litter box. What a huge pain for the brothers.

"You owe me, cat, so don't give me that judgmental look." Kane glanced at Muffins who was sprawled on the sofa and staring forward listlessly.

Kane wanted to sprawl across the couch as well or at least take a seat, but was well aware that doing so would end in a range of hissing noises followed by more than a few claw marks. Nobody moved Muffins. Ever. Not even Sue.

How long did it take to get a vacuum? Kane pulled his envious eyes from the cat and glanced down the hallway.

"Sue?" He raised his voice a bit without effect. Not a mumble nor cough nor whisper in response. The two-bedroom apartment his sister rented wasn't large, so if she wasn't in this room, and she wasn't in the kitchen, there weren't many other places left to look.

"Sue?" he called towards the bedrooms. "You doing okay?"

The silence that followed was wholly different than a general lack of response. It was so deep, it enveloped the whole apartment: city sounds filtering upwards from the street below, the light hums of chatting neighbors and even his own heartbeat.

Kane walked through the kitchen towards the narrow hallway. "Sue?" he called again, albeit with less conviction. "You in the bathroom?" If she was, her response wouldn't be silence, and Kane could expect a loud, faux-British *Bugger Off!*

He tilted his head forward and listened. Nothing. Only a creeping silence and an odd feeling that something was amiss.

Slowly, his feet moving as though caught in deep in sand, Kane dragged himself forward into the hallway. It was longer than he remembered and stretched endlessly towards a front door who's bright outline was getting dimmer and dimmer. The silence increased in depth until he felt it encase his ears.

"What the hell is happening?" he asked aloud amongst growing unease, but his voice was hollow and muffled. From behind him, Muffins hissed relentlessly, but even this faded into obscurity.

"Sue!?" he croaked, his voice having vanished with the rest of the world's noises. As the sounds dissipated, the world around him grew dimmer as well. It wasn't merely the door lying at the end of the eternal hallway—rather, color from the walls, details in the hanging pictures and even his own emotions. He should be terrified now, right? His heart should be leaping from his chest as he turned around and bolted towards the nearest phone. *911. Caller emergency. Yes, our apartment has been possessed and / or I've gone insane.* A strange numbness flooded over him, and any will to change direction evaporated.

Oh gods, not again, was his last clear thought before a deep sense of apathy overtook him. Kane didn't feel like turning around, he didn't feel terrified and he sure as hell didn't care that he was no longer walking. He had stopped moving his legs an eternity ago and was being dragged forward involuntarily. Where was his sister? Did it matter? There was a bedroom door right in front of him, but as he turned to peer into it, the door slammed shut. No, no, no! That wouldn't do. There was only one path, only one exit from this place. Kane wasn't sure if he believed that, but a familiar prickle above his throat felt desperate to convince him of that truth.

Kane's head swiveled forward, stopping as his eyes met the door at the end of the hallway. It wasn't far now; either he had misjudged the distance or he truly had been drifting here for an age.

The bright outline had been entirely replaced by a darkness that was ready to leak through its seams. Only a dim light on the floor remained, but this too was slowly covered by an encroaching shadow. In that moment, the journey ended and Kane found himself face to face, not but a nose length apart from the closed door. The perpetual shadow and silence formed a cosmic monstrosity that both spanned the entirety of the universe and yet was concentrated in each atom drop of nothing washing around him.

Tick, tick, tick. Even though the sound was as gentle as a fingernail rapping on a wine glass, the reverberations in this amaranthine hollow erupted into a chorus of chaos and disarray. Kane pressed his hands to his ears, but the noises leaked through skin and bone.

Tick, tick, tick. It was coming from the door; it must be coming from the door! Was someone knocking? The sound was forcing him to bend over, his body ready to heave at the relentless echo of that horrific sound.

Tick, tick, tick. "Ah!" he cried, but his own sounds were gobbled into oblivion. He couldn't wait for another knock. If he heard that vile cacophony once more, that symphony of discord, he knew he would die. He forced his hand to the knob, clenched and turned with a forced grunt.

*Tick, tick, ti—" T*he door swung open, and the abyss of darkness was transformed into searing light. His flesh smoked as the light washed over him like the birth of a star. A stark internal pain erupted. It was so intense, Kane felt his atoms rip apart and reset in an infinite loop. It was beyond his comprehension—thin as a sunbeam and yet containing the power of stars.

Right as he readied his eyes to close for the last time, a shadow stood before him. It was a blur as Kane could hardly see through popped vessels and melting synapses. *He would die,* his body screamed at him. Then, the shadow's mouth moved as silently as the *ticking.*

"Tim?" Kane gasped before blacking out.

TWO

A VOICE REACHED AND PIERCED THROUGH THE DARK VALE enshrouding him. "Oh fuck, what's all this blood?"

"Kane! Kane!"

Kane's vision suddenly melted to reveal his sister violently grasping his shoulders and throttling his body.

"Kane!" she screamed as his eyes fluttered to life with a moan.

Man, he'd rather be rattled awake by King Kong. He heard a popping sound from his neck. For a moment, he struggled to force down a lingering nausea and dizziness. The next layer on a shit cake. What's the cherry on top?

After a few deep breaths, the sweating stopped, his vision cleared, and the dizziness abated to a manageable level. As he awoke, his sister gave him an aggressive hug before standing and pulling out her phone.

"Thank god," she whispered. "Kane, stay calm, I'm going to call an ambulance."

All at once, Kane's stupor evaporated in a flash of adrenaline. No, no, no—she couldn't do that! There was no way he could afford that type of luxury medical transport.

"Sue, you know I don't have insurance." He fell over and grabbed her ankle, looking towards her with a weak smile. "Would you like me to starve in debtor's prison?"

Her look swayed between yes and no as her eyes vanished behind a scowl of frustrated concern.

"Please, dammit, Sue!" He gave a weak shout with his hand remaining firmly locked in place.

A tense moment passed as Sue's eyes bounced between her phone and bleeding brother. "Oh fine, have it your way!"

Sue collapsed against the adjacent wall and stared at him as though he were an open closet door in a dark room: a monster creeping directly beyond the boundaries of a living imagination. Kane could see that if he so much as moaned the wrong way, Sue would be screaming for 911 before he could stop her.

Her concern was more than understandable. It wasn't that he had simply collapsed or had some freak seizure caused by stress, too much wine and a mild cat allergy. No, Kane had bled. A lot. Not only from his nose—which had come from banging his head against the door. Oh man, he wished it was that simple: a nosebleed. That would be easy, understandable. Besides, a broken nose was as dangerous as a broken toe in his experience. This type of bleeding was far beyond that, however. Kane was glad it had stopped after he had awoken and that his sister had reserved telling him about it till after he looked stable. If not, he would have stood and called the ambulance himself despite him being *as broke as the shattered half of a homeless toy*, as his father used to say.

His head looked like someone had tossed a grenade inside and sealed the doors. Blood was sprouting from his nose, sure, but also from his mouth, his eyes, his ears and even his sweat.

If he believed in some divine stigmata, which he definitely did not, this would have fit perfectly—minus the bloody palms. At one point, he must have bled so rapidly, there were little puddles near the front door where he had collapsed, and his shoulders felt like he was wearing crunchy padding. Why the hell hadn't his sister called an ambulance?

Kane lightly panted as his sister stared forward. Neither spoke nor moved, each embroiled in their own thoughts. Had that really been Tim? Or was he merely a dream or subconscious form of penance? Even as he focused on his experience, the entire scene melted away. Eventually, it was too distant to be real. This didn't bother him much, though. The less he thought and saw of his brother, the better.

Every few minutes, Kane watched his sister's hand shift towards her phone. She would take a long, loud breath, touch its screen and withdraw her fingers before closing her eyes with a scowl. Kane couldn't be sure, but it seemed the idea she could use it at any moment brought her a mixture of comfort and guilt.

As no one spoke, another deep silence befell the apartment, although this one more in line with a normal lull in sound. The honks of cars remained mixed with spirited, sometimes threatening hoots and cries from the cauldron of the city below. Kane heard the familiar hum of conversations in adjacent apartments and a slight echo when passersby walked near the apartment door. Even amongst the gentle noise, he and his sister remained completely motionless, breathing shallowly without disturbing a quiet that could easily be mistaken for peace. Even Muffins, who had been lying in his owner's lap moments before, scampered off at the droning sound of its own purrs.

"I better go and wash my face," he said, pressing his hands and butt against the wall and shimming upward. How long had they been sitting there? Twenty minutes, an hour? He finally felt strong enough to stand, and although a bit drained, his dizziness and overall exhaustion abated as he stretched out. He expected his sister to leap up, make sure he was okay and help him go to the bathroom. Instead, Kane saw her anxiety had been swept away by utter exhaustion (and an unhealthy dose of sociopathic-level compartmentalization) as well as something else. Her eyes were staring at him as if inspecting some exotic creature in a zoo, waiting for it to reveal the truth about its essence and place in our universe.

"I thought you said the episodes had stopped." This was accompanied by a light sigh she probably hadn't expected him to hear. But he had heard it, so instead of verbally responding, he shrugged as nonchalantly as he could and walked directly towards the bathroom.

Brother's death celebration. Or better said, "Day of Remembrance." Check. Destruction of sister's property. Check. Loss of sanity and complete physical breakdown. Check. "And how could this night get any better?" he mumbled to himself as he opened the door.

For starters, he realized too late that *making the night better* meant not looking in the mirror as he cleaned himself off. It would have been difficult, sure, but at least he could have tossed some water on his face before assessing the damage. Before he had that revelation, however, he walked directly in front of the large, dirty mirror his sister hated cleaning and found himself staring into what could only be described as death incarnate. Even knowing who it was, Kane nearly toppled backwards in shock. It was no wonder his sister was so apt to call an ambulance, and he marveled that she'd let him avoid medical treatment. Why hadn't she called 911 even after he begged her not to? That must be the type of mental fortitude you needed to work in a kill-shelter.

If Kane wanted to summarize how he looked, he would have used the following: the lovechild of a zombie, the elephant man and a victim of domestic violence. That blood was caked in each orifice, each pore, was an understatement. Beyond that, his skin was puffy and swollen, small clumps of hair were beginning to fall out and his teeth hurt. Why the hell did his teeth hurt? The only good news was that his symptoms were going into remission, and he knew from prior experience that the hair would grow back to normal in a day or two.

Oh, God, if you exist and give one flying crap, please don't let my teeth fall out. Reaching towards his cheek, Kane sighed as if all the sighs from his entire pitiful life had come together for one last hurrah. "I thought I was done with this," he said aloud before submerging his face in the sink. No flare-up for a year and now what, it was suddenly worse?

Instead of making his way into the hallway, Kane took an extra moment in the bathroom to catch his breath. And why not? He knew his sister would be worried, sure, but he needed this. Besides, she could knock if she was so concerned.

"I thought you said the episodes had stopped," he heard his sister's voice ringing in his ears.

"Stopped?" he mumbled, plopping himself on the toilet and leaning back. "More like a sabbatical."

There was another small round mirror directly across from him above an overfilled clothes hamper. Why were there so many mirrors? It was a house of horrors. Did his sister watch herself pee? Were there so many guests in the bathroom at once that she needed auxiliary reflection? As Kane sat there, staring at his puffy face and mangy skull, the placement of the mirror brought him more and more discomfort.

"Why is this happening again?" He moaned, recalling the last occurrence.

He had been with Molly at the time but couldn't recall if

their relationship was already on its last leg. Last leg? Not a table, more like a marathon.

"It must have been summer," Kane muttered silently, remembering intense heat beating down on his face after awaking in their garden. What had the *episode*, a mocking nickname his therapist had given these occurrences, been that time? A living vision, some crooked nightmare where eternal spirits haunting his dreams leapt into reality for a demonic bacchanal? Maybe. Or it could have been a quick glimpse into a scene his mind had forced itself to forget.

Often, no matter how hard he focused on remembering the details, most of his episodes were forgotten moments later like the wisps of a dream. Even what he had experienced a few short moments ago was beginning to fade. Fortunately, although Kane often thought of it as unfortunate, the evidence of these occurrences weren't simply boarded up in some holding cell in his subconscious. Every incident left physical marks on the world around him as well. These marks were sometimes subtle and sometimes terrifying.

During the last time, the time in the garden, the marks had been—he strained to conjure the memory. As more time passed, the larger his mind blew a bubble around the event until he could hardly remember the city he was in, let alone the finer details. Hadn't this particular case been different?

Normally, a bad episode made him lose some hair or bleed a bit from his face. There had been a few times, precious few, where objects had shifted around him slightly. The changes were almost imperceptible and Kane would have hardly noticed save for a few trail marks in windowsill dust. When Molly had come home after those, she had told him she didn't see anything amiss or moved. This was followed by twenty minutes of accusing him of playing a prank on her until even he believed he may have been making things up. Times as severe as those had only been once or twice in the years since they had begun.

And the one in the garden? Kane recalled how the heat had struck his face upon awakening, how his entire body felt made of Styrofoam and rattling with beads. The sun was hot, sure—he could feel that on his forehead. Although, it wasn't nearly as hot as whatever had overtaken him.

Insects were whirling around, and the faint smell of rain floated by. Heat. Insects. Smells. Pointless details in a mind keeping him off the scent. None of those things were relevant if he couldn't recall the most critical aspect.

"What the hell happened to the flowers!?" He suddenly heard Molly's voice ringing in his ears. The flowers? He forced his mind deeper into the memory. Something had happened to the flowers.

He strained to picture more of what had happened, but his surroundings went dark. Kane glanced at the mirror, half in thought, half in frustration at his inability to remember the rest of the story. If his face hadn't been so puffy, it would have shown a wild contortion as he struggled to grasp the threads of his unwoven past and bridle a rage at watching them slip through his fingers.

What the hell had happened to the flowers?

Although he and Molly had been together for several years, she wasn't in the habit of taking even a single episode lightly, often screaming and accusing him for hours of being on drugs or having some involvement in the occult. The fact that these occurrences only began after his brother died was completely lost on her. Truth be told, he couldn't blame her much. Even for him, that coincidence would swing hard between meaning nothing and meaning everything.

Of course, the episodes were the least of their relationship problems. Verbal abuse, theft, late nights without explanation.

None of it equaled a healthy, loving couple. Kane often imagined their love like a desert flower, bursting from a decades long slumber only to find a barren, acrid wasteland. Wilting was the only option, right?

"Wilt!" he screamed both in his head and aloud. The flowers, all the flowers in their garden, had wilted as though they had recently experienced the worst drought of their haughty young lives. Most were blowing into dust; some were rotting where they stood. And Molly? When she had found him on the ground in the midst of that circle of death she had—

"Kane!? Kane!? Are you ok?" That wasn't Molly's voice. There was no shrill intonation on the end of each word that was both threatening and conciliatory.

"Almost done, Sue," he said, forcing himself off the toilet and reaching for a towel to wipe his face.

"Kane, I—" she said in a tone that he didn't like one bit.

"Sue, please, I promise I'm okay. I just need a moment."

"Kane, it's Muffins. He, they, I." She paused. "I don't know what the hell is going on here."

A few moments later, both Kane and Sue were planted in the kitchen, staring with open mouths.

Meow.

Muffins sat on the couch and stared at a horrified Kane whose dizzy head pounded. The aches had started to subside, and after washing his face, he looked more and more human. Thank god, since he was human.

Although the physical aspects of the episode were subsiding, Kane was beginning to think the mental complications had just begun.

Meow.

Kane looked at Muffins before turning to his sister, who was watching the scene from a safer distance in the kitchen. Her breathing was shallow, and her eyes bulged a bit as she strained to comprehend some inexplicable mystery before her. But there was some inexplicable mystery before her.

Meow. This one from a cat across the room. Muffins. Or was it Muffins?

Meow. This one from a cat on the couch. Muffins, right?

"When did you get two cats?" Kane asked as the uncanniness of the scene penetrated his exhausted mental state.

His sister glanced at him with a look that asked how stupid he could be. "I don't have two cats, you ass!" she growled, taking another step backwards.

CHAPTER

THREE

"DON'T HAVE TWO CATS," KANE WHISPERED WHILE THE WORDS burned through his synapses. It wasn't merely two cats, either. Both were a spitting image of Muffins.

One cat jumped down and sauntered toward Kane with that vapid sociopathic egotism all cats exhibit when they intend on forcing you to rub against them. As if you could only delight at providing them pleasure.

Kane stepped backward and nearly tumbled to the floor as his heel buried itself in the corner of a rug. The cat, unamused and unswayed by this poor display of coordination, continued its relentless, prowling approach towards him. The creature might as well have been some eldritch monstrosity lurking within the darkest reaches of the cosmos, considering how much fear it provoked in Kane. Although he recovered gracefully from his initial bout of clumsiness, he now found himself pressed against the kitchen counter, nowhere to run, as the strange cosmic horror rapidly approached his leg. For his sister's part, she was in an even worse spot: standing inside the kitchen with the only option for escape being to leap over the counter and run into the claws of the other beast stationed on the couch.

Kane thought back to the layers of the shit cake from earlier and realized this must be the cherry on top. Right as he thought his heart was too weak to take any more of this slow-burn torment, the beast's tail swaying while it inched itself towards him on paws of madness, a loud "ppppppuuuuurrrrrr" emerged. At that moment, the feline's velvety fur worked its way up and down his leg like a fluffy wave.

"Ahhhh," Kane gasped silently, his head swinging towards his sister, who's only retort to this fearful display was her own look of terror. This open-eyed fish stare continued for several seconds until Kane realized with step-off-the-cliff-relief that his leg was not being devoured. No searing pain, no shreds of flesh or sharp fangs consuming him amongst an ethereal darkness. With a moan of relief, he collapsed on the floor.

The cat used this opportunity to rub itself against the rest of his body.

Kane and his sister took the better part of an hour to return to their senses. Before their own shock had dissipated, the cats had long grown bored with merely rubbing against unwilling humans and had retreated to differing spots on the couch. From time to time, a cat's head would pop over the edge of a cushion and stare for a moment at the two frozen humans, its eyes asking *Why aren't you over here petting me?*

But that was truly the last thing Kane and his sister wanted to do: pet the "cats". In fact, upon regaining some semblance of composure, his first move was to jettison himself towards the front door, forgetting his sister, his sister's cats and the rest of the occurrence. If it wasn't for Sue's hand grabbing his arm, his plan would have succeeded.

"What the hell are you doing?" he hissed at her, staring at the couch behind which the two nefarious apparitions slumbered.

Odd, but his sister had somehow regained a certain level of her normal confidence. Although the uncanny situation would have driven most anyone else to run away, his sister was staring at him with a new intensity that said: *We can't back down.*

Kane had no idea who or what they were backing down from. Not running was akin to refusing to back down from a burning building when there was no one inside to save.

Glancing over to the couch with a jerk, Kane turned towards his sister, and with his finger buried in her chest said, "You're the person who dies first in every horror movie."

"No, the coward dies first in those movies," she retorted in a whisper.

"I'm not a coward, I'm just cautious."

"Cautious? It's just cats!" Her whisper was bordering a soft, hysterical yell.

"Cats? Are you some weird emotional light switch? Why are you suddenly forgetting what happened to me a few minutes ago? Those aren't just cats, they're horrific beasts from the beyond."

The look his sister gave him wavered beyond an overwhelming sense of mockery and sardonic wisdom. "If those cats, things, weren't cats and wanted us dead, we'd be dead. Have you considered that?"

"Some creatures play with their food first."

"What creatures do that?"

"Fucking cats, for example!" His voice leapt from a whisper to a muffled yell.

"Then they're just cats!" his sister responded with equal volume.

There was a slight scratching noise on the couch's leather, and in spite of her sudden overconfidence, Sue's head darted as quickly to the source of the noise as Kane's.

"See, you're scared too!"

"I'm not scared; it startled me."

"But they're just cats," he said in a mocking tone.

"They ARE just cats," she replied with a sudden coolness that gave Kane pause. Sometimes, when she truly wanted to, Sue could stop arguments with the same tone of finalité their mother would employ.

"Yes. Exactly. Cats. Plural. Two of them. The fact is, that's one more than you ever had. Besides, if you don't remember, Suzannah (in a normal argument, employing her full name would have been the ultimate offense) I just had—"

"One of your visions. An episode." Her voice suddenly became milder. "It's exactly like the flowers." Her face turned pensive as she stared over towards the couch.

Had he told her about the flowers? Man, his mind really did force him to forget the details. Hopefully, assuming he made it out of this one alive, it would be rapidly erased from his memories like the others.

"No, this isn't like the flowers."

"Kane, you're amazing. You've somehow made another Muffins like you made those flowers wilt." Although still thoughtful, his sister's gaze became more earnest.

"Firstly, it's not something I do," he responded with a sense of disgust and defensiveness. He had never felt in control of what happened, ever. He described it as being like a tunnel, or a filter, rather than a conduit or switch. "Secondly, life won't suddenly burst from nowhere. Matter can't be created or destroyed"—a textbook phrase shamelessly ripped from his junior high science class. "Maybe," he rationalized in an attempt to downplay the episodes he despised so much, "maybe a cat jumped in through the window."

Sue looked at him with less and less interest.

"We're on the third floor" she responded numbly.

"Maybe it came in from a neighbor's balcony!" That sounded pretty good. Even he was starting to believe himself. Doubting the weird things which happened around him was a balm on a quivering wound. If he didn't accept or understand them, would it heal on its own?

To do this, explanations through his minimal scientific knowledge and advice from his therapist were par for the course. Anything to avoid delving deeper into a terrifying mystery. Kane often thought that, worst case, the episodes were a jumble of psychotic experiences with physical manifestations, and each person involved was suffering from a form of mass hysteria. The fact that his mind quickly drove memories of these occurrences away helped immensely.

Now that Kane had thoroughly rationalized his world, he also looked over to the cats with a sense of inebriated purpose. Mystery be damned, none of this was absurd, none of this was surreal and none of it had to do with him or what he had experienced. He wasn't crazy, and that damn second cat had leapt in from a neighbor's apartment. It wasn't a monster, and the only special circumstance at play was his own budding insanity. He would prove it. Marching over to the couch, he took a running leap and sprung over the edge to land right between the two—what Kane hoped were—felines.

"Ow, careful!" Kane yelped as Sue finished putting a Band Aid on his forearm. As it turned out, both the creatures had not only been cats, but those of the variety that despise large humans almost crushing them.

Kane had sprinted forward, diving ass first towards the cushions amidst angry hissing and outstretched claws. The second he had landed, both took a swipe at his jeans, but quickly moved to his arms because—and Kane was sure of this —they knew that's where blood could be drawn. Nothing that a few bandages and a packet of tuna couldn't rectify.

Kane had a way with animals, unlike his sister, on whom they could smell constant blood. After they had scampered to a dark living room corner to inspect their injured prey, he only needed a few gentle words and the smell of processed fish to lure them to the couch once again. After a few seconds, Muffins number one (or was it number two?) sat on his lap, joyfully licked tuna juice off his fingers and purred deeply.

"See, just cats," Kane croaked, his heart still pounding so desperately, he thought it may work its way out of his throat. His sister only responded by rolling her eyes and returned to the kitchen to throw away the bloody paper towel she had dabbed his arm with.

Muffins number two (or was it number one?) was more than happy to lick tuna juice off his sister's fingers, although it was much more hesitant to plop itself on her lap. For several minutes, Sue stretched her fingers out and let the cat nibble on them as though feeding grapes to Caesar. This gesture finally satiated the king, and after a while, both cats were lying comfortably prostrated across their legs, purring softly, as the humans pondered them in silence.

Clearly, the cats were real. At least, that's what Kane kept telling himself. If they weren't, they definitely had no desire, or ability, to seriously harm him and his sister. Then again, how could he be so certain? As Kane cringed at that terrifying, unknowable mystery, he repeated the following in his head like a mantra: *Purring means safety. Purring means safety. Purring. Means. Safety.*

But safety here or there, the problem of the second cat's existence was extremely troubling. Could it be related to his recent episode? The connection was so obvious, and yet the idea so egregious, he frantically rationalized other possibilities. His episodes were long gone. He had taken care of them, dumped them outside to rot months ago. How could they return after the intense suffering he'd gone through to remove them? But the connection was so obvious, Kane bit his lip and cursed under his breath.

"It definitely leapt in from a neighbor's balcony." He flung this wild theory to his sister, who regarded him with silence. Her fingers moved through the silky fur as she furrowed her brow and opened her mouth. Something was clearly on the tip of her tongue.

"Kane," his sister said softly, "even if that were possible, the balcony door is closed."

"Ok, so it came in earlier and hid."

"It's winter, you ass." Her face reddened. "The door hasn't been opened in weeks. You think I've had two cats living in this tiny apartment without knowing since November?"

"They *do* look alike."

"Don't. Be. Stupid."

"Well, what about—" At this, he realized that the whole thing could be some kind of sick prank: a joke his sister had spun to rile him up. Or she was punishing him for completely abandoning her this past year. Then again, the entire thing hinged on him having an episode. Also, his sister could be a monster, but she never mocked these incidents.

"What about what?" she mumbled, her focus completely engrossed in the cat on her lap. If he didn't know any better, his sister was either bewitched by the feline or studying it in mind-numbing detail.

"Muffins had a baby, hid it from you under the guest bed, and it finally decided to make an appearance and socialize today."

With the non-petting hand, his sister flipped him the bird. Not bewitched after all.

And so, the conversation ebbed into silence and Kane's mind steadily spat up logical, yet desperate, scenarios. Had she left her door briefly open and one darted inside? Or had the cats used a hole in the wall to scamper between apartments. Or they were both experiencing a mass hysteria. Kane imagined that's what his therapist would have chalked this experience up to. This didn't feel like a mass hysteria, however, nor did it feel reasonable to say there was a giant hole in the wall that cats passed through: *secret catacombs.*

The more he considered it, the less and less rational his reasons became: aliens, a government conspiracy, Jesus invisibly wandering around her house, dividing things when he couldn't find bread and fish. Kane rubbed his face. The most obvious reason was that he had superpowers and the ability to create, or at least divide, life at will. Oh man, it sounded even more insane when he said it aloud in his head.

Kane shook himself free of his thoughts and found his sister still intensely focused on the cat on her lap. She had stopped petting it and was instead grabbing its paws and inspecting each one of them in turn. When she made it to its right hind leg, she stopped, bent in closer and lifted it a bit.

All at once, her eyes shot open so wide, Kane thought they would pop out. Standing up abruptly, she flung the startled cat off her lap.

"What the hell's wrong?" Kane said, moving an annoyed Muffins-number-one to the side.

In place of fear, his sister stumbled back and held her hands to her mouth. Tears streamed across her cheeks as she whimpered breathlessly. In a flash, Kane grabbed her by the shoulders. "Sue, Sue, are you ok? What's wrong?"

Head down, hysterical, she pointed over to where she had flung the cat. "That's not Muffins?"

"Not Muffins?" Kane was so exhausted, the meaning of the words ricocheted off him. "Not Muffins," he repeated.

"Kane." His sister wiped her eyes and stared at him with a strange mixture of fear and bewilderment. It was as though she had recently watched the threads of the world unravel before realizing it was all made of yarn.

"Kane," she repeated, "what was your vision?"

CHAPTER
FOUR

"AND THEN, I DON'T KNOW, THERE WAS A TICKING, AN AWFUL ticking, before the door opened. Someone was there, I think, or maybe it was a shadow. The light was so bright." Kane's face contorted as he struggled to remember the details. It had only been a few hours and already the color, texture and contours of the experience were beginning to soften. "There was someone there, behind the light and pain so deep, I couldn't think or feel. In that moment, a voice emerged." Kane's mouth opened, but no words followed.

He knew he had heard words at the end of it, knew they were buried in some far-flung corner of his mind. However, in the final, furious moments, his surroundings blurred as though looking at a picture through a bottle: the closer you got to the edges, the more opaque and blurrier the scene became.

"And the voice?" His sister attempted to jump start his thought train again. "Who was, or what did it say?"

Her face was scrunched together, eyes glazed and unblinking. He hadn't ever seen her like this. Whatever she had seen on the cat must have shocked her deeply—her face swayed between a grimace and stoic nihilism.

"I'm sorry, Sue, but I can't remember and, honestly, it really isn't worth getting so worked up over one of my stupid episodes."

"They're not stupid," she hissed. Her earnestness and intensity caused him to flinch back. Not stupid? They were his and he could call them whatever the hell he wanted.

"Listen Kane." Sue sighed with a tremble. "That's not Muffins. I never told you this, I never told Tim this..." She trailed off a bit. "Muffins doesn't have a little black diamond shaped patch on his hind leg."

No diamond shape patch? Kane turned to find non-Muffins number two sniffing around where drops of tuna juice had fallen on the floor. "So, it is another cat. How the hell did it get in here?"

"No," his sister said firmly, albeit with a slight shiver. "It's my cat. I mean, from before."

"From before?" Kane was lost. There was no before. Muffins was the first cat his sister had ever had. Even if there had been another one, how the hell did it wind up here?

"But you've never had a cat besides the one Tim and I got you."

For a moment, his sister shirked away from him, too frightened to continue. Her head shrunk into her shoulders, and Kane could see a few more tears welling in her eyes.

"Sue." Kane reached out to grab her arm, although he wasn't entirely sure he wanted to hear the rest. As his fingers touched her skin, it was too late. His concern brought her back to reality.

"You had gotten me the cat, Muffins, ten or so years ago," she peeped out, recoiling from his touch. "Right as I graduated college and was looking for work."

Kane remembered this well: his sister, in line with her usual passionate self, screaming at the sight of the little fluff ball in the cage he and his brother had brought.

"He was so cute. I was just so immature at the time. I had no idea what it meant to care for more than myself. Sometimes, I would go to parties that lasted the weekend and would forget to put food and water out."

At this, Kane smiled weakly. There were precious few of those first few months where he and Tim didn't constantly check on Muffins. His sister had been learning what it meant to be an adult outside the confines of academia, and in retrospect, giving her a cat was the worst welcome gift into adulthood imaginable. In the end, Muffins had survived, and his sister was the better for it.

"Well, there was one weekend. Do you remember when I was living in that trashy little duplex?"

"Sure, over by McVale Road."

Instead of responding, his sister sighed. "I had left to go with some new work friends to a stupid themed party. Hanging with acquaintances was better than waking up alone," she said, more to herself than to Kane. "I had chosen the perfect costume."

"Oh yeah, that stupid french fry getup!" Kane interrupted. "I used to wonder where that ridiculous thing came from. Tim thought you—"

"Oh you asshole!" Sue yelled and pushed him away. "I left the fucking door open, Kane, that's what I'm trying to tell you! Somehow, I took off for that stupid party and left the front door wide open!"

Kane recoiled, completely shocked at her reaction.

"And what, Muffins escaped?"

At this, his sister leaned back and wiped her eyes again.

This wasn't the response Kane had expected, and his attempts to reach out and console her ended in failure.

"Don't. Touch. Me," she hissed, swatting his hand away.

After a few deep breaths, Sue froze in place. Kane couldn't tell if she thought ending the story would mean opening some Pandora's box. *Riddles in the dark,* he remembered reading in a book somewhere. And these riddles had to be solved. He would give her time, even a glass of water, but he couldn't leave her story untold with the implications settling in like a slow-motion fist striking his face.

"I'll get you some water," he mumbled.

But as he leaned on the couch to stand, her hand shot out and held his arm with an unreal strength for her petite frame.

"Sit. Down. Kane." Her voice was a gentle contradiction to her steely grip. "Please."

"I don't know how long it took Muffins to realize his ticket into the wide world had been bought and paid for. I don't know how long he ran in and out, chasing birds, playing with other cats. Watching traffic go by. But when I returned, he was already dead. Hit by some car or truck or motorcycle. Either one, it doesn't honestly matter. No one had stopped. Not one of my neighbors had called me. I was driving in and saw his body." She paused and strained to continue. "And—"

Oh, shit. "And what, you found a perfect replica? Another Muffins so Tim and I wouldn't know?"

Her sister sunk into her seat. Kane hadn't meant for it to sound accusatory.

"Kane, I thought it was a miracle. He was staring at me from a cage in the shelter the next morning and everything—everything—was the same."

"Except for the diamond."

"Except for the diamond. Even without it, I hoped, I

convinced myself that he had been reborn for me. That I'd been given another chance. Now I truly have been."

At the word *reborn*, Kane's eyes darted over to non-Muffins number one. This was impossible; she was wrong. She had to be wrong. Kane could hardly breathe.

So what, somehow he'd made a zombie cat—was that it? They'd rename him Lazarus; his sister would get her chance at rebirth and forgiveness, and they'd move on with their lives. But Kane knew cat afterlife was utter bullshit. A more likely scenario was that he'd pulled it over from a parallel universe or was granted God-like abilities to create life at will. At these insane thoughts, the same uneasy, helpless feeling from before seeped into his mind. Kane wasn't in control. Kane could hardly claim to be a small part of what he experienced. He was a thin wire running out of a nuclear power plant, a speck of dust struck by the light of a thousand suns. Control? He'd be satisfied knowing he mattered at all.

"Kane, I don't know why this happened, but I know there has to be a why." His sister wiped the tears from her eyes and stood abruptly. "I've decided I'm not going to let this chance, this miracle, go to waste." As if on cue, non-Muffins meowed and came trotting over. Sue reached forward and stroked it gently. "Muffins, the original Muffins, is here again and needs someone to take care of them. However it happened, whatever you experienced in that episode, it doesn't change the fact that I've made my choice and won't mess this up again."

Well, wasn't that nice for her? Kane was irritated at how positive his sister was spinning this. Kane wasn't a vending machine she could press for spiritual salvation. Especially since he was the one who'd paid.

In spite of his own frothing indignation, Kane gave the hint of a smile at his sister's renewed energy. This was the Sue he knew: the one who could rebound from anything. Even if that *anything* was a supernatural adoption. He wished he could have her blind optimism, and that pissed him off most of all.

"Go to hell," Kane sneered. He'd drag her into the mud with him if it was the last thing he did.

His sister had been so captivated in her speech, she hadn't even noticed the dark shadows forming across his face.

"Excuse me?" Her hand abruptly stopped petting non-Muffins number one. It was clear she couldn't decide if he was joking or not.

"I said: Go. To. Hell," Kane repeated, this time reaching for his jacket, which had been haphazardly tossed on the couch. "You get your second chance, and I get jack shit. This is so nice for you, Sue."

"Kane, that's not what I meant."

Kane wasn't listening. His rage was a wall to the world.

"This is fucking looney, but oh, thank the gods you've been redeemed. Thank goodness, we don't have some evil demon parading around in a flesh catsuit." At this, Kane made his way to the front door, backwards so he could continue to look into his sister's eyes. "I could have died, Sue. Or this is a mental breakdown. So, you tell me. Should I feel crazy, terrified or fucking ecstatic for your zombie-cat?" He passed by a photo of his brother and on an enraged whim, grabbed it and tossed it into the kitchen. "You piece of shit, you did this to me!" he screamed at the picture as the glass shattered across the linoleum.

Huffing, he braced for a fury of verbal blows. Regardless of their circumstances, he knew he was acting like an asshole. Worse, like a child of their parents. Sue didn't deserve this, but then why was he so angry?

Kane felt his gut drop as his sister responded with a weak smile and eyes filled with pity. She truly had changed. Even if

Kane misread the compassion as arrogance, what he saw fanned the flames of his rage.

"You should toss that cat out the window into traffic," he said coolly, aiming for his sister's heart. "That's where it belongs."

And with those final words, he slammed the door shut into the night.

"Ah, fuck!" Kane huffed into the cool air, kicking a roadkill-esk plastic bag strewn on the sidewalk. Why had he said those things? Why had he left?

And boy, how he'd left: machine gun spraying his anger on the walls in a tizzy. He was such a child. Disgusting.

"Comfort my emotionally scarred sister?" Check.

"Protect said sibling from the mysterious cat creature?" Check.

"Apologize for hurtful words and atrocious behavior?" Check.

Kane deserved the brother of the year award. He was such a piece of shit.

And Sue hadn't even defended herself. Although horrendous, she took the abuse with loving stoicism. Of course, that only fed his guilt. He should have stayed with her, but he didn't.

Instead, he found his regular dealer on 9th street.

"Drop me a *teenager*."

"Damn, man, you look like shit."

"Good thing it's not a fashion show. I've had a rough night."

"Hey, bro, no ill will intended. I was only looking out for my boy. You sure you don't wanna *hit a goofball?*"

Soon, he was so loaded that his surroundings evaporated

into the night air like smoke from his pipe. In his dreams he saw the shadow behind the white light again, although this time the burning brightness had vanished. In his mind's eye, the shadow had been his brother who unfurled an arm and whispered words Kane could barely hear. *What is it?!* Kane wanted to yell, but his body felt numb and gummy. His brother read his thoughts, however, and wiggled and squirmed around as if to undo himself from unseen chains. Kane furiously stretched towards him as well. This was his last chance.

As the face of the shadow burst into light, Kane had to avert his eyes and recoiled. The face of his brother. *My god,* it had become so unbelievably hideous that Kane could only recognize him through his emerald green eyes. Pockets of flesh were folded over themselves and bunched together. In the midst of deep gashes and purple stretch marks, porous holes were wriggling around with small maggot-like creatures. The skin around his nose had been torn off and was pierced to various parts of his face and neck by a thick sinew and slime.

As Kane tilted in closer, his body revolting at the thought of coming into contact with whatever lay before him, his brother's blistered lips touched his ear while a hand worked its way around his throat. "Get out," they crunched before darkness collapsed over them.

CHAPTER

FIVE

KANE GROANED, ROLLED OVER AND FELT AROUND TO FIND PURCHASE on the coffee table he had slept next to. Sleeping was the wrong word; moribund coma was a more apt description. After whatever that dream was, he had dived headfirst into a deep, empty slumber with only wisps of sensation and light caressing his mind. "Twas but sound and Fury," Kane mumbled sardonically, pressing firmly into the tabletop.

Unfortunately, his palm slid forward on some long-forgotten bill, and all the objects atop came crashing down. "Ugh." He wearily inspected the damage.

He felt like a tornado; bottles were strewn around, papers, pills and a blackened pipe scattered across the floor. Remediating the pile of chaos was easier said than done as the clutter blended perfectly into the larger disaster in the rest of the room. Old pizza boxes, dirty clothes, more bottles, chunks of drywall which had broken off during some *punch-the-wall-rage-fest*. There was no way he was getting his deposit back. If a poet were to describe the ambiance and feel of his apartment, he would land on the following haiku: *This place looks like shit.* Not much of a haiku, but what competent self-respecting poet would ever want to write about this armpit of the universe?

Kane moaned louder, ignoring the symphony of popping joints as he forced himself to wobble upwards. Water. He needed water. He went to swallow but his throat was dry and grated together.

Tottering groggily towards the kitchen, he found the cabinets open and not a single glass in sight. "Seriously?" He sighed, unsure who exactly he was asking. Where was his drinkware? Kane peered throughout the room and found his answer: every single usable piece lay shattered on the floor with shards sprouting from the torn linoleum haphazardly. Another sigh, this one accompanied by an aggressive forehead rubbing with his palms.

"Oh, man. Whatever." He was so desperately thirsty. Luckily, his midnight routine didn't involve removing his shoes, and so with a bit of caution, he crunched over to the kitchen faucet and, cupping his hands, sucked gulp after gulp of the metallic tasting tap. Water dripped from his chin as the dire state of his apartment came more into focus. Kane hadn't ever been the cleanest person, but this was outrageous. Had he done all of that last night?

Kane suspiciously eyed the pipe, which lay innocently on the floor like the forgotten toy of a child, and caught the residual smell of meth. If ever there was a time for self-prescribed intervention, it would be now. Was it really time to stop though? It had only been a year since he'd begun. Honestly, even if he broke every single item in his home, Kane was confident the pros would outweigh the cons. Even if it got worse.

"What do I have to lose?" He chuckled at the irony of the walls being the last possible thing to break. "Just the deposit,"

Kane huffed out, sauntering over to the living room and being careful to avoid broken glass and a few skittering cockroaches.

As Kane collapsed on the couch, *what he had to lose* slowly came into focus. This place was a disaster. Not only the trash and broken glasses, but his own body as well. He felt like shit, as the medical term went. Kane's eyes drifted over and rested on the pipe again. "A few broken toys ain't no reason to cry and go home," Kane remembered his father saying.

All around him were *broken toys* in one form or another, smashed to bits through rage or intoxication: job, money, relationships, soul. In that order. Compared to those, the wreck of an apartment was insignificant. If his dad were still alive, would he be bent over his knee, pants down for the thrashing of a lifetime? Kane doubted it. He outgrew the beatings as soon as he outgrew his parents. It's no fun to hit someone who hits back.

"Especially when they hit harder," Kane mumbled.

But if he wasn't in for a pounding and he wasn't going to clean this mess, why would he quit? Go dry. Get clean. Lay down the heavy load. These broken toys weren't his anyway. They were garbage in a garbage existence and belonged to no one. They were lost, as shattered as him. Clearly, the only sensible thing would be to forget them like the trash they were and move on. *With scaly eyes, swinging around the piñata till you taste the candy.* Another glorious, worthless pseudo-religious saying from his father. What the hell did that even mean: scales and candy? Where did the piñata come from? If his father's wisdom had been a little wiser (or at a minimum, intelligible) he would have avoided treading down the long, heavy road that only ended in pain.

"Pain." Kane snorted. Pain was familiar, like a comfortable blanket or a well-worn shoe. Sure, there were a variety of holes. Sure, it smelled of vomit baking on asphalt in the middle of

July. Oh, but going back to it sure did feel oh so oooey gooey warm. Kane was sure his father would quip about him being a dog.

His eyes remained locked on the pipe, longingly, and with a certain revulsion. The black crust around the chamber reminded him of how his entire body ached and burned. If his mouth wasn't so dry, he knew he'd be tasting burnt charcoal and tangy, metallic dried blood. "Oh, fucking hell," he grunted, feeling each syllable reverberate in his pounding head.

This shit would kill him eventually. He knew it the second he'd taken his first puff. Not directly via some wretched over-dose where he contorts and wriggles around until his heart decides it's had enough. Indirectly. Soon rather than later, he'd catch some disease or wind up homeless and starving to death. A victim of his own apathy. Kane knew the risks. Even his dealer had tried to dissuade him when he first approached.

"You a little goodie-two shoes fo' this stuff, ain't ya?"

But Kane was not the type of man to be put off and he sure as hell wasn't wearing two good shoes. And afterwards, the blanket sure was warm.

"So warm." Kane turned away to face the backside of the couch. Since he'd leapt from the bandwagon and sprinted away, he hadn't had a single episode. Not one. Well, until yesterday. Who cares about saving a few toys when he's the piñata, screaming as the universe pelts him again and again with a spiked bat. Had that been what Dad meant? He was tasting candy because he was the candy.

Kane covered his eyes and let his fingers spread enough for a trickle of light to come through. The fact that the drugs hadn't prevented last night's occurrence was extremely concerning. Had he not taken enough? Or did his schmuck dealer jack over the stuff and give him a cold round? Who knew? Definitely not Kane and that bothered him to the core.

He only trudged along this drug-fueled path because of its magical ability to halt his episodes and alleviate his miserable life. Drugs he could count on whereas the other healthier exits had been blocked or circled right back to the beginning. Parents? Dead. Friends? Non-Existent. Love life?

Molly. Kane's eyes instinctively scanned the room for his phone. It would be somewhere around here and drowning in her messages like a puppy under her steely grip. Hopefully, the battery had died so he wouldn't have to see the notification screen. Better yet, hopefully, she'd died.

"Molly." Kane cringed as her name accidentally invoked the image of her face. She was the real horror.

In a healthier family, Sue would have been his lifeline. Unfortunately, Sue was a nuclear bomb and not the type of person you indulged emotional topics to unless you were ready for years of fallout. *Daddy sure did make certain we fell apart after he died. Like broken toys. I guess we all belonged to him in the end, didn't we?*

In a failed attempt to help him work through his shit, Kane's therapist had employed some redundant psychological phrase to describe his broken family. A term that was worthless, German and overtly Freudian: Famlienroman. Funny thing was, even if his therapist had manufactured the entire concept, it would have meant the same thing: his family was jacked. As broke as the shattered half of a homeless toy. "Thanks, Pops, you were a real treat."

Kane rolled over once again. The pipe lay before him, unmoved. What, had he expected it to float into his hand? The thought amused Kane so much, he snapped his fingers, flicked his wrist in a faux-magic way and chortled. If he had the power to do that, he sure as hell wouldn't be here. He could have followed in Tim's footsteps and capitalized on this strange power.

"Tim." Kane abruptly stood up and went to cup more water into his mouth. "Uggh."

To be fair to his little brother, Tim, little by three minutes, couldn't levitate objects either, and he had still amassed unending wealth and billions of followers. Meanwhile, poor Kane, whose visions had only been triggered after Tim's death, watched his brother's growing popularity with a deranged covetousness.

"Look at Little Tim riding with big boy tires," Kane would mock, infuriated his brother was so far ahead he couldn't even hear him.

Turning off the faucet, he made his way to the fridge. Completely empty. Not even moldy take-out. If only last night's episode had predicted he should have bought pizza.

"That would have been the level of Little Tim's fortune-telling-vision-bullshit," Kane snarled. "A worthless, minor and so fucking specific vision of the future it was its own miracle people gave a flying fuck in the first place." Kane slammed the fridge and continued his diatribe to an audience of skittering roaches.

"There is a woman in red, and she will burn her husband's t-shirt with an iron tomorrow in Milwaukee. Her name is Dee Dee Horton, and she lives on—" Kane spun his fingers around his head as though unscrewing his brain. "And no, you can't do anything to change it!" The only satisfaction Kane ever got was that his brother's predictions could never alter the outcome of the event. "Making your gift the most pointless ability to ever grace the supernatural world, you pompous schmuck."

Kane returned to the couch and collapsed atop it, his puckered face a mixture of bitter nostalgia. Obviously, if Little Tim's range of predictions remained so mundane, he wouldn't have been able to rise to prominence. He would have been condemned to some forgotten corner of a circus show, reading palms and tea leaves for the few dollars he was able to pluck from suckers. The thought of Little Tim desperately struggling to please customers by telling them when they would burn shirts or forget tea amused Kane to no end. Unfortunately, that's not what happened.

"Throw enough darts, and eventually you'll hit red." Kane recalled the Kabul bombing and shuddered.

His eyes fell on his phone, which was dangling precariously off a large fold in his jacket on the floor. The face was lit which could only mean one thing. "Messages," Kane moaned, forcing himself upward.

Message from: Molly—10:04 pm

Message from: Molly—10:08 pm

Message from: Molly—10:10 pm

There were dozens of them, but Kane expected nothing less. Although she had broken it off, for some odd reason, Molly felt compelled to check in on him. Unfortunately, as she was a complete bitch, her loyalty manifested itself in a *nagging semi-stalker behavior with sadistic manipulative tendencies* (straight from the mouth of his therapist). Also unfortunately, she knew yesterday was the fifth anniversary of his brother's death and was even more apt to bombard him with what he imagined were subtle criticisms thinly disguised as condolences.

"I know it's hard for you today, so you should really consider how to move on from that shithole." *Click.* Nailed it. Kane rubbed his face.

Tim's followers were eerily similar to Molly before she broke it off: knowing her partner was a mound of dirt but somehow able to find a few nuggets of gold. For her, it had been his sense of humor, his ambition and his unending patience (gone, gone and way gone). For Little Tim's followers, it was the few major predictions that always came to pass.

Well, almost always. His final grandiose vision, the one which would change the world, remained elusive to this day.

However, regardless of the one glaring gap, his zealots were more than happy to swarm his words like ants covering a discarded piece of chocolate. And Little Tim had been more than happy to keep tossing candy at his feet, delighting in each medal, book and special guest status at various parties. He had become the founder of his own worldwide religion with hundreds of millions of followers. All in a matter of five years.

But Kane saw Little Tim for what he actually was; not a phony—that obviously wasn't true. No, Little Tim was worse than fake.

Kane removed his shoes and threw his feet on the recently emptied coffee table. The odor from his socks would have been unbearable if last night's meth-rager hadn't completely obliterated his sense of smell. Looking at the greasy-brown, filth-rags covering his feet, Kane recalled his brother's pompous interviews, expensive cars and dinner dates with the wealthiest people on earth.

"Scared little Oz behind the curtain." He ground his teeth together and swallowed hard.

Fear was the truth, the awful truth, and Tim was loaded with it. For all his ramblings on what his visions meant and how they fit into the universe, Tim had no idea what was happening to him and the world. Little Tim wasn't a fake; he was a liar.

And only Kane knew. Only Kane saw: Little Tim was as in control of what was happening to him as Kane. Bloody stigmata and all. They were a couple of piñatas, tasting candy as the universe bashed them over and over. The act, the facade, that Tim put on wasn't only for his zealots, but for Little Tim himself.

These visions, the only documented supernatural miracles

to take place in the modern world, a wonder of science, religion and philosophy, was not a gift at all. It was a horrendous curse.

Only Kane knew.

If he hadn't despised his brother so desperately, he may have felt pity. Just a little bit. They were twins to the end and suffered together, even if Kane's was slightly belated.

After deleting dozens of messages left by his ex, Kane forced himself upwards. There was one message he hadn't deleted. One which caused him more stress than the whole lot left by Molly. It was from his sister, Sue, at 7:47am. What, she thought he was going to be awake?

"I'm not a wretched morning vulture catching maggots." Kane bit his lip and wondered at his overreaction. Throughout the night, he had convinced himself over and over that he didn't owe her anything, that she was merely another broken toy tossed away in the garbage heap left by their father. Although, even when he was flying high through the clouds, puffs of smoke disintegrating into hallucination as he made his way above the stars, his guilt continually weighed on him. It was a constant gravity and had nearly brought down his entire experience. "Stupid old hag." The shame bubbled upwards as the words rolled off his tongue.

He knew she didn't deserve it. Of those in his family, she was the best of them. Sure, she worked at a kill-shelter. Sure, she had an explosive temper and was flakier than burnt toast. Even with these traits, Sue was somehow normal. She had made it: escaped her father's grasp and written herself out of their *Familienroman*.

"Ugh. This is why I hate coming down." Sentimentality. Kane shooed away a shame that threatened to bury itself in his chest.

Opening the phone, he found the voicemail to be only five seconds long.

"What, lose your nerve, Suzannah? Can't think of anything nice to say so you won't tell me to eat sod and die?"

"Kane," Sue whispered excitedly, "it's on TV; they found it."

With those few words, the embarrassment, negative feelings, hurt and hatred Kane felt vanished in an instant. Even if it was temporary, it was the climax he wished the drugs gave him but constantly proved to be just beyond his reach.

"Well, looks like Little Tim was always right after all."

CHAPTER
SIX

"They found it," Kane mouthed, standing up abruptly and almost tripping on a pile of dirty clothes. "Tim was right." He felt the world spin and crashed on the couch.

Kane gawked at the TV and recalled watching Little Tim being laughed off a niche public television show at the start of his career. He had no idea he was the butt of the show's joke and had been insultingly christened Prophet Keller.

"A nuclear bomb in Kabul? Who cares about Kabul?" the show's host chided. "Why don't you tell us—actually, why don't you show us how that would even happen?"

Unfortunately for Tim, he could neither explain the events which led to what he saw nor explain why he was unable to adjust their course.

"We're all floating down a river," he had stuttered amongst boos and snickering "and even though I've seen a bit farther downstream doesn't mean we can paddle against the falls."

For weeks afterwards, the overwhelming majority of commentators had mocked and heaped load after load of shame on Tim's head. In Tim's words, it felt like whatever supernatural power had afforded him this gift had gaslit him.

Then, October 31st came and upended the world. The bomb was small and dirty, like a water balloon filled with piss. As it splashed on the people of Kabul, their lives became a living nightmare: a packaged inferno wrapped in flames and tied together with a radioactive bow. For Tim, it was as though he were strapped to a catapult and the ballast holding him down was cut at once, propelling him to unfathomable stardom.

It hadn't mattered that he was unable to change the outcome, nor that he was able to see who was responsible or if there would be any subsequent attacks. For those looking to him for wisdom and guidance, those things were mere inconveniences.

"Fat trimmed from fattier meat." Kane rolled over and dug through the couch cushions before triumphantly thrusting a TV remote into the air. Luckily, that last piece of functional electronics in his apartment remained undamaged, although Kane grimaced as it flickered to life and revealed a large sticky-looking brown stain. There were no soda cans or cups nearby, so where the hell did it come from? Instead of dwelling on the unsettling possibilities, he clicked through the channels looking for a news program.

"Even I can change the channel"—Kane released a nervous laugh—"which is one better than you could ever do, bro."

Being unable to change the outcome of his visions was more than a mere inconvenience for Tim. He constantly struggled with the implications of an immutable future right until the bitter end.

And the end had been bitter, if not acrid. There had been one final prediction, one so unbelievable and contrary to his brother's typical specificity that it could have as easily been echoed from the shouts of a main-street schizo or painted in blood and feces on the bathroom wall of a serial killer. In the end, Tim, poor Little Tim, abandoned the chance or will to explain a prediction which, years later, hadn't come to pass.

"Until now," Kane mouthed breathlessly.

Kane clicked past a morning talk show and landed on cartoons. It was an enticing option to heave himself up, grab his pipe and spend the rest of the day zoning out, high as the moon and enjoying the whimsical, animated situations so contrary to the wreck of a life around him.

"Uhhhhh." He sighed, shooting a dismayed glance towards his phone before clicking onwards. After another four channels, he finally landed on a news program. It was vehemently discussing Tim's unexpected death five years ago, causing an unwanted bombardment of memories.

"Hours," one of the members of the discussion group spoke up, "or minutes, before his final second death, Tim had scribed the following on a plain sheet of paper in his study:

I can't see past it. I've struggled, dreamed and wept into darkness but none of this makes it through. There is no other side. It doesn't exist, so I can't see past it.

And humans will find this monolith of twilight and edge buried deep below. An umbra on the dark side of the moon. And humans will see that it has no end because it has no beginning.

And now, that's it. There's nothing else. I can't see past it, so I have to get out.

. . .

"And as you know, directly on the neatly folded envelope, placed to the side so no blood would douse the letters, a name was written: Gabriyel Stver."

Holy hell. Kane shook his head, remembering the first news reports of his brother's suicide which splattered across international news like Tim's brains over his study. The whole thing mimicked a deranged scene in a Lovecraft novella.

Presently, the news channel was playing old footage of Tim's demise as a prequel to today's events. 'Incessantly' was the word. If he gave one flying crap about his brother, putting his death scene on repeat would be offensive. As it were, Kane wasn't offended, just annoyed. He was as shocked and interested as when the occurrence had first happened. The only thing that bothered him, though, was the thought that Sue was being forced to watch the same thing. She wouldn't just be offended, but sickened as well.

Somehow, only CNN had gotten exclusive rights to stream the discovery live. *Final Prediction Unearthed! Tim's Edge Discovered!* (the name his followers had bestowed). As their station prepared to broadcast, and the remaining news programs prepared to intercept and interpret what was occurring on CNN, the only option to raise ratings was to inform their audience of old news. Kane's guts clenched as he watched pictures of Tim's life and death flash across the screen; stories of his visions, old footage of debates between his followers and other religious figures popping in and out with unnecessary rapidity. It was flooding the major networks like God forgot his covenant when it came to journalism.

"Whose are the animals and where's my ark?" Kane sneered.

Sue's message remained on his phone, her voice a thin dew of emotion caught on a perpetual digital web. He had no intention of erasing it. Who knew, one day he could retrieve and sell it to some overeager journalist.

"This is where it started." Kane did his best impersonation of a newscaster, imagining Sue's message playing as the intro.

But in reality, he was too scared to delete it. He had been so awful to her last night, what if she refused to speak with him again? Kane rubbed his forehead and gnawed on his thumbnail. It had only been a few weeks since he'd come back into her life, and he couldn't imagine being cast out so soon. *Throw away the lock and key. Ain't nobody gonna come for me.* Was that from a Johnny Cash song?

"Ah, for fuck's sake, show us something already!" Kane exclaimed towards the TV in desperation.

As if the newscaster was hardwired into the audio of his home, the screen momentarily went black. A mental sigh of relief. *Finally.*

Kane leaned forward, staring into the darkness. After a few dozen seconds without video, Kane thought there must be a misfire with his connection. Standing up, he charged over to perform the only technical activity he knew how: pound the box and curse in tremendous volumes.

However, right before the first blow landed, the screen flickered to life, revealing a tense newswoman in front of several pieces of heavy machinery. She was inside a cavern, or large cave, and silently waited for the green light to begin the broadcast.

To be so young and the front person for such an event. With a certain envy, Kane imagined how unbelievably capable and ambitious she must be. A heck of a lot more than he was. Although he meant it as ridicule, the words filled him with a certain sense of shame.

The newscaster must have been given a signal as all at once

her restless features relaxed into a poise of perfect calm professionalism:

"Exciting news on the scene of the dig today. Five years after the original prediction, Tim's Edge has finally been found. I'm here with Gabriyel Stver, head of the Timothy Lamm foundation and Senior Operations Officer at the dig site."

At this, the camera panned slightly over to the left, revealing a pale apparition of a man with deeply receding blonde hair and small circular glasses. Kane took on an air of exaggerated revulsion. His appearance was akin to a bond throwaway villain or a psychopath who etches ancient scripture into human leather for fun.

"Mr. Stver, it's been five years since the search commenced and four since the massive efforts around this dig. Before you divulge what exactly it is you've discovered, please give us your thoughts around this exciting journey."

"Come on!" Kane threw the remote at the screen and pressed his body into the couch. "Get to the point already, you ass!"

"Well, Miss, may I call you Miss? Or is it Mrs?"

In place of further response, he stretched a hand towards the confused newswoman who, for her part, squinted a bit as she gently shook the tips of his fingers. Kane was sure they'd met before and wondered if he had a social impediment or was merely the embodiment of awkward. Many of Tim's leading zealots were typically rough around the edges, but this was a bit much.

"It's been exciting. Terribly exciting. A terribly exciting adventure, these last five years. I was as surprised as anyone when my name was found on the envelope of our great founder's last prediction. Tim! On heaven, Earth and Down below!" He clasped his hands together and shook them like he was ringing a large bell. "Once I was informed, rather found, my work inside this mine became all the more evident in the location, I mean locationing. No, wait, finding of—"

The newswoman suddenly cut him off, clearly aware his ramblings wouldn't bode well for her career and the success of this broadcast. If she didn't keep him on track, the entire interview would be relegated to the dusty shelves of sound bites and highlight reels on obscure streaming platforms.

"Mr. Stver, if you could share a bit more on the details leading to today's events?"

Mr. Stver dropped his hands suddenly and whipped his head upwards and downwards.

"Ah yes, yes. Some history. Well, you see that." He paused and looked confused. "Did you know before they found me, our group was planning to dig on the moon? Noble and yet with vastly misplaced guidance! That was the actual start, wasn't it. The letter was so specific. 'An umbra on the dark side of the moon'; who knew this mountain was actually what he meant?"

A weak smile worked its way across the side of Kane's face as he saw the tense features return to the journalist's eyes. Small lines formed as the muscles of her head slowly contorted and pulled her skin taut in a grandiose display of stress. However, as a consummate professional, she also forced a weak smile and through gritted teeth began once again.

"Yes, and you were the one working in this mine who told the world how it tied to the prediction rather than some 'lunar lunacy', in your words."

Mr. Stver was clearly missing the tone of the reporter, who was pushing things along to today's occurrence as opposed to providing history of things people already knew.

"Oh, right! I did say that, didn't I? One has to admit though, it was lunacy, right? And lunar went so well with it, I thought it would make a great little bit to put those two words together. In his all-knowing wisdom"—at this, Gabriyel clasped his hands together in the same bell-ringing motion as earlier—"Tim brought me into his holy circle of prescience to put his sheep on the right path."

Kane already knew this. Hell, the world already knew this: Tim's followers fundraising to colonize the moon while simultaneously searching the census and phone records of every country on Earth in search of Gabriyel Stver. Crowdsourcing information with a billion people meant finding Gabriyel was easier than shooting fish in a barrel with dynamite. What a shock: he had been the lead safety engineer of a small mining operation in Moon Mountain, Arizona. Demolishing an entire mountain was child's play after that.

Surprise. Surprise. Kane clenched his lips together until they were white. The not so specific prediction must be cut from the same cloth as the others.

On the screen, the newswoman continually, and desperately, steered the conversation in a way that would get Gabriyel to describe how they'd found the object without giving away the whole list of details at once. Gotta keep the tension. Faucet not firehose, Kane read in her eyes.

"Ok, so walk me through how you found the object today, Gabriyel."

Oooh, that was a subtly passive aggressive comment if Kane ever did see one. She had stopped using *Mr. Stver* and replaced it with an intonated first name like a mother scolding a child. Although Mr. Stver was impervious to her nipping tone, he also seemed generally excited to make it to the point of the story himself.

"Yes. Uh. Well. Uh. Last night one of our workers reported that a large drill bit broke in a small section of the lower mine. Normally not an issue, but when a second bit broke, we decided to have our senior geologist investigate. Could be that we'd found something, right?"

Mr. Stver spoke in agitated waves and the reporter, who had clearly given up the ghost, simply nodded in resignation.

"We waited a long time for him to return, several hours if I recall, but after various attempts to reach him on the radio, we decided to go investigate."

This statement made the reporter's ears perk up.

"And what; had he vanished?"

"Vanished?" Mr. Stver looked confused. "Oh, no, no, no. This isn't some poorly contrived horror novel, Mrs, I mean Miss—"

"Laila. We've met. Tell me, Gabriyel, what exactly did you find?"

"Oh that's right, we have met." Gabriyel stared into the distance and let his mouth open a bit. Kane could see the reporter was close to snapping. A fraction of a second before she popped, however, Gabriyel abruptly shut his mouth and continued speaking as though his momentary pause was a well-placed staccato.

"It didn't take us long to find Mr. Comena. He was bent over where the drill bit had broken, staring into a darkened patch we couldn't quite see from a distance. The drill car isn't a small object, as you well know, and through various RF readers scattered throughout the mine, we have an extremely good sense of the specific locations of the equipment. Funny thing, prior to the advancement of that technology, the safety of the workers relied on—"

"Mr. Stver!" the reporter belted out. "What did Mr. Comena find!?"

Mr. Stver shifted his glasses a bit. Even a person as socially inept as him could sense a direct frontal assault. Frankly, Kane expected him to cross his arms and pout at the televised rebuke, but instead he smiled sheepishly.

"Nothing."

The reporter nearly toppled backwards. "Nothing? What do you mean, nothing?"

The same sheepish smile lightened a bit as his eyes took on a bewildered, ten-mile stare.

"Like I said. Mrs. Miss Laila. Mr. Comena found nothing. Perfect, endless, incomprehensible nothing."

CHAPTER
SEVEN

ARE YOU WATCHING THIS WHIRLWIND? -- MESSAGE FROM SUE AT 1:03 pm.

Kane stared at the message for a long time, not able to tell why there were tears in his eyes. Relief flooded every limb and caused him to collapse backwards into the sofa cushions.

Clearly, Sue had gotten over their little fight. Good for her. How mature. Kane suddenly became indignant. Crossing his arms, he set his phone on his lap and decided he would wait for *her* to text *him* again.

And what was he hoping for, that she would panic and realize how important he was? That she would come rushing over to his house to see if he was ok? Kane was so out of tune with his own emotions, they passed by with an extreme Doppler effect.

Kane, I know you're awake. Stop being an a-hole and text me back. The stuff on CNN is nuts, right?

. . .

More tears, which Kane shook away as he relaxed his clenched throat.

Obviously, she's desperate. He should respond.

"After some more water." He forced a yawn.

As the cup situation from before had not magically improved, it took a few minutes to quench his thirst. Once he had finished lapping water from the faucet, he found a string of text messages.

Are you seeing this? -- Message from Sue at 1:15

Kane. What is this? -- Message from Sue at 1:34

If you're not going to write me back, at least turn to CNN -- Message from Sue at 1:39

Kane stumbled into the living room once again and placed himself a few feet in front of the TV screen. It was clear the tone of the scene had shifted dramatically. The reporter and Mr. Stver had stepped outside the confines of the typical interview format and had made their way towards the lower levels in a Jeep. As they wound their way through the bowels of the gutted mountain, the pixels of the camera caught less and less of the surrounding light. Although there were numerous bulbs encasing the walls, none of them made a dent in the encroaching darkness. Soon, even the vehicle's own headlights and dashboard dulled.

Kane could hear a rough voice from behind the lens. "Hey, Mrs. Laila, the camera isn't working."

If Mrs. Laila had responded, her words were lost in the cacophony of static. The video fidelity was rapidly decaying, and Kane felt he would have better luck gluing together the scattered remains of the broadcast's transcript than understanding the pieces of their conversation.

All at once, the screen cut out. At the rate the quality of the picture was failing, Kane had expected no less. Even so, the sudden darkness caused him a start.

What the hell? Kane reached for his phone and made the decision to text Sue after all.

Did you see that? -- Message from Kane at 1:48

Oh, welcome to the party. I guess a visit to the lost and found siblings box isn't in order.

Sry—was sleeping

Apparently not anymore

Kane didn't respond at first. He was weighing his words wisely.

F-off -- Message from Kane at 1:53

*Lol **and** you woke up on the wrong side of the bed. How much of this have you seen?*

Enough

And?

And what?

And what do you think? It's nuts, right?

Fits Tim's MO

.   .   .

The reply from Sue took longer to arrive than Kane was comfortable with.

You mean another miracle? -- Message from Sue at 1:56

Kane didn't know how to respond. Was that sarcasm or piety? He never would have expected Sue to be devout to anything, especially Tim. Although, since last night, he had a growing suspicion she may have joined the fold. How far they'd both strayed. Originally, his response was going to be *If by miracle, you mean turning water to piss, then yes,* but he decided against it.

What do you think happened to them? he sent instead. *It's like the entire network went dark* -- Message from Kane at 1:58
      The other channels show the same thing. Everyone's confused. They're saying it may be some sort of electromagnetic interference. -- Message from Kane at 1:59

Kane could imagine the mass panic taking hold across the globe. Some people may buy the elementary school scientific explanation of electromagnetic interference, but for many this would equate to the end of the world. And why not? Whatever *nothing* Mr. Cominena (or whatever the hell his name was) had found appeared to be no longer confined to the bowels of the mountain. Kane rolled his eyes at the idea any of this could be supernatural.

And now, people had disappeared within it. What a recipe for hysteria. Since it had happened so suddenly, Kane doubted most governments would be able to censor the event. *Electromagnetic interference.* That was as believable as saying they'd driven up Atlas' ass and gotten stuck.

Kane -- Message from Sue at 2:00

Kane waited for the rest of the message, but when it didn't come, he responded with the only appropriate reply:

Sue -- Message from Kane at 2:01

Another long pause. As he stared into the dimly lit phone screen, Kane felt as though he had tossed a stone into a deep well and was awaiting the inevitable thud.

Do you think Gabriyel is aware of the end of Tim's note? The end of his prediction? -- Message from Sue at 2:05

No. No one is. How could they? Kane had torn it off the page and burned it before anyone could take a look.

Will you tell me what it said?

Kane's response was instinctual, pure reflex: *No, Sue. I won't.*

His mind unwillingly flashed back to the day he had discovered his brother's corpse rotting in his study, brains flung across the wall and caked on the paint. Afterwards, he read the note and...

The memory caused such a dizzying feeling, his phone nearly slipped from his hands. *What the hell?* Clenching his head, pain arose from his throat, drew across his forehead and cleaved his consciousness in two. He blinked and the sensation vanished with the same abruptness as its arrival.

With blurring eyes and a tingling weariness, Kane glanced around the room. Whatever that was, it hadn't been another episode. He was about to pat himself down for blood to make sure when he spotted another message from Sue glowing on his phone.

I understand -- Message from Sue at 2:08.

Kane collapsed in relief, although he couldn't tell if it was due to Sue's reply or the fact the intense sensation had completely disappeared. Had it been nerves?

I understand. His sister's words were tiny and pathetic to look at. Yet he couldn't stop staring at them.

The old Sue would have come over to fight him for disagreeing. K.O. Down for the count. Kane pictured her petite frame forcefully twisting his arm around his back as she buried her knee in his spine. Sadly, this image was more than his imagination. If ever there was a city-sized asteroid heading straight for Earth, Sue was it. Kane shook his head yet again. What happened to her?

Thank you, Kane replied with faux-reluctance, meaning every word.

. . .

Right after the TV screen had flickered out, it flashed on. In an epic display of shock and surprise, Kane rammed his feet into the ground and nearly tipped over the couch.

Oh, it's back on -- Message from Sue 2:09

"I, I, I," Kane could hear the words repeating amidst the static on the TV screen. Oh no, here it was. Some nameless horror is going to be tearing the guts out of that poor woman as she chuckles at the pretty little red worms.

As much as he hated to admit it, the surreal situation was gripping him more and more. The reality, the truth he was compressing into a neat little compartment in the no fun section of his brain, was that the electromagnetic interference explanation was most likely accurate. Or the connection sucks underground.

The other option was an encroaching nothing, some stygian realm where the monsters emerged to live under your bed. Kane knew it was madness, blatant lies of the imagination. At the same time, he had also given it a wisp of life, quietly acknowledging its presence for the same reason others had: entertainment. For Kane, a little validation may have been in the mix as well.

"It was amazingly vast." He heard the woman stutter again, the static dissolving from the screen. "I can't even imagine what's on the other side."

Looks like they made it. Electromagnetic interference it was.

It was obvious the reporter had completely forgotten she was being filmed (or the camera hadn't worked for so long, she thought it was permanently defective).

"What do you think is on the other side, Gabriyel?" Her tone had completely lost the distaste for him she had been chewing on earlier.

"Mrs. Laila, I don't think you understand. There is no 'other side'. If Tim couldn't see past it, what makes you think you can?"

Mrs. Laila considered that question for a long time. Even after they had arrived at the main lobby, the group remained in pensive silence—heads down, unblinking and stationary within the vehicle.

Their faces reminded Kane of a group of circus performers he had caught a glimpse of backstage as a child. In his young mind, he had pictured them being the same as during their performance: happy, energetic, full of life and whimsy. Instead, he found them spiritless marionettes whose strings had long since been cut. A few were smoking, with one taking quick sips from an obscured object. One was staring at a rope dangling from a rafter with such intent, Kane knew this would be his last show.

Those faces, those human masks fitted atop corpses, were being worn by this group as well. Even Mr. Stver, who was shaking his head gently with the same sheepish smile as earlier, was powerless to start the performance. Would it be his last?

Kane -- Message from Sue at 2:32

Oh no. Gently placing his face into his palms, Kane rubbed until his head felt like tacky dough. He already knew what Sue was going to ask and didn't want to give her the satisfaction of a response. Even if he replied *no*, it wouldn't do any good. Sue would fight him on this, violently, no matter how much she'd changed.

Besides, he didn't want to say *no*. If he did this, the episodes may stop. He could quit the drugs and get his life together. Heal. Those were enticing prospects, but the actual reason he wouldn't say *no* was the chance to finally rid himself of his brother. Tim. Little Tim, the broken toy he could finally toss out.

Kane glanced at his phone. He didn't need to predict the future to know the next message would be short and swift.

Kane, let's go see it -- Message from Sue at 2:32

Pick me up tomorrow.

CHAPTER
EIGHT

KANE PROMISED TO MEET HIS SISTER THE FOLLOWING MORNING AT Little John's Big Meals Diner. The place had been christened with this pathetic wordplay in obvious reference to both the Robinhood story as well as the not so small stature of its owner: Little John Borowski—whose not so little boy used to frequently beat the stuffing out of a truly little Kane. Why in the hell Kane's parents, who knew the bullying was happening, had dubbed this the family rendezvous point was beyond comprehension. Some form of subtle taunt to grow a pair by his father, no doubt.

After the interview with Stver had been cut short and Mollie's forty messages had been deleted, Kane felt an oppressive boredom take root. He could pick this trash up but felt a not-so-subtle sense of revulsion at the idea. Eventually, his hand drifted towards the pipe. A few puffs later and the afternoon became an odd time warp. Abbreviated eternity. Hours, minutes, seconds—they blended together into the same rotting black sludge you get sloshing every color of paint around in a bucket.

"Visions, visions go away, come again another century," Kane muttered at one point in the evening. "And bring pizza; I'm starving."

"Oh, shit!" Kane suddenly flung himself off the couch, unsure of the time. Did the soft blue sunlight mean morning or evening? His drug-fueled afternoon had slammed headfirst into a drug-fueled evening before he had blacked out and awoke entirely disoriented. "Oh shit," he pressed his fingers into his face. His phone read 8:05 am.

One frantic packing session and a few gargles of water later, and he was groggily stumbling towards the diner. Kane wasn't sure what was fuller——the suitcase in which he had stuffed a week's worth of mismatched clothes or his throbbing skull. He was late. Real late. *Later than a gator who ate'er,* as his mother used to say.

After jettisoning himself off a city bus, he spotted the diner: a small corner spot on the intersection of two decrepit streets. Kane hadn't been here in a while, and the first thought which came to his head was, *Place has seen better days.* This was only reinforced as he stepped inside.

Behind a counter which ran parallel to the entrance of the door sat a box TV which must have been older than Kane. Surrounding this antique apparatus was a backdrop of old bulletin boards which hadn't had a single flier removed since Reagan was president. Kane was confident that if more seasoning was needed on the specialty of the house—heart-stopping bacon-crunch-scrambles—the patrons could rub the little grease pockets directly on the oil-splattered windows. To accompany the ambiance, each round leather seat facing the bar was flaking as though it had a bad case of pruritus and Kane thought this must be a result of the well-seasoned fumes emanating from the kitchen. This was disgusting, sure, but

Kane's mouth was sopping wet. Clearly, he wasn't alone, as the joint was packed to the brim.

Sue sat on one of these peeling stools and was positioned so her back was to the entrance.

"Uh oh." Kane closed his eyes and tensed up. She was probably pouting. He felt his heart skip a beat in terror. The prospect of a multi-day road trip with an angry Sue was as appetizing as eating those window-goo egg pockets.

Kane dropped his luggage (if you could call such a pitiful display of drugs and dirty clothes luggage) near the door and gallows walked towards his sister. He was confident no one would steal his stuff; the bag was too disgusting to be readily handled by human hands. Worst case, a worker would put on rubber gloves and throw it in the dumpster, assuming it had been left there by some nameless transient.

As Kane approached, he noticed Sue was on her phone scrolling through an editorial entitled *Tim's Edge and the Edge of Faith: Ten Reasons He's the Devil.* Although he was close enough to touch her arm, Kane weighed if he should wait until she was finished. Better to disable a sleeping bomb than a ticking one.

Before he could say a single word, however, Sue loudly said, "Oh, did *Littler John Jr.* catch you in the alley and beat you up?"

"What?" Kane was confused. His sister had spoken so loudly, the entirety of the diner piped down and strained their ears towards the excitement.

"I said—" Sue took a deep breath, clearly intent on belting out her previous question with heightened gusto.

"Sue, I heard what you said," Kane cut her off. "I just don't understand what you're getting at."

"That's the only reason you'd be this late, right?" She turned around to face Kane with a look that said *Draw, partner.*

"Sue, I—" Ooops, Kane felt his metaphorical fingers slip off the sandalwood, causing the pistol to tumble to the dusty earth.

"No, it's ok!" Her voice was raised. "I'm sure you were busy having the living daylights kicked out of you by the owner of this diner's child!"

Kane's face was so red and burning, the next order of bacon-crunch-scrambles could have been cooked on his forehead.

"Sorry, Sue." He put his hands in the air in a calming gesture and ignored the eyes of the dozens of onlookers peering in his direction.

His sister stared at him for a moment and said, "Uh huh," before abruptly turning around to continue scrolling through her phone.

Kane didn't know what to do. He felt like a complete putz. The voices of the diner had slowly reemerged as the prospects of live entertainment had dwindled, but Kane remained standing, unmoved behind his sister.

After a short time, her voice emerged again. "Sit, Kane." Her tone was cold, although the fiery accents had been extinguished.

He was starving but didn't dare order anything. The waitress's face grimaced slightly as she sensed the tension and silently brought cup after cup of coffee without asking if they were ready.

"What a professional," he mouthed into the dark brown liquid.

Kane nervously gnawed on the rim of his cup, completely forgetting he wasn't three years old. For her part, Sue still thumbed through the same article on Tim. What would it take for her to forgive him? Kane was at a loss. He sure as hell didn't have money for a gift. Did she want him to get down on his knees? In front of everyone here? He took a deep breath thinking about touching the floor and realized that may be exactly what was needed. A bit of begging, a bit of not-so-figurative shoe licking.

The last time he had seriously upset Sue, she made him wear a diaper while they went shopping. And that was merely for smashing her car into a stop sign during a street race.

"If you want to act like a child," she had hissed, "then you might as well dress like one."

And with a sense of remorse, Kane had agreed. He had removed his pants and donned the comically large diaper while they strolled around the mall. This wasn't nearly as dramatic a situation, but he knew if he didn't hit the brakes now, there was no way in hell the apology train would be able to stop before derailing.

"Sue, I," he started, ready for the ass-kissing of a lifetime. To his surprise, his sister cut him off.

"No, I'm sorry, Kane." She placed her phone on the table with a *thump* and met his eyes. "I shouldn't have done that. I shouldn't have embarrassed you in front of these people." Taking a deep breath, she grabbed his hands emphatically and pulled him towards her. "Kane. I'm sorry. You didn't deserve that. I'm sure you had a good reason for being late." Sue held his gaze while shame burned around his cheeks.

A good reason? Kane thought back to the previous night, to the drugs, to the meaningless string of events which had led him here today.

"I don't know, Sue," he said, averting his eyes from her intense stare. "I think it's my fault." All at once, she flung her arms to her waist and twisted her seat around till she was facing the bar.

73

"Nonsense, dear brother," she replied in a poorly contrived British accent before adding with her normal voice, "It was pretty shitty of me to bring you here. This was the same diner our parents dragged us into so they could taunt you for being such a pansy, right?"

"If you can't grow a pair, you may as well cut them off." Kane did his best impersonation of their father.

"You're getting the stuffing beat out of you because you're such a turkey," Sue continued.

"Gobble, gobble." Kane smiled and flapped his arms around limply.

"Guess I'm raising two little girls," Sue said, but winced as she noticed a pain flash across Kane's face. "Sorry, I shouldn't have said that."

Kane took a few deep, calming breaths and stirred his coffee with his finger. "It's ok. Guy was a complete prick, huh?"

"Rotten, green and oh so mean," Sue mumbled.

Kane had spent his entire night floating around the cosmos on puffs of smoke. His worries, his cares vanishing threads of a dream weaving into a waking reality. He had wanted this high yesterday, bad. Boredom, fear of the episodes and some invisible hand throbbing and pushing on his insides had joined forces and run amok. Today though, in this very moment, Kane felt a stronger craving for a fix than he had in his entire life. His only option was to race to the bathroom or tell Sue he'd meet her outside. Licking his lips, he glanced over to his suitcase before feeling the weight of the little bag of powder in his jacket. His luggage sat there, unmoved, a stained and reeking monolith anchored in place by human disgust.

"Hey, Sue." His shaking knee made his entire body tremble in a soft convulsion. If he wasn't careful, she would get suspicious. And like a wolf on the trail of a scent, if Sue got suspicious, she wouldn't let go until each morsel from the prey's bones had been licked clean. Kane gathered his strength and steadied his body. *Still as a knight*, a saying his mother would espouse to reprimand her rambunctious children.

Before he could continue, she stood up with a jolt. "You're right, Kane."

"I'm right?" he repeated blankly, forcing down an approaching shiver as Sue gathered her things.

"It's getting late. Let's jet before traffic gets crazy. We'll have plenty of time to talk in the car."

Kane's stomach emitted a vicious growl. "Can I at least order something to go?"

His sister's smile was as cold as it was devilish. "I have a few snacks in the car. That'll have to do till lunch."

And without another word, she tossed a twenty on the counter (what Kane was overly thankful for as he had no cash beyond drug money) and rushed toward the door.

"I need to use the restroom," he said weakly. "I'll meet you out there."

"That took a while," Sue said from the driver's side door. "You ok?"

Kane approached the car with his suitcase, looking despondent and clutching his belly.

"Yeah, the diner coffee didn't sit right with me. I think I got it out though." Although he had only taken the smallest hit possible, one he knew would fade in fifteen minutes but provide enough oomph to shelter him from the approaching storm, the after-effects had his head buzzing.

Sue eyed him up and down, and looked poised to launch an interrogation. To Kane's relief, however, she simply nodded, started the car and winked for him to hop in. "That's what happens when you get older. I have some Tums in the glove compartment if you want some."

Tossing his pitiful luggage in the trunk, Kane went around to the passenger side door with the intent to sit up front.

"What the hell?" he screeched, flinging the door open in surprise as two small feline heads popped up from the window.

"Hey, what are you doing? Close it before they escape!" His sister belted out, struggling with her seatbelt as she leaned over to block the cats.

"What am I doing? What in sweet hell's name are you doing?" With a coordination he hadn't thought possible for having such a heavy head, Kane lunged inside the car and shut the door.

Wait. Why had he done that?

This thought struck him as he turned to find two felines staring at him from the back seat.

"You're bringing those things?" The cats' eyes followed Kane's pointing finger like it was a mouse on a string.

"Bringing those *things*?" His sister glared at him. "If by *things* you mean Muffins and Muffinz, then yes, I'm bringing those *things*."

"Muffins and Muffins?" Kane stared at his sister aghast. "You gave them the same name?" That was a bit twisted, even for Sue.

"No, the second Muffinz has a *z* on the end. It's cute, right?"

This was anything but cute. Kane had believed his days of playing around with fiend number one and fiend number two were behind him. If he ever went to his sister's apartment again, he would have requested she lock them in a closet OR that she provide complimentary holy water and a church approved ward. Of course, she wouldn't have agreed, but it would have been worth a shot.

But now, even though he was mired in processing the last few days, his sister had brought these abominations along for the beginning to every road trip horror film ever made.

"Meow," one of the cats uttered, leaping into the seat of a petrified Kane.

CHAPTER
NINE

"DON'T FEED THEM THAT!" SUE PULLED A HAND FROM THE STEERING wheel to snatch a chip from Kane.

"What? Thing one and thing two love them," he responded sheepishly, leaning over so the chip was directly beyond her reach. Suddenly, he gasped as Sue swerved into the opposite lane.

"It's Muffins and Muffinz," she responded with a squint, refusing to look ahead while both her hands slipped from the wheel and into her lap.

Since they had left Chicago two days earlier, Kane had constantly referred to both cats as thing one and thing two. Sure, this had been partly done to spite bringing the creatures along in the first place. More, though, the Dr. Suess reference had added a bit of levity to an absurd, and potentially terrifying, situation. At least for Kane.

Although his sister had taken the first few remarks in stride, her annoyance ballooned rapidly.

"Jeez, Sue, I'm sorry." He shoved the chip in his mouth and swallowed with a single *crunch*. "I'll stop, I'll stop."

His sister's hands fell to her side as she closed her eyes. In a split second, the vehicle drifted dangerously close to the edge of the other lane.

"Are you?" she asked as the familiar hum of the rumble strip shook the car.

"Yes, yes. Shit. Yes!" Kane replied, looking between his sister and an oncoming truck.

A second before they dived headfirst into their own obituaries, Sue's eyes flung open as she deftly swerved to safety with a yank of the steering wheel. "Well, ok, then." She smirked as though her insane behavior had been theater.

Kane didn't know what was more terrifying: the prospect of winding up devoured by fiendish claws or leaping into a pit of Sue's wrath. Obviously, whatever smoothing out she'd experienced over the past year required a bit more sanding to remove the splinters. He would have to be careful and treat her like he did before: *tippy tip toes on a shark's nippy nip nose,* as his mother used to say.

Oddly enough, although terrifying, Kane often found pleasure in locating Sue's buttons and pushing them until a meltdown was imminent. Afterwards, instead of escaping, he would mash the console over and over, watching his surroundings glow green. Why did he behave this way? It was a game of chicken or Russian Roulette. The closer he got to death, the closer he got to life. Was that it? A condition so contrived and common as living like a sadist? Kane hoped there was more to it than that.

Sue's angry stares also bolstered an odd sense of community he felt between them. He simply didn't want to feel alone, and his acting out gave him the only weapon against a deep isolation: attention. Or it was just fun and he was a huge prick; Kane stuffed a handful of chips into his mouth and stared at his sister's content face. *She thinks she's won, but she doesn't even understand the rules of the game.*

Deep forests mottled with patches of snow gave way to rolling hills which stretched beyond the horizon. They were caught in an ocean of green, sailing placid waves in search of a distant land.

To pass the time, Kane imagined they traveled across wrinkles which cut through the palm of a slumbering giant. It was childish for him at first, but as they rode up and down hill after hill, the idea gradually took hold. They were near the center, and this dip was his lifeline. Kane wondered how much longer he had. The giant would awaken right before the end and fling them off.

There were a few times Kane wouldn't have minded being flung off. He'd crash land somewhere he could finally get a little privacy. Although Sue didn't appear suspicious of him, being cramped in a car together for three days meant Kane didn't have many opportunities to *hit the fix*. Obviously, he could only fake having a stomach ache so often, and one or two small hits a day was only rubbing his itch, not scratching it. Kane was thankful the trip was nearly over. Sure, the rest would be tough, but with a few small "walks" in the morning and evening he could pull through without getting overly jittery. If not, Kane figured he had one stomach ache card left to pull at their lunch time restaurant. Hopefully, his ace in the hole would plug the leak. He shuddered.

Soon, the green of the rolling hills abated into sparse pockets of grass bunched together amidst scraggly rocks and trees. Kane hadn't seen the desert before and imagined it as the Sahara with endless dunes under a vast sapphire canopy. This had nothing in common with what he expected: rocks stacked like poorly contrived castle turrets and scarce patches of trees filling the ravines of the brown earth like pockets of unwanted hair. Even the blue of the sky took on a slight dusty tinge as the landscape dried and withered under the bleak winter heat.

"Someone forgot to water," Kane said, staring at an outcropping of brown rocks.

"Someone watered with acid," his sister replied, bringing both a smile to her and Kane's faces. "Another day, and we'll be there." She peered around, half focusing on her surroundings. "But I don't think it'll get any better. I think it's gonna get worse."

"Where the hell are we again?"

"New Mexico, according to my GPS. An hour or so from Albuquerque and around a day's drive from Lunar Village and Moon Mountain."

"Albuquerque? Lunar Village?" Kane asked rhetorically. What stupid names for places in a miserable wasteland. "That's a helluva long way from Chicago."

Tall mountains approached, taller than Kane had ever seen in his life. They stood out conically from the caramel landscape. Even at this distance, Kane could see snow on top and splotches of green drawing thick lines amidst the dull browns. They were like the giant's teeth, jutting into the beyond.

"No wonder Moses didn't want to live in this shit," Kane said, more to himself than to his sister.

"Forty days in the desert is forty-one days too long." His sister lowered her voice to mimic their father.

Kane smiled. He had completely forgotten that stupid saying.

"You remember," his sister continued, "how he used to scold us with that whenever we'd act without planning first?"

Oh, he remembered. A dull pain struck his chest.

"Do you know why it's forty-one days, Kane?" He

mimicked his father's baritone. "One was wasted not planning and the other forty were the consequence." Brilliant, Pops. Kane grimaced as a picture of his father's face flashed before his mind's eye. His father had taken an unrelated biblical story and twisted it to fit his ridiculous lesson. Square peg, round hole. Ball gown on a pig. Whitewashed tombs.

His sister sighed. It was clear she had received her fair share of that lesson as well. "Why do you think he did that?" Sue asked. Although her eyes were on the road, Kane could tell she was staring elsewhere.

"Because he was a prick." This caused Sue to laugh so loudly, Muffinz, or Muffins, poked its head from behind the seat to see what all the ruckus was about.

"Well, that's obvious," she said with a snort. "But I mean, really. Why all those stupid sayings? Why all the forced pseudo-religious lessons and verbal lashings? I've spent years mulling it over and I still don't get it."

A small gas station shot by on their right. As Kane glanced through the window, he could see an old man standing in front, wiping the windows of a pickup truck that had no wheels.

Sue and he had discussed the topic of their father frequently before Kane had disappeared, especially in the days and months after his death. Years earlier, Tim had been there as well and lamented: "We'll never know. When Dad died, the secret recipe of his insanity died with him. Glad he didn't put it in the will."

The truth was, Kane had no idea why his father would stuff twenty pounds of unrelated Bible stories into a five-pound sack o' lectures to beat them with. Was he trying to validate his beliefs? Find footing on solid ground to prove to himself and the world how right he was? Kane imagined his father was so insecure, this biblical glue was the only thing keeping him together. Or that was simply the way he was raised. Kane gave a mental sigh.

If his father had screamed, "spare the rod, spoil the child!" as he whipped Kane with an extension cord, that would have made sense. Even grabbing Tim by his long hair and shearing him with a hearty, "Does not nature teach you this is a disgrace?" would have at least been relevant. The way it stood, his comically twisted usage of biblical stories was absurd. "David and Goliath clearly show the evils of tall people," Kane recalled him saying once at the dinner table.

Unfortunately, his father was deadly serious about his entire interpretation. The comical had morphed into the terrifying as light wordplay became both verbal and physical abuse. Too bad it wasn't only for the three of them. They could have grown out of it.

"If only," Kane's pursed lips grew pale as his fingertips clenched a wrinkle on his jeans. There had been more than a few times he had returned from school to find his mother with thick globs of makeup or long sleeves in the dead of summer. "Bastard," Kane growled.

Sue reached over to touch his forearm. Kane felt his eyes blur and grunted. He hadn't cried in years, and he'd be damned to do it again this week. "I gotta pee," he blurted out, brushing Sue's hand away before turning towards the window.

His sister didn't say anything for a long time. Although Kane couldn't see her face, he knew she was looking at him with frustration, empathy and arrogant love.

"Sure, Kane," she finally said. "Let's get past Albuquerque, and we can hit the next rest stop."

After Albuquerque, the desert morphed as though their quick jaunt through the mountains had moved them through a curtain onto the next stage. In place of stone behemoths, jutting from the sharp mountain contours, the desert had become flat, soft, with distant mountains gnawing through the endless blue sky like rancid teeth. With a certain fascination and pleasure, Kane had watched these mounds come together and separate, dancing in the distance to the rhythm of time and speed.

Unfortunately, both he and Sue were so enthralled with such a dramatic change of scenery, they completely missed the rest stop.

"Next stop 43 miles," Kane groaned, reading a passing sign. "Sue, the next rest stops gonna be three feet in the back if you don't find some ground to wet." At this, he grabbed an empty water bottle and jiggled it in her face menacingly, only yanking it away as she swiped at him.

Luckily, finding *some ground to wet* wasn't nearly as challenging as he imagined. As the highway drew closer to the mountains, small dirt roads cropped up that led to structures on their sides. Mines? Often, the hills were of such pale color, the small brown buildings could have been moles or freckles. *Probably cancerous,* Kane thought to himself as Sue turned onto one of these dusty paths.

"Make it quick," his sister chided. "I want to get to Lunar City by dinner."

At the word dinner, Kane's stomach growled a bit. They had only eaten nuts and chips since breakfast and the prospect of a solid meal was enough to make Kane bolt towards the desert in sheer joy. Although brief, he had weighed the option of taking a quick hit while his sister waited in the car but had decided against it. There's no way in hell she was gonna believe he took a fifteen-minute piss.

It took a minute, but eventually he found a scraggly looking bush with enough branches to temper the stream. Piss on his shoes was the last thing he needed. If Sue found out, she'd make him go barefoot the rest of the trip.

Kane reenacted the great flood by staring into the sky and around at the worn hillside structures before focusing on his own feet to make sure there was no accidental splashing. This activity went on for a while without him feeling any less full than he had at the beginning. Odd. Water must've really done him in. His gaze danced from bush to bush, rock to rock, upwards to the forlorn sky and downwards to his shoes. No matter how much he expelled, he simply couldn't remove the sensation there was more inside—circulating, permeating, an endless reservoir fed by torrents of rain and powerful rivers. He jostled around a bit to see if that would loosen whatever tingling feeling was flooding around his waist. It was like he was pissing in a dream.

All at once, Kane felt a scratch at his throat, gentle at first, like the wings of a silken gnat were being birthed from his tonsils. The feeling grew, twisting and whirling, until his entire esophagus felt coated and stuffed by a swirling warm velvet. The fabric writhed within him, wriggling around as it slid and scrunched its way into his belly. Kane looked down, a peaceful frenzy enveloping him.

"Oh no!" He torpidly pulled his shirt up as streams of water gushed from each pore in his waist.

Kane could feel the force inside him change, contracting and expanding with rotating gusts of hot and cool air. It was making its way through his guts, lower and lower, dancing towards escape and tearing through him in the process.

The shaggy, pissed-covered bush hissed and screamed as the liquid splattered across it. Wisps of smoke transformed into raging fires which mushroomed upwards and consumed each branch in red ember, vanishing into dust as the tips disintegrated and scattered. Kane blew in a frantic attempt to extinguish the flames, but pushing only caused more water to splash onto the ground. Soon, the entire desert was engulfed in a firestorm, circling and spreading outwards.

The thing was close now, so close to leaving Kane. It passed across his belly button and fluttered throughout his guts. In a series of frenzied jerks, Kane forced his hands towards his gut and pressed. If the thing was going to escape, it would have to rip itself from him. As his hands touched the twisted bulge, Kane thought of a hard stone.

"So chiseled," he mumbled to himself, pressing on his belly more furiously. If it escaped, if it left him and went out into the world, what would happen? Kane didn't know the answer. It simply felt wrong. Premature.

As his fingers prodded into his flesh, the tips pressing into the solid void of his gut, Kane felt them brush the top of whatever was inside him. All at once, the water stopped. The hot and cold blasts squirming around him faded and the object contracted so rapidly, it was a wonder it had ever been in him at all. If Kane wanted to describe the feeling, he would have said it felt like the second after a good puke.

With a sense of warmth, the writhing vanished, although Kane could feel it skimming the surface. In its place, a strange sensation of being watched overtook him. It was as though an autopsy was being performed from the inside out, dissecting and stitching each atom together in turn. In this moment, Kane felt himself in two different places at once. Split and observed through blurred vision. He was a mirage, an illusion—smoke, mirrors and hot sand. The blurry vision was sharpening, and Kane was drawing closer and closer to himself.

He didn't know what would happen when he came into focus. He didn't know if he would be torn asunder or melted down to be cast into a grand sculpture. Is this what Tim felt before the end?

Kane didn't know why he thought that. Tim should have been the last thing his weary mind conjured. However, as the blurry shapes gradually moved together, the image of Tim, of himself, didn't allow him to think of anything else.

What if they remained unjoined or were split into eternity? The thought was like a nuclear detonation on his chest, so recklessly violent he collapsed where he stood.

CHAPTER
TEN

"Hit the spot like a bat to a piñata," his sister's voice thrust him awake. If he hadn't been buckled in, Kane may have leapt from the moving car's window. Where was he? He peered outside to find a canopy of stars dimmed by the headlights of oncoming traffic.

"Hey, are you ok?" Sue gave him a puzzled side glance.

"W-what?" Kane stuttered between heavy, panicked breaths.

Sue turned and eyed him up and down and, after a moment, slowed the car to pull over. The bright midday desert had been swept away by the cover of darkness, and Kane could hardly see ten feet in any direction. Where the hell was he? What the hell had happened?

"No, really, are you ok?" His sister unbuckled herself and furrowed her brow. "Was it the dinner? I told you not to get those nachos. The cheese alone—"

"What!?" Kane's elbow struck the door as he flinched back. "Dinner? When?"

Sue's cheeks went flush with frustration. Her eyes

narrowed and read, *This is hardly time for a joke.* Kane wasn't joking, however. If anything, a joke was being played on him. The last thing he remembered was taking a leak in the desert. Water gushed all around him before something snuck up inside and—

"Kane?" This time his sister's voice was threatening. She had caught wind of a scent and was hot on the trail.

"What, what?" he replied, rubbing his face while attempting to get his bearings. He had been in the desert peeing when a thing arose in his throat, directly beyond his tonsils like silken gnat wings. With a slight tremble, Kane twisted and wriggled the base of his tongue, feeling for any hint of its presence. Oh no. Kane gave a mental gasp. It was there, unchanged.

He took a deep breath and felt the sliver of something press against his soft flesh, burrowed in and protruding. His eyes must have taken on an exaggerated bulge because Sue's angry look softened as she wrinkled her nose and eyed him up and down curiously.

Kane had no idea what to do. Should he yank it out with tweezers or leave the slumbering entity be. Feeling around the flesh of his throat again, one thing was for sure: it wasn't dormant. Although minor, it trembled slightly as it wriggled around, pressing miniscule incisors into the surrounding tissue as it slowly made its way backwards. Where was it headed? In that moment, the same sensation of being watched overcame him, although it was only a flicker and distant flash.

As the feeling rapidly fled, the silken object tunneling into his throat halted as well. It drifted away step by step until Kane was left with a tickle and a peculiar notion he had made the whole thing up. Obviously, he hadn't, right? His tongue swabbed back and forth, prodding around for any hint of what he had experienced. Nothing.

"Kane, are you having a e-episode?" his sister stuttered.

"What!?" He turned to her. "No, I mean—of course not."

This was true. Kane knew this from the moment he had woken up. No puffy skin, no mangy hair or blood. Whatever had happened to him was not an episode. Or at least not a typical one.

Should he confess to Sue that he had no idea how he'd gotten here? But how could he? The entire memory of the past few hours had vanished, been ripped from his head or torn to pieces. Clearly, he had done things, eaten things. Kane felt around the flesh of his throat again. Still empty.

"Sorry, I just..." Sitting upright, he struggled to regain his composure. "I fell asleep and forgot where we were." With a swift motion, Kane turned his head to the window. "It's so dark," he said against the rhythm of his beating heart.

What did she want him to say? Kane didn't have a handle on what was happening, and explaining it would be like asking a child to write Tolstoy. If he felt up to it, he would tell her later, once he'd figured it out for himself.

Kane twisted nervously in his seat as he pondered the idea that the drugs had finally gotten to him. Did he take a hit in the restaurant? With a subtle motion, he felt around his jacket, and to his utter panic, the pipe and little white baggy had disappeared. Frantic, he pretended to keep his cool while searching the rest of his pockets. *No. No. No.* His hand darted this way and that, pretending to itch, pretending to straighten his clothes.

"Kane?" The threatening tone had returned to his sister's voice. "What the hell are you doing?"

"What?" Kane shot his sister a glance but avoided her eyes.

"What are you doing?" she repeated, her voice lowering menacingly.

"I'm, well—" He had to think fast, fabricate a lie. There would be time to tell her later. *Later than a gator who ate'er.*

"Sue, I'm so sorry." The deception rolled off his tongue. Kane had often lied for drugs, for money, to himself and those around him. Now he was reaping what he'd sown. "I lost my wallet at the restaurant. Must've slipped outta my pocket. All my fucking money was in there!" At this, Kane slammed his fist harshly against his knee. "Shit!"

Of all his lies, this one was impressive: awaking in a panic, confused, not wanting to give away the fact that, like a toddler, he had left a valuable object somewhere it could easily be stolen. Kane knew she'd buy it. He knew she'd act on it. In a few moments, they'd be buzzing back to the restaurant, begging the owner and patrons for any tips on a lost wallet. He knew it and hated himself for it. What else could he do? He needed time to get his head right and figure out what was happening. Explanations, apologies and a few harsh words could come later. Sue was a nuclear bomb. If he didn't wear protective gear, the fallout would kill him.

As Kane expected, within seconds they were speeding towards the restaurant, begging the owner and patrons to look for the wallet.

"I think we sat there! Or no, wait, was it over there?" His sister tugged him around hand-in-hand. Kane didn't remember any of it and merely nodded as she suggested looking in each corner and bathroom stall.

After returning to the car, and as Kane expected, he hated himself for what he'd done.

"It's ok, I know money's tight for you anyway. I got this, *big bro*, don't worry." Smiling weakly, he gave a slight nod before turning to peer out the car's window. He'd slip Sue a few bills when she wasn't looking.

But that was a lie, wasn't it? Any remaining funds he had

were headed straight towards the first dealer he found. Although he fought against this idea, told himself how disgusting he was and how much better Sue deserved, in the end he knew he would lose. To himself. To the drugs. To the world. Perhaps, he deserved everything happening to him.

CHAPTER

ELEVEN

As they approached their hotel in Lunar City, Kane strained his eyes to see if he could spot Moon Mountain. He had read online that the name was in reference to it being bent over like an eclipse. Apparently, the native Sinaguan people believed it to be Kokopelli's back and considered it a sacred place.

A moon and the back of some god. Kane rolled down his window and stuck his head into the rushing wind. *Or a load of nothing.*

Beyond the faded lines drawn by the car's headlights and the distant misty glow of the approaching city, the darkness around them was a pure, unadulterated void. Even the beams from the stars reflected off this impenetrable shell of blackness. Growing up in the Midwest, this intense dark was nearly impossible, and Kane came close to forgetting himself as he peered into the onyx canopy.

"It's like I'm witnessing the collapse of the universe," he mumbled.

Moon Mountain was nowhere to be seen. It was no surprise. Kane felt he could be a nose width from it and not see a single speck of dust. For a moment, he closed his eyes and let the wind stroke and caress him. To his wonder, the darkness beneath his lids was less intense than when his eyes were open. What amazing nothing. No wonder Tim's Edge was here.

After he had his fill, he plopped into his seat and rolled up the window. They were nearing Lunar City, a town of 900, and the encroaching darkness swayed and retreated as the bright bulbs of main street radiated outwards to strike it. It was getting late, and Kane was surprised to see the hustle and bustle on the streets. He smirked at the idea that trash bags full of humans had been ripped open and were scattered litter around crowded eateries, motels and bars. As they drove past the park, carefully avoiding several dozen people moseying across the street, so many tents came into view the scene formed a living mosaic.

"What's going on here?" Kane nodded towards the front window.

"No idea," his sister responded weakly, shaking her head in disbelief. It was as if Coachella, Lollapalooza and Woodstock had birthed a disjointed population bomb.

As for the town itself, Kane would have described it as quaint under normal circumstances. On par with typical Route 66 vibes, the buildings were western, most with adobe stylings and often low and flat. Most locales were surrounded by flashing signs which shot into the air like electric popsicles: *Moon Base Bar, Spaceman Hotel, Moe's Lunar Landing, The Apollo.* There were dozens, each sporting some moon-based theme and paraphernalia. Under normal circumstances, Kane had no idea why anyone would travel out here. It was hours from a proper city and apparently had no redeemable landmarks other than an oddly shaped mountain. How it drew such a crowd was remarkable.

"You think they're here for Tim's Edge?" his sister asked as they drove past a large crowd of RVs in a parking lot.

"No idea," Kane responded. Even as he said it, the truth was obvious: the masses here were on a pilgrimage to see the monolith. "Unbelievable," he muttered.

After reaching the opposite end of town, Sue pulled into the last spot in a dusty parking lot. "Dark Side of the Moon," Kane read the glowing popsicle aloud. "Sounds like someone's a Pink Floyd fan."

Sue grinned at him before hopping from the car. "I didn't think we'd need reservations, but I made one just in case."

Peering around, both she and Kane spotted numerous people in sleeping bags beyond the main road. A few tents dotted the parking lot as well, although *Camping Not Permitted* signs were placarded across the gate. Kane also saw multiple *No Vacancy* lights dotting the building.

"Good thing I'm the smart one." Sue winked, yanking her luggage and a plastic cat crate from the trunk. Soon, she was walking towards a small building with a faded red sign atop the entrance which read *Office*.

Kane reached for his luggage as well but paused for a moment, glancing over at Sue. She was clearly on a mission and had left him to gather the few things he had brought. Without realizing it, his sister had given him the opportunity he'd been waiting for all night. Opening his bag, he frantically, efficiently searched for the one thing that mattered most to him: his pipe and that little white baggy.

"Shit!" His hands scurried through his clothes, darting this way and that. Each pocket had to be checked, each nook and cranny. And in short order.

He released a muffled cry. "Ugh! Where did I put that thing?" His mind strained to see the events before he awoke. He was peeing and a scratchy feeling grated at his throat. Or had it? Kane thrust his tongue as far backwards as he could manage and prodded around. He felt nothing but a fading memory and the lingering sensation he had dreamt the whole thing.

To his therapist, this would have been referred to as a *psychogenic fugue state*, caused by an underlying mental disorder or more than likely, his heavy drug use. Kane wanted to believe that desperately. He had blacked out before, but only for short periods, and always in conjunction with some debilitating physical injuries. Beyond collapsing, he couldn't recall actually doing things during those blackout episodes. The thought he had an utterly forgotten, hours-long road trip preceded by a mental breakdown caused him to shudder.

Previously, when the episodes were happening week after week, and meth had yet to save his life, his therapist had recommended he get an MRI. Kane had adamantly opposed this on simple grounds: he didn't want to know if anything was wrong with him.

"A dead bird in hand is better than two skeletons in the bush," he had joked.

But not wanting to face his own mortality was only half the truth. In reality, he was terrified that the results would show a specter or otherworldly visitor inhabiting his flesh or a dark lesion in the shape of Satan's face. Cancer was one thing, but suddenly realizing the validity of religious dogma he'd spent years neglecting was wholly different.

But since none of that was possible, the old coot may have been right. Kane decided an MRI would be his first stop once he returned to Chicago. Assuming he could steal enough money.

After the last pocket had been unzipped, he knew the entire search and rescue endeavor was a lost cause. Whatever stops he had made along his trip through amnesia town had ended with his most valuable item taking a cue from his sanity and vanishing.

This was his chance to stop. The thought caused an electric jolt to shoot through his gut. What did that even mean: *stop?* Would the episodes reappear? Would the blackouts continue, cutting through his consciousness and filling it with holes? Kane had no idea. What he did know was that to stop was to die. Meth was the only thing which had made life tolerable after his brother passed—after the visions started. *Drugs were great advice, Tim, glad you were the trailblazer.* Kane believed he owed the delicious crystals a debt of gratitude and was hell-bent on maintaining the relationship.

"Thank you for your service." Kane's mind eye saw a grimy wad of cash lining his wallet. With a weary grin, he zipped his bag shut and closed his eyes. They'd find each other again real soon.

Moments later, his sister emerged with an arrogant smirk and a key dangling from her finger.

"What took you so long?" Sue asked, glancing at him from the corner of her eye as they sauntered towards their room.

"Sorry, thought I'd check my bag one last time." Kane sighed heavily and looked at his feet. He was good at lying, but he recognized there was also a kernel of truth to his down-trodden demeanor. Taking advantage of Sue was unbearable.

"It's honestly no problem," she said with a grin. "I know you'd do the same for me." And although Kane knew it wasn't true, he mirrored her smile. He was a piñata, and there was a gash in his face where the smile should be.

The hotel room was bleak: unsimulated 1950s retro style because its last refurbishing was from that decade. Normally,

Kane kicked off his shoes in hotels, pretending a shabby $30 a night inn was a luxurious four-star suite. With stains mottling the floor and walls, however, his imagination was strained to conjure more than the words *crack den*. Kane would be sleeping fully clothed tonight. Sue didn't make a single comment towards the room's hygiene and proceeded to strip bare and beeline for the shower.

"Dibbsies." She said to a blushing Kane, who, despite their joint parentage, hastily averted his gaze with a well placed turn. Sue, entirely unfazed by this odd display of prudishness, continued her strut.

Kane knew this was a quirk of hers but refused to dive too deeply into its origins. He could only imagine the personality trait or underlying trauma that drove this behavior. Although both parents had been incredibly conservative, guarding the flesh with a religious fervor, his sister was unconcerned about these voyeur displays—well, at least around those she knew it didn't matter. Kane recalled more than one reprimand from her mother when an open bathroom door, a forgotten towel or some other childish mischief had led to familial horror as Sue streaked through the house.

But they were older now. That's just not done. He was grateful he had taken long "walks" the past few nights to avoid this tick.

After he knew she was in the shower, Kane turned off the lights and hopped into one of
the double beds. Even without his sister's shenanigans, his exhaustion canceled any plan to move. Indefinitely. Brushing his teeth? Hard pass. Taking his shoes off? Harder pass. Telling Sue to grow up? The hardest of hard passes.

Within a few minutes, Sue's shadow re-emerged from the bathroom. Although he pretended to snore, Sue wouldn't be fooled. Kane wasn't one to fall asleep that fast, no matter how exhausted he was. *Sleepless in Lunar City,* Kane's restless mind blurted out, *starring Tom Hanks' cousin and a few homeless zealots we found in an alley.*

Kane heard the covers of the other double bed shift around. He guessed she wasn't brushing her teeth either. This went on for a while until Kane imagined his sister must be kneading the blankets with cat-like obsession. What the hell was she doing? It was difficult enough for him to fall asleep, let alone with jarring rustling sounds

Kane peered into the darkness but couldn't find purchase on a single speck of light. The desert's darkness had crept into this room and erased each trace of its existence. For a moment, Kane became horrified he may be having another episode. As silence spread across the room, the idea grew to such proportions, he considered bolting for the door.

From the void, his sister's voice emerged. "Kane?" she asked softly, melodically.

"Uhhhh, yeah?" he responded with weary gruffness. Please, Sue, he needed sleep!

There was a slight pause, and Kane regretted being so harsh. After a time, though, the silence felt right, pensive, urgent and yet deliberate and precise.

"Do you believe this?" Another brief pause. "Do you believe *in* this? In Tim?"

Oh, man, she wanted to discuss this now? With a certain frustration, Kane pondered her question. Did he believe Tim? Did he believe when his brother spoke of god and having purpose through destiny? Did he believe it when Tim interpreted his gift as a cane fitting the shepherd's hand?

Kane considered his answer for a while, waiting for his sister to break the silence with a drawn out, "Welllll?"

But as time dragged on, it was clear she didn't mind waiting. Kane knew that for her, slow answers were like slow cooking: filled with juicy honesty. For several minutes, she remained still, her breathing so light the air between them dampened the noise.

Kane struggled to manufacture a good answer—either a lie or the truth. What was he going to say? Or better yet, what did she want him to say? The truth was that he didn't know. It was so easy to chalk the episodes up to a psychotic breakdown, textbook schizophrenia or drug-related mental illness. Even an inherited superpower would be palatable. However, placing the entire ordeal on some coarse supernatural explanation was not only oversimplified, but offensive as well. Let go and let God so he didn't have to drive anymore, so the universe wasn't an unknowable chaotic mess and he had some value. If he had told Sue his thoughts, she would have laughed hysterically and said, "That's a philosophy major for you."

Did he believe in this or in Tim? Did he believe they were anything more than spinning atoms—each collision the tick on a cosmic doomsday clock? Did he believe Tim's gift was more than the amalgamation of trillions of statistical improbabilities masquerading as clairvoyance? A million monkeys, a typewriter and Shakespeare. Aliens. Evolution. Quantum mechanics. Government conspiracy. Pure luck or Krishna. Honestly, Kane had no idea. Each path was easily tread, and easily tread upon. And for Kane, they felt utterly lacking in substance and flavor, directionless and as void of light as the surrounding darkness. There was also the problem of those damn cats—living evidence that some part of these occurrences lurked beyond the confines of his own existence and sanity.

He was moments away from admitting his doubts and worries to Sue, but passed into a dark slumber at the sound of her rhythmic breathing.

CHAPTER
TWELVE

"Wakey, Wakey, eggs and bakey." Sue's voice pierced the delicate flesh of Kane's groggy mind. In place of a response, he simply groaned and smothered his face with a pillow.

Sue, entirely unabated, pressed an elbow into the soft part between his ribs and laughed menacingly. For whatever reason, his sister felt it necessary to wake him each and every morning. Judging by the amount of sunlight filtering in through the curtains, Kane could see today was vastly earlier than usual.

A second elbow landed on his ribs, causing his previous groan to become a screech as he squirmed away from her grasp.

"You awful morning person!" He had intended on yelling in a faux-angry manner. To his surprise, it had more seething than comical undertones.

"Oh, I'm sorry, Jesus. Has it not been three days yet?" Sue retorted. This was the same thing their dad would say to them as kids before sunrise service. In response to her comment,

Kane hopped up and chucked a pillow at her, relieved to find Sue fully clothed.

After dodging two revenge pillows and a shoe, Kane noticed two plates of limp bacon and watery eggs had been placed on a small table next to the door. A third plate with either bread or stones (Kane wasn't sure) had been set between them.

"So, literal eggs and bakey." Kane rubbed his temples and avoided looking into the dim light behind the curtains.

"Yup. Included in the price of admission. Although they'll soon be figurative if you don't wake your ass up."

"Can I at least go to the bathroom first?" A yawn as he combed through his hair with his fingers.

"No," Sue said with a flinty stare.

Kane replied with a customary flipping of the bird as he sauntered towards the toilette.

Why he had expected it to be any less shabby than the rest of their room was beyond him. No matter how cheap the motel, Kane held the belief that the bathroom was a pillar of light: porcelain and tiles, ceramic tub and sink, cleaned with harsh chemicals to keep the blight away. It may be tarnished, but rotting would be out of the picture. At least, if the business was concerned with staying open. *La Toilette*, a beacon of gentility in the dim world of bargain hotels. As a junkie, Kane thought he knew a thing or two about those.

Obviously, he needed to travel more. Kane cringed, peeling back some of the vinyl with his shoe and plopping himself on the toilet. The bathtub had been completely removed, replaced by a few cement stones which made a border around what could have been a functioning outhouse hole. Pools of dingy water lay atop the tile from where Sue had taken a shower. The sight of his sister's hair wallowing in them like dead fish made him consider bathing in the sink.

Unfortunately, the sink wasn't much better. Kane didn't know that metal could peel, but he guessed it became possible as filth and mold uprooted and disintegrated everything in its path. The state of the bathroom didn't seem to bother Sue, but Kane instinctively checked off another place where shoes would be mandatory. The irony of his own filthy home wasn't lost on him. At least he had a functioning drain. Kane looked around with an odd sense of pride.

After he had finished his business, he tiptoed to the sink, careful to avoid stepping on the sticky flooring. Kane mentally groaned. Only the cold water worked and the mirror had an impenetrable layer of filth on it. There was no way in hell this place was thirty dollars a night. Kane doubted they could charge ten by the looks of it. The A/C was broken, the front door looked to be coming off its hinges, the beds were filled with potholes and lumps. This place was a crack house without the crack. Sleeping outside may not be a bad idea after all.

Wiping away an inch of grime and dust on the mirror, Kane amused himself with the idea the hotel had actually paid Sue to stay here. He was feeling less and less guilt towards her "sacrifice" of paying for his room. Thank god this place was a trash heap.

"My going rate sure as hell wouldn't be thirty a night," he mumbled, skimming away layers of dust with his forearm. All at once, his eyes glanced in the mirror, and he stumbled back, landing ass first on the vinyl with a crunch. "What the hell was that!?" he gasped.

Kane peered around at the dingy bathroom as though it was the mouth of some beast. However, nothing odd lurked in its dingy details. No creeping silence, dripping darkness or the sense of being watched. The walls blistered and flaked away, but that was unrelated to having an episode.

Kane's mind raced. In the mirror, there had been a moving splotch of cloudy darkness which didn't belong. Had it even been real? He'd only caught it for a split second before collapsing backwards. Glancing around himself once more, he slid his hand across the sticky vinyl and shifted his body against the wall.

The bathroom remained unchanged.

The walls, tile and sink were so disgustingly normal it was uncanny. Had he been mistaken and an odd reflection of light had caused an optical illusion? Kane was already on edge after his bout of amnesia, so a drug-less, stress-induced hallucination wasn't beyond the realm of possibility.

After a few deep breaths, he regained his composure and slowly crept upwards to the mirror. "Oh, shit!" he gasped silently. It was still there. How could that be? Everything felt so normal! There were no signs of an episode. He could hear Sue talking to the cats outside the bathroom door and chewing on her food so loudly, he was sure it was audible from space.

The rest of his reflection and body were normal, his hands, his chest, the surrounding walls dimly reflecting in the low light. However, in place of his right eye, there was a hole. It wasn't just any hole, rather a spinning black mass which increased in depth and darkness the closer it moved towards the center. Placing his fingers on the mirror again, his hand moved in front of the abyss. It wasn't an illusion.

"Not an illusion," he said aloud, bobbing his head to the beat of his breath. Careful to avoid direct contact, Kane took a napkin from his pocket and led it to his eye. "Ow!" he gasped as it poked him. To his surprise, whatever spinning wheel of darkness had drawn itself over his face wasn't tactile. Kane dropped the napkin, bit his lip, and led his fingers to the same spot. His fingers touched skin, and he felt blood pumping furiously directly beneath. Beyond that, no strange sensation was perceptible.

Kane stared at his reflection with a growing numbness and curiosity. Was he going into shock? The thing wasn't as alarming as a few moments ago. Sure, it maintained a sense of horror, but the perpetual, smooth circular churn provoked a sense of calm. An odd tingle caused his throat to contract.

"It's not that bad, right?" He chuckled silently, leaning in closer to watch the ever-darkening swirls of black caress the borders of some ethereal pool as they swiveled and swirled towards an unknown focal point beneath its surface. The worming black distortion serenely huffed and puffed, breathing clouds of obsidian miasma into midnight air. Kane shifted in closer and closer, the terror wholly replaced by fascination and wonder, when he heard a loud pop from the sink. "Ah!" he croaked out, leaping backwards as the rusty pipes slid into their original position.

In his head, Kane expected to look up and find the encircling anomaly gone, vanished at the flash of adrenaline and panic. To his bewilderment—and oddly enough, to his relief— it hadn't moved a single iota. Briefly, Kane teased the idea this object was his spirit animal. In the next moment, the octopus would appear once it was done shooting its ink.

"But what if it never leaves?" A tremble shook him from the inside out. What did that mean?

Staring into the onyx coil, he had no idea. Whatever his trickster mind or deranged otherworldly powers had in store for him, he only knew one thing: his singular relief would be meth. *And pronto, Dante, it's hot in here.*

Kane prodded the cloud again with the same lack of effect. Was this the pivotal moment when he would realize he'd finally snapped? That somehow, the insanity had evolved beyond his episodes like a fish flopping on the beach as its gills desperately sucked in air. That metaphor made no sense, and Kane knew it. He was too nervous to think straight.

Kane felt a certain draw to gaze more deeply into the unknown. Wasn't that why he had come here? To get answers? What good would it do him to surrender to mysteries, cower away from chances to finally take a step closer towards the truth? Even if that meant a step closer towards a ledge. *Or edge,* Kane thought sardonically.

With newfound resolve, his hand swung towards the mirror and wiped away the rest of the dirt. He stared for a moment before calling, "Sue?" on a whim. As he spoke, the numbness intensified throughout his body. His throat felt so dry and tight, he instinctively reached towards the sink and took a handful of water. "Ugh," he cringed. It tasted like a lead marinade.

Within seconds, his sister was in the bathroom, mouth crunching on what he imagined to be a biscuit rock.

"What's up?" she asked, crumbs scattering from her mouth to the floor. Kane watched as she peered around the bathroom. "Oh," she said, "you cleaned the mirror. I was wondering how I was going to do my make-up."

In her sparkling green eyes, there wasn't a single hint anything odd was occurring. She was looking at the same thing Kane was, probing its depths with human eyes and processing the information with a human brain. The second he saw her face, however, he knew she was somehow looking past it. Or was she unable to see it? Perhaps it was similar to an autostereogram—one of those pictures where you can only view an image from certain focus points. That was an oversimplification, but Kane had no other explanation.

"Did you need me for something?" Sue mumbled, swallowing the last bit of bread.

"Yeah. I saw a roach." He pointed towards the outhouse hole.

His sister scowled at him, crossing her arms in disapproval. "Oh, really? And what's your point?" she asked gruffly. "I killed five of them in my bed last night, and you don't see me complaining."

With a twinge of disgust, Kane realized that's what last night's rustling was.

"Hey, Sue, I'm not complaining."

"Beggars. Can't. Be. Choosers," she snarked, whipping around and stomping off.

Normally, Kane would have been annoyed at this taut attitude. However, the second she left, his mind was drawn to the mirror and his own reflection once again.

"Finish your odyssey, Odysseus?" His sister was stuffing the last forkful of his eggs melodramatically into her gullet. "I'm not sure when you decided taking forever in bathrooms was a good life choice, but consider this an intervention." Sue glanced at him, clearly annoyed, and took a sip of her coffee with an audible slurp.

"Sorry, Sue," Kane said half-heartedly, glancing over at a small mirror beside the TV. "I'm slowly turning into a sloth in my old age." The whirling darkness was visible in this mirror as well. Kane sighed and shook his head. "Am I going to have to starve this morning?"

His sister was staring at him curiously, deciding whether or not to dig into his odd behavior. "Well," she said, drawing out the "e" until the entire word was a taut string at the point of snapping, "there's more at the front desk. But don't tell her you're my brother," she added with a wink.

Now it was Kane's turn to give his sister a suspicious look. "Sue, why can't I tell her I'm your brother?"

"Let's just say this place is cheaper than the mud on dirt's shoes. They charge extra for additional occupants."

"Ugh," Kane moaned, rubbing his face and giving a slight start as his hand brushed by his right eye.

"Unless they're married. I could have told them you were my kid, but I don't think that would have worked out."

"Sue," Kane began, weighing telling her how disgusting he found this place and the idea of pretending to be her husband. "What type of hotel did you book us?"

"Hey, now." The threatening tone from before had returned. "It wasn't that this one was the cheapest, you know. You think I want to stay somewhere I can shit and shower at the same time?" This made Kane chuckle. She wasn't as blind as he'd thought. "Listen up, big bro, this was literally: The. Last. Room. In. Town. I checked everywhere. Called. Websites. Booking sites. There was zilch, ok. So, back off."

At once, Kane understood. This wasn't some rash decision. Well, not completely rash. She truly had tried to find them somewhere better. That made this hotel the best place in Lunar City. Kane was unwilling to divulge he would rather have camped under a bridge for a week.

"Sorry, Sue," he said with honest remorse.

His sister looked at him with a renewed sense of pity. "It's ok. I'm sorry I ate your food." She glanced at her feet for a moment. "Good thing we have the same last name, or I don't think we could have pulled it off."

"And it's a good thing we're not twins." Kane heard his stomach growl and opened the front door. "Be back in a bit."

. . .

The front desk was better than Kane expected: retro with a thin veneer of class. Of course, the shabbiness remained, but the floor, wall and counter were spotless. Even the plastic plants were entirely void of dust. He should request that whoever cleaned here be put on duty in their room. It was worth a shot, although he doubted anything less than TNT would be sufficient to muck out the filth.

The fifties style persisted here as well, although there were quite a few haphazard moon paraphernalia scattered across the walls. Kane was surprised to find a paper mache astronaut guarding a small path, which led to a smaller hovel where the complimentary breakfast was kept. Clearly, it had been placed there to dissuade patrons from entering.

Kane peered around, looking for either whoever was working at this hour or a way to signal them. No bell, no phone, no buzzer—just a crude life-size pinata of Buzz Aldrin extending his flag hand and bouncing for what the people of this town must consider a three-star buffet. He wondered if the cardboard was stuffed with candy. By the looks of it, the entire thing could have as easily been a life-size voodoo doll, or some effigy made by an overzealous stalker.

The smells emanating from behind the figure were less than appetizing, but hunger was the best spice. Kane's mouth filled with saliva while he frantically looked for a way to get past the object without tipping it over.

He'd have to move it to the side. Right as his hand grasped the figure's buttocks, the other wrapped around its waist, a woman's voice croaked from behind the counter. "Can I help you, sir?"

CHAPTER

THIRTEEN

"Can I help you, sir?"

The *sir* wasn't part of the question. Kane's face took on a shade of moon-white as he gingerly peeled one hand off Buzz and turned around.

"Just getting some food," he stammered towards a mousey little woman with tattoos and piercings sprinkling her gaunt face and neck.

"Really?" she whipped her response back. "Is that all you were getting?" Kane's pale-moon-face turned sun-red as his other hand slipped off Buzz's cardboard buttock.

"Nope. Just the food."

An odd smile danced across her milk chocolate eyes. "I'm pretty sure that thing weighs a total of five pounds. Even I can move it."

Kane stared at her deeply, perplexed by the sudden coquettish tone. Even as their eyes met, she didn't flinch or avert her gaze.

"See something you want?" Her grin widened.

Mousey wasn't quite the right word. Her face was sharp,

hawkish with thin creases working their way up her cheek-bones like the run of a bow. Her jagged eyes were oddly misplaced and accentuated the disproportion of her features. If God was Picasso, this would have been the perfect specimen. It wasn't to say she was unattractive; rather, the odd proportions gave her an exotic mystique and allure. And she was smiling at Kane, a rare occurrence.

It was difficult to tell if she was thin from hunger, sickness or genetics. Her face was lean, delicate but with an odd haggard aura that was as imbalanced as the rest of her appearance. She was dressed in odd mixtures of gray and black, akin to spilled ink on cement or steel cast in onyx. Although it was going to be ninety degrees today, her sleeves traveled to her wrists before culminating in knit gloves. She must be burning up.

Her smile, plastered to her face, was starting to make Kane feel uncomfortable. "I should grab some food." With a gentle heave, he moved the paper-tiger-bouncer to the side.

"Yeah, you should." Her voice echoed behind him, somehow more flirtatious than before.

Kane wasn't in the habit of getting talked to by women and definitely not since losing his job and sinking into the depths of slob-dom. Years earlier, Molly had made the first move and approached him aggressively and with purpose. Who could say why, although at the time Kane had been fairly well off and wasn't dressed like someone living in their parent's closet. Was he only a buffet dish? An amusing pot of nondescript food you grab moving through life's line?

Even though he was wearing his last bit of clean clothes, his hair was unkempt and he hadn't brushed his teeth in over two days. His weight had fluctuated wildly, so his shirt was too baggy and his pants were too tight. They were washed, but Kane knew there was more than one visible stain and a few holes where the pipe had slipped through his fingers and burned his shirt. If she was looking for a tip, the joke was on her. He didn't have any money.

"Well, if you need anything. Really. *Anything*. Don't hesitate to call." His back was still turned to her as he nervously piled mountains of disgusting eggs on his plate. "And don't worry, I got you," she said, and this time the coquet overtones were replaced by an odd camaraderie. She was talking to Kane like she had known him his whole life. Like she was a fellow soldier knee deep in battle or a best friend before a bar brawl. Her tone reminded him of his dealer.

"Wait," he mouthed breathlessly as her odd appearance caused him to do a mental double take. He knew tons of junkies who dressed normally and tons of sober people who were bathed in piercings and tattoos. Covering her arms with those sleeves in the dead of summer was curious, though.

There was a small mirror behind the coffee station. As Kane looked into it and the churning black mass, he made a mental note. He'd return here soon. If she was his ticket to drug-induced freedom, he'd find out. Had to find out.

"Well, we can't leave them in the motel!" Sue was seconds away from a meltdown, but Kane refused to give in.

"And why not?"

"Have you seen the roaches here? They'll eat my poor little *Muff-twins* alive."

"Muff-twins?" Even with their anger reaching critical levels, Kane laughed. How the hell did she come up with this crap?

Clearly not amused, Sue swiped at him with a closed fist. "Hey, hey, hey, now!"

He hopped beyond her reach.

With his hands in the air in a conciliatory posture, he countered with, "Sorry, it caught me off guard."

In an instant, his sister was inching closer, hand cocked to her side and ready to strike.

"Sue, listen. Weren't you the one who said this place is fine? If the cats were going to be eaten, it would have happened last night."

"No," she responded sharply, "because I would have heard them meowing."

Kane was retreating two inches for each inch Sue moved in. Unfortunately, he was only a few feet from the wall and rapidly running out of space. "Can't we see if the front desk will take them in for the day? If we lug them around with us, we'll have to leave them in the car. It's supposed to be ninety-five later."

This caused Sue to pause. Since it was only March, and the Chicago freeze had yet to thaw, his sister hadn't thought there would be such a drastic temperature swing in the desert. He imagined her plan was to haul them around in the backseat and leave them inside as they went from place to place. Same careless Sue.

But honestly, Kane could care less if the Muff-twins lived or died. He was more concerned with avoiding a single second more with the unholy vermin, especially considering the new issue with his eye. Kane had yet to determine what to make of the cats, but he knew being locked away with the two purring triggers couldn't be good for his mental health.

"Sue, let's at least look for a daycare or—"

"And who's gonna pay for that?" she barked as a red struck her cheeks. "You, Mr. Forgetful?"

Ouch. Even though he deserved it, the comment stung. Because of his lie, his sister had been forced to pay for everything from the hotels to food. Even worse, she was happy to do it. Of course, the actual problem was that Kane had no intention of paying her back. Sue's kindness was a one way street, and he deserved all the nasty comments she could ever make.

But Kane still cringed as her words stung him with guilt and remorse. He had been doing so well before his brother died —job, a house, money, unbroken toys. Sue's comment was a painful reminder of how far he'd sunk.

"I guess not," he said with a frown, hiding how deeply her words had cut him.

"Exactly, you guess not." Putting her hand on her hips, she followed with, "They're my cats, so here's what we're doing: we're gonna take them, park in the shade, roll down the windows and if need be leave the car running with the A/C on."

What a terrible plan. Kane smiled weakly.

"What, you have something to add?" Sue shot him a look that said: Your answer is *no.*

In reality, she didn't have to tell him anything. Kane's answer was already going to be a *no.* Per usual, Sue was a grinding stone, and he was simply too worn down to continue arguing.

With how well she'd been treating him since he'd reemerged into her life, Kane truly had thought she'd changed. She'd even apologized. Sue—apologizing! But if being bound together for hours on end had shown him anything about his sister, it was how much of her old self remained. Although, if he was honest with himself, he didn't mind it much. This was merely another comfortably warm blanket to wrap himself in: Sue treating him the same way his father had.

After a quick packing session, Sue and Kane departed for *Moon Mountain.* To his surprise, even more people were roaming the streets than the previous night. Streams of human crowds swarmed the town like a roach nest had been shattered on asphalt. The local infrastructure was overwhelmed as people crammed into the few existing buses or had to wait in football field sized lines to enter a fast food joint or a grocery store. Was this a recent development as more people made the pilgrimage to see Tim's Edge? If the influx didn't stop, Kane was sure Lunar City was a few short days away from becoming a filthy shanty town. Dozens of delivery trucks forced their way across the roads amidst the backdrop of an increasing number of make-shift stands peddling their wares.

"Someone has to make money off this," Kane mumbled.

"Reminds me of Burning Man," Sue said, petting a cat which had positioned itself on her lap.

"Burning Man?"

"Yeah, you know, that festival in the desert where they build an entire town for a few weeks, burn effigies of different things and tear it down before repeating it the next year."

Kane looked around and wondered what would burn before being torn down. Dozens of RVs were pulled over on dirt roads, and a few tents in the park were more grandiose than Kane would have expected for a quick camping trip. "You might be right, but that sounds insane."

Sue shrugged. "Makes a lot more sense once you've taken a crap ton of drugs."

Kane swallowed heavily. "Excuse me?"

"Well, there's a lot of freedom in the middle of nowhere. After a few days, the entire thing morphs into a gigantic psychedelic rager."

Kane swallowed again, but his throat was tight and dry. He quietly promised himself he'd become an active Burning Man attendee in the future. "Where are we headed, Sue?" At the word *drugs*, Kane visibly shook and forced his mind to focus on something—*anything*—else. Luckily, his sister was gawking at the crowd of people and didn't notice.

"Tim's Edge," she muttered.

"What? Now!?"

Kane felt the earlier shiver ripple up his spine.

"Yeah, why not?" Sue continued. "That's why we're here."

"Sure, I mean." With a quick glance to the side, he saw Moon Mountain jutting upwards from the landscape. It didn't look like a moon; it looked like a claw.

"I was thinking we'd take some time to settle in or whatever."

Kane had no idea what that meant: settle in. Or whatever. They weren't here for a spa day; they were here to see Tim's Edge. Why he hadn't expected his passionate sister to make a beeline for their singular goal was silly. Worse, deluded. Even so, Kane couldn't shake the desire to procrastinate.

Obviously, they would go to Moon Mountain eventually—hell, it was even the right thing to do—but at the same time, he desperately clambered onto delaying the inevitable. It was as if he had been standing at the bottom of a ravine, watching reality career at him like a distant avalanche. At first, it had been meaningless, theoretical. Then a point was reached where the colossal wave of ice and snow broke through his imagination and tumbled into life-threatening significance.

"Settle in?" his sister asked slowly, drawing in the words with flared nostrils, "or whatever."

"Or whatever," Kane repeated, doubling down in a tenuous plea for mercy.

His sister turned onto Main Street, ignoring his begging eyes. They had driven past a couple of crossings when she suddenly asked, "And what does *whatever* mean to you?"

Relieved, Kane blurted out a series of suggestions.

"Breakfast, maybe."

"We already ate that."

"Brunch!" he replied, causing his sister to frown.

"Ok, well, what about a drink?" The prospect of seeing Tim's Edge sober was as appetizing as food served right off their hotel room floor.

"Kane, it's eight thirty in the morning."

"Actually, it's closer to eight forty-five." At this, his sister's hand flung over and thwapped against his shoulder. The cat on Sue's lap hissed and sprung into the back seat.

"Ow!" Kane rubbed his arm.

"Spare the rod." His sister smirked.

"Can we at least get some water bottles?" And in one final act of desperation, he added, "For the cats." If his sister didn't bite at this, he was at a loss. He couldn't very well recommend they return to Chicago, although that was his preferred option.

"Nice try. There's two in the glovebox."

Kane moaned as Sue pulled onto the highway. Moon Mountain appeared even sharper from this angle.

CHAPTER
FOURTEEN

"It's weird there's no news, right?" Kane was fumbling with the old radio dial, twisting it right and left. They had been on the road for close to an hour and Kane had come to terms with the fact that there was no stopping the freight train that was Suzannah. They were going to see Tim's Edge today, come hell or high water.

You want to know how to stop a giant? Kane recalled his father asking him before a little league game. The answer hadn't been a stone, a sling or a herculean throwing arm. *If you wanna stop a giant, get God on your side,* his father had continued with that pompous smile Kane knew all too well.

"Thanks, Dad," Kane mumbled, sure that only God could stop his sister. Although, since he didn't believe he existed, it was gonna be tough to pull him off the bench.

"What do you mean, no news. Didn't you see that article I sent you on how Tim's Edge might be a parallel universe?"

Kane acknowledged her question with a nod, remembering his terror as she fumbled with her phone to send him the link while driving twenty miles per hour over the speed limit.

"But I don't mean analysis news. I mean real news. Updates, new events, new footage. Anything."

With a slight tilt of her head, Sue visibly processed Kane's words.

"I thought after three and a half days, the media would have more than days old info."

"Mmmph." His sister pursed her lips. "That is odd."

"You think it's the government?" Kane paused. "Like, censorship or a complete information blackout?"

"Or aliens, or ghosts, or shady men in black." Sue was unamused. "Whatever it is, we'll find out soon enough."

Even as she said it, Kane could tell there was a flicker of doubt. If some nefarious entity was behind the lacking coverage, getting in to see Tim's Edge may not only prove impossible but dangerous as well. The fact that neither of them had considered this until this very moment was baffling. Goes to show a powdered nose and a powder keg don't make a good team.

Flipping from station to station, Kane finally landed on a local broadcast. The voice was scratchy, covered in static and stupendously monotone.

"And the town council has also imposed a curfew on the inbound highways to stem the rampant increase in newcomers. Additionally, a petition was recently sent to the county to request increased police funding and extra deputies to help deal with the uptick in petty crime."

Kane's ears perked up. A local station would know more. If anyone was in tune with the rumor mill, it would be them. Hopefully, this wasn't being censored as well.

. . .

"And in more news—"

Here it was. Kane leaned in closer to the old speakers in the dashboard.

"Your local Roadrunners have made the single A playoffs and are headed to Phoenix for the tournament. If you are interested in attending, there's—"

"Roadrunners?" Kane mumbled.

"It's the local high school basketball team," Sue replied as if it were the most obvious thing in the world.

How could she know that information? Before he had a chance to ask, Sue suddenly shot her finger in the air and exclaimed, "Oh, look Kane, a deer!"

"A deer?" he repeated slowly. "Where?"

"Over there!" With a squint, Kane followed Sue's outstretched hand to the right. "By those flowers!" Her finger wagged frantically. *What a child.* Kane's face bunched into a slight cringe.

Sue must have believed there were guidance lasers bursting from her fingertips as she chopped towards the general area of the creature with an increasing flurry of thrusts. In reality, her overly boisterous gesturing was as useful as spitting in the direction. At least with spitting, she wouldn't be so dangerously close to thwapping him in the face.

All he saw was high desert, with a few stubby trees and sickly-looking shrubs mottling the brown dirt like patches of mangy fur.

"Where the hell are you?" Kane whispered, hiding his own

childlike excitement. Then, he spotted it moments before it whizzed by. However, its passing speed was meaningless. As Kane glanced at it, time slowed into infinitesimal pieces, breaking apart and scattering before their hovering descent.

He hadn't only caught sight of the deer. He had glanced into its eyes—hollow, dark, rotating and worming with an obsidian cloud of pitch black dust. It was eating some odd-looking flowers: drooping, ashy-green petals streaked with coal gray.

Whooosh! It hurled past and Kane had to fling himself around to catch a final glance.

"Did you see it!?" His sister's hand was centimeters from his nose. She had stopped watching the road and was twisted around looking through the rear window

Kane was straining his neck backwards as well, although his childlike excitement had morphed into bewilderment. There was no way he had imagined that, right? The onyx abyss, the wriggling clouds of torn reality worming into an inverted paradox of contrasting antithesis.

Even as his mind concentrated on the memory, the image blurred. It had been a real deer, right? The flower had been a normal shrub: Bambi's brunch in an acrid wasteland. Soon, the memory was overlaid by images of what an actual deer should be: black, swirling eyes replaced with adorable charcoal stones. What about the onyx colored flower? The dark steel petals were simply sheets of discarded metal with greenery growing in between them. Deer did have black eyes, right?

Likely, he'd imagined the entire experience. His mind had exaggerated and bent what he saw to make sense of what was happening to his own body. Kane instinctively assumed the tone of his therapist: *Your deep subconscious panic has overlaid perceived physical reality with your darkest fears.*

"Prick," Kane muttered. At this point, the memory of the

creature had faded. He was mistaken, no doubt. He had only seen it for a second, not even a second, and so who could say if the image had been real or not?

He knew if he caught one final glimpse of the deer, it would mean looking in the rearview mirror. If he did that, he would see his own face, his own shroud of inexplicable mystery. His universe was sinking, and it was all Kane could do to shovel water overboard to keep it afloat. Of course, there was the option of asking his sister for help, but that meant he would trap her on the boat with him. Did he actually want that?

Glancing over towards Sue, he knew there was another option: float. Ignore the water pooling around him, ignore the call of the hungry gulls from above, ignore the rushing wind and darkening sky and simply lay down. His body would be gently carried away by the rising water and who could say where he would land? Maybe at the bottom of the ocean. At this thought, the previous numbness ballooned and encased his whole body. Just float. This was entirely his problem, and none of it was too serious. He meant to touch his face, assure himself the patch of darkness either didn't exist or posed no danger. Instead, he shut his eyes and drifted into a dreamless sleep.

"You have got to be kidding me!"

Kane was yanked awake and instinctually thrust his arms forward in defense. "Wha-what!?" With a sudden surge of adrenaline, he glanced around himself, expecting to see dark, rolling clouds which signaled the end of the world.

"Look at this." His sister finished her sentence by swiping her hand forward. In front of them, a line of cars snaked into the distance. Not only in their lane either. Clearly, someone had become frustrated with the wait and pulled into oncoming traffic. A large swath of followers had mimicked this behavior and created an impressive jam on both sides of the road. Each lane was so crowded, Kane felt like they had purchased a one-way ticket into a sardine can. How the hell were they going to return? Kane glanced at the progressively steep incline which led to a mountain on his right. Could Sue's car ascend that grade of monster slope?

"Oh man, it must go on for miles," Kane whispered. He grabbed his phone and opened the maps application. "Ten and a half miles. J-eee-ee-ze." Kane internally chuckled as he imagined this being the reason why no updates had appeared on the news: the reporters couldn't even make it to the site.

How long had this line been growing? Judging by the number of people going car to car to sell water and food, and the faces of their patrons, it had been a while. There were also several abandoned cars positioned directly beyond the road. Kane mused that, rather than deserting their car to finish the pilgrimage by foot, they'd been raptured—plucked from the Earth like an unwanted weed. Or eaten by a deer.

Sue watched the scene in silence, her face turning beet red. It was so bunched up, Kane worried it may collapse in on itself. Without warning, Kane felt the car jerk as his sister flipped the turn signal on, put the car into low gear and veered off to the right.

"Oh, shit!" Kane grabbed the handle above his head and pressed his body into the seat as Sue's bumper struck the bottom of the hill. Kane clenched the door handle and held his breath as the car worked its way up.

"Sue, Sue, uh, Sue." Kane jostled around as the wheels bashed into rocks and shrubs. The engine gave off a menacing rumble as it strained under the unexpected load and Kane hoped they wouldn't have to wander forty years through the desert to make it home. Behind them, the cats hissed and clung to the seat's fabric in a hopeless attempt to avoid becoming furry ping-pong balls.

Several cars had attempted to follow, but didn't realize that Sue's success wasn't achieved by human will and determination. His sister's car was an old Subaru, and the four-wheel-drive was the only thing keeping them from digging their own grave in an epic stall. None of the cars who followed in their wake looked to have similar capabilities, however, and after a few seconds they had their wheels buried in the dirt and spitting rocks.

"Fu-!" Kane yelled as they neared the crest of the hill and vaulted over a small craggy depression.

Sue didn't reply. At least, not verbally. She merely swiveled her head around and gave him a deranged smile like she was a psycho lover driving them off a cliff.

Kane nearly slammed his head on the dash as the roller coaster came to a sudden halt. The car lunged over the top and landed precariously on a semi-flat surface. To Kane's utter horror, the other side didn't slope in the same smooth decline; rather, it was a hundred foot cliff plunging into jagged rocks below.

"Holy shit, another few yards and we would have been toast." Burnt toast. Or a smashed piñata.

The cats had stopped hissing and instead cowered together in a corner; claws dug into the cushion in preparation for the next horror-coaster. Sue breathed rapidly, her eyes slightly glazed as she lifted her foot off the brake pedal. What she had done had been nothing short of insane, even for her. He watched that realization work its way across her face. Kane didn't dare question her motives. His sister's eyes had squinted in a look of determination. If Kane spoke up, he was sure his questions would be assessed as threats. Instead, he took a sharp breath and asked, "That way?"

. . .

They had both remained silent for the rest of the ride. There were things to discuss: how they would get in to see Tim's Edge, how they would get back, how far they could travel atop this crest. As Sue swung the wheel back and forth, gingerly working her way around stubby pines and tufts of underbrush, it was apparent that neither of them wanted any break in concentration. Hills morphed into hills before finally ending in another sheer drop and a steep decline leading to the highway. Sue leisurely pulled over under a tall pine tree and shut off the engine.

"Kane," she said, causing him a start.

"What, end of the line?" he retorted, once again opening the map application on his phone. The signal was bad here, even worse than before. It was no wonder; they were deep in the boonies. Moon Mountain had looked so close when they had left town, but Kane could see it remained a couple of miles away. To his chagrin, the sun was creeping its way over the hill like spilled fire, and Kane knew it was going to get real hot real soon. Contemplating walking in those conditions made him wish they had plunged over the cliff.

"2.2 Miles," Kane said, looking at a squiggly line the map had drawn in an attempt to find a route off the hill." The thing was probably as confused as he was.

With a rush of energy, Sue threw open the door and yelled, "The Moon Mountain Ferry has docked! Please collect your belongings and make your way towards the exit!" And with this, she practically exploded from the car, trompsing around the area and performing unnecessary stretches.

"2.2 Miles isn't too bad." Kane stretched a bit as well as he stood up from his own seat, finding a tree to lean against in a fight to not to collapse. "You ready to get walking?"

Sue came around the car, opened the trunk and grabbed an object from the inside. Kane couldn't see what it was, but he heard a rattling impact as it struck the ground. Then, another object was removed with the same metallic rattling. An uneasy feeling worked its way up his gut.

"Sue, we're leaving those cats here, right?"

As the words left his lips, Sue stepped around the car, two small wire frame pet carriers in hand. Where the hell did she get those? Did she make a run to the local vet before he woke up? They were cheap, heavy and although much sturdier than her small plastic one, clearly not intended for long hauls. With a morbid curiosity, Kane wondered if Sue employed a similar cage during her animal Green Mile.

"Uh, obviously not," his sister shot back, throwing one at his feet. "What if there are bears around?"

Kane's imagination flickered to an image of a slumbering horror bursting from the flesh of Muffinz to devour the bear whole. "I'd be more worried about the deer."

His sister shot him a glance which swayed between confusion and reproach before shaking her head and opening the car's back door. Although he wasn't sure how, the cat's were both impeccably trained and darted into the open cages. Kane was sure the backseat was thankful to be rid of them.

"Ok, let's go," Sue said, yanking one of the carriers upwards and starting down the hill with a huff.

CHAPTER

FIFTEEN

UNDER NORMAL CIRCUMSTANCES, DESCENDING A HILL OF THIS GRADE would have been a cake walk. To be fair, it still was, only the cake and icing were both made of shit—and that of the quicksand variety. Carrying Muffins, or Muffinz, lent this trek a feeling more akin to a descent off Everest. Even worse, if that was possible, the sun beat down upon them until little beads of sweat forcibly worked their way into Kane's eyes and caused him to squint uncontrollably.

"Shit!" he yelped at a menacing hiss from beneath a pile of rocks. He nearly lost his balance while stepping away and swung his body around to avoid chucking one of the Mufftwins down the rest of the hill. Only sheer willpower, and the obvious truth that his sister would gut him alive, gave him the wherewithal to fling a leg forward and halt his fall.

Sue was struggling with her cage as well and continually heaved it upwards so it didn't drag on the ground. The cage was so large compared to her petite frame, it looked like an oversized-clown purse. If Kane was in a better mood, he would have gone over and helped. Watching her struggle was so satisfying, though. If he was lucky, she'd be the first one to lose her balance and send one of the creatures flying into the great, horrible beyond.

In true anti-climactic form, both he and Sue made it to the bottom safely. What Kane believed to be a menacing final decline revealed itself to be a gentle sway into the road. After making it to the bottom, he dropped the carrier and fell onto his knees.

"I'm alive!" He panted towards his sister. Sue didn't concern herself with his grumbling, however, and wordlessly trudged forward, leaving Kane to cringe alone at the thought of the hike back up.

"Monster," he groaned, rubbing his arm gently before wrenching the cage upwards and scurrying after her.

As they reached the road, Kane saw people inside and outside their cars staring towards them in awe. It was as if they believed themselves witnesses of Zarathustra awakening from his long slumber to descend the mountain. Kane also spotted more than a few small hands pointing at them from behind tinted windows.

"These people brought their kids?" He felt a sickly lump work itself into his throat. What kind of monsters would bring children somewhere like this? The answer lay in multiple stickers dotting the bumpers of most vehicles: *Lamb of God, Modern Miracles, Forseeing is Believing.*

"The religious kind," he muttered, grasping the cage more firmly. How close had his sister gotten towards this fervent madness? The lump in his throat transformed into a boulder.

At this proximity to Moon Mountain, Kane saw dozens of patrolling vendors peddling their wares car to car. Food, water, snacks, gasoline. Kane watched as an older man in a seemingly older pickup held out twenty dollars in exchange for a small red can of gas. How long had these people been here? Why couldn't they walk to the mountain?

"Staying overnight?" Kane nearly toppled over as a booming voice erupted from his left. "Staying into the apocalypse?" Kane turned to find a large, red-haired man maneuvering through the cars with a wheelbarrow filled with tents. The man was smiling; his light-brown locks, greasy with sweat, were plastered to a freckled forehead which rose from prominent onyx eyes and a delicate yet pronounced jawbone.

Into the apocalypse, Kane mentally parroted the man but found himself unable to mirror his impossibly low baritone. When had finding Tim's Edge equated to the end of the world?

"You there!" The tent-man's deep voice thundered. The cats hissed, but Kane pretended he hadn't heard.

"Oh no." He moaned as Sue turned around to face the shrewd merchant head-on.

"Sue, ignore him." Kane went to grab his sister's arm but found her out of reach. "We're almost there."

"Kane, we don't even know what *there* means. Look at this place; it's a madhouse. Don't you want to know what we're getting ourselves into?"

With a bit of shock, Kane withdrew his outstretched hand. Her comment was so out of place, it caused him to freeze. Their roles weren't supposed to follow this pattern. He should have been the one to recommend caution while Sue haphazardly marched forward without a plan.

But honestly, if she was so worried, why had she left town without asking around or plunged them into danger at the first literal roadblock?

"Weirdo." Kane watched Sue saunter away as she waved at the grinning merchant.

"I don't even know you anymore," he meant to say but fell

silent. It was as if he were staring at a painting, squinting to see the artist's original sketch through layers and layers of color. Could a year really change a person so drastically? Or had he never actually known her?

Kane wondered if that's why they had been fighting more than usual: he treated her as though she were the same person even though she had obviously grown. Grown and left him behind. Kane licked his lips, walked towards his sister, and ignored a sudden feeling of loneliness.

"Six hundred dollars?" Sue's hearty laughs didn't dissuade the merchant's smile. It was greedy, haughty, but held a tender flirtatiousness.

"I know, it's crazy right? I purchased these tents at Wal-Mart for less than fifty dollars a pop." He pushed his wheelbarrow farther to the side of the road and leaned against it. "But it's extremely expensive to schlepp them here, and it would be a miracle to find any stock left in a three hundred mile radius."

"But who the hell has six hundred dollars in cash? I doubt any of these people"—his sister made a broad sweep of her hand—"thought they'd be here for more than a day."

"True," the tent-man responded, reaching inside his cart and fumbling around. "But you'd be surprised how many of them don't expect to leave. Besides"—he finished retrieving a small device with a long antenna attached—"you could always pay by card." His grin was ear to ear, stretching across his face and exposing overly-white teeth. The man was sketchy, but Sue was smiling in reply. Was she enjoying this guy's company? Kane was so uncomfortable, he forced himself into the conversation.

"What do you mean, they don't expect to leave?" He wasn't sure if the man actually hoped to make a sale or was simply filling time before moving on, but either way, his openness and ever widening smile aroused a wariness in Kane.

"Take that car, for example." He pointed towards one with kids inside." They believe Tim's Edge is the mouth of God and will whisper secrets only to nearby children before closing forever.

Mouth of God? Whisper secrets to children? Kane felt his back tighten and neck hair prickle.

"The man in that car"—this time his finger was pointed at the man in the pickup who they'd seen purchase the gas canister—"believes that it's an entrance to heaven kept secret by the government for years. Apparently, right before the rich and famous die, they send them here to pass through without suffering."

"But the mining company only found it a few days ago. That's insane!" Kane responded with disgust.

"Insane?" The man's grin stretched farther. "He bought one of my fine tents, so he couldn't be that crazy!" Kane wasn't amused. He was getting as restless as the caged cats who meowed in unison. They clearly liked the man as little as he did.

It was sickening. Mouth of God, gate to heaven—where the hell did people come up with this shit? The worst part was: these theories held as much weight as any other idea, and that was a problem. If this wasn't in his head, aliens, or the government—if it was spiritual or supernatural—what did that mean for him? For his life?

The past few days had flown by so fast, Kane hadn't had the time to consider what Tim's Edge might actually be. He had been so wrapped up in his drugs, in his tenuous relationship with his sister, leaving town and his own mental issues that secondary concerns had been relegated to a dark corner of his mind. Of course, he knew the meaning of Tim's Edge was out there—hell, they were headed right for it—but its essence and the myriad of implications had yet to be explored. If he was honest with himself, they were better left that way—not that he could drum up enough emotional stability to process them in any case.

But whatever was happening, mouths of God and gates to the afterlife were insane. That he knew.

Right?

Sue was pensive and didn't partake in the guffaws of the tent-man. Her face was serious, her brow furrowed and her lips pursed. As Kane looked at her, he realized his fear of Tim's Edge paled in comparison to the idea his sister may buy into one of those crazy theories. A more mature person would have made a mental note to discuss it with her later. But Kane knew broaching the topic of his sister's beliefs meant begging to be proselytized Auto-da-fé style. He should leave it alone. She'd mention it anyway.

"I think we're good without your tents, Ezra." His sister gave the man an awkward wink before whipping her cage in a circle and causing a feline shriek. "Maybe we'll see each other later." Sue grabbed Kane's arm, spun him around and dragged him along in the opposite direction.

"Hopefully, Suzannah. It was delightful to meet you." Kane heard the man chuckle. "Perhaps we'll see each other in the eye of nothing."

The eye of nothing—that's what Tim had said in the last part of his message. Had he heard that right? Kane frantically glanced over his shoulder against the forceful tugs of his sister. The tent-man had vanished—vaporized by words spoken from the mouth of an angry god or raptured to heaven. Or he was just making his way through the cars.

CHAPTER
SIXTEEN

"No way," Kane mouthed, placing the cage on the ground and collapsing next to it. Most of their journey had been filled with the impossible, the unlikely and the absurd, but what now lay before them was, "insanity," he huffed out.

Sue slowed her gait and plopped herself beside him. Her mouth was open, her brow furled as she stared forward. Exhaustion was an understatement. They had traversed through a miles-long line of cars only to find themselves facing a gigantic parking lot filled to the brim with even more. Kane grimaced at the thought of hoisting the cage into the air as he squeezed through.

"There are hundreds of them." Kane rubbed his strained arm muscles and felt the blood return.

Moon Mountain was so close, he could see gigantic cement openings, surrounded by piles of tailings, plunging into the mountainside. Large vehicles buzzed around, racing back and forth through herds of workers in a grand corporate ballet. The miners were distant enough to appear as little specks—ants frantically searching for twigs, leaves and discarded candy to feed their queen. This wasn't what left Kane and his sister aghast, however.

Thousands of cars were pulled off the road, building a huge parking lot that spanned the hills to their right and across the acrid wasteland to their left. The sheer quantity of vehicles crammed next to each other could have easily made each a mosaic tile spanning the whole of the Sistine Chapel. Where the cars stopped, a few hundred meters from a large gate surrounding the mine, thousands of people, tens of thousands, were interwoven like colorful fibers of a carpet strewn across the caliche dirt and sand. Each was swaying gently, some with raised fists, yelling curses, pleas or blessings at a dozen guards set to hold the masses at bay at the gate. For Kane, the crowd's cacophony held the energy of an uprising.

"How the hell are we going to make it inside?" Kane muttered towards his sister who stared into the crowd and aggressively rubbed her forehead. With each passing minute, newcomers arrived and added to the overflowing masses which already threatened to spill atop the cars and into the desert around the mountain.

Sue's mouth opened and closed a few times before weakly uttering, "This is why we should have bought tents."

Kane stared at her in disbelief. "Sue, if this gets much worse, we'll need an entire settlement."

Without so much as a grunt in reply, Sue heaved the cage upwards and ventured forth into the churning mass of bodies. The cat dropped flat to avoid getting jostled and Kane couldn't help but grin.

Making their way forward proved more challenging than even Kane expected. The cages kept bumping into people while the Muff-twins swiped through the bars at the children who scampered towards them for a pet. At one point, he had to lift the carrier above his head to avoid a crowd of adolescents who had gathered around.

"We just wants to pet 'em!" a little girl screeched, jumping and waving her hands threateningly towards Kane's head. The Muff-twins were obviously a balm to the tension around them. Although the parents arrived after a few moments to yank their kids away,

Kane lashed out at the complete lack of apology. "No, it's fine. We weren't bothered at all."

A few meters later, the crowd became so thick, Kane wished he were born Moses instead of a worthless drug addict. This would allow him to part this sea of people instead of feeling bad about drowning in it. Chiseling a "ye shall not gather in crowds of more than a hundred" would also make a great commandment.

"The Bible says: Thou shalt not kill," he recalled his father proclaiming upon hitting a complete stall on the Kennedy Expressway. "But it doesn't say anything about maiming."

But Kane wasn't Moses, Sue wasn't Zipporah, and this crowd, teeming and turbulent as it may be, was no sea. If it was, Kane would settle to simply walk atop it rather than perform some pompous display of supernatural might. Even being heaved forward mosh pit style would have been more than adequate.

This close to the gate, the crowd was thick and tight, strung and laced together. Each person was pressed so hard into their neighbor, they may have well been one continuous person. The worst part was, they were swaying in unison, screaming at the guards across the fence and pumping their fists in righteous anger. More than once, Kane had to duck as an elbow flung itself towards him. Man, this was awful. Was there really no other way through?

Sue had disappeared into the crowd, although Kane knew

she couldn't be but a few dozen feet ahead of him. Obviously, her petite frame had made moving through this tumult much easier. With a sense of caution, he peeled back person after person to make even a few feet of headway. Each time he touched someone, he worried they'd turn around and punch him instead of the air. At least if that happened, he could justify getting the hell out of here. No luck.

Right as Kane thought he'd have to drop his cat cargo to move forward, a ruckus flared up a few dozen meters to his right. Kane had completely lost sight of Sue and grew tense at the thought it could take him hours to find her. He could yell, but his voice would be drowned out. Should he head toward the main road and look for her? Although he twisted his body and anchored his feet to turn around, he found himself being shoved and thrust forward. Muffins(z) must have sensed the anxious helplessness of his chauffeur as it hissed and swatted through the bars with each jostle.

"Why don't you drop dead like your better half," an annoyed Kane growled towards the cat.

The heightened cries were muffled by the reverb of the crowd, but Kane still heard more than a few f-bombs, shouts of pain and calls for help. Although he struggled against the current of the group, he eventually found himself front and center to a large clearing. Was Moses here? Kane clutched the cage tighter and stepped into the parted crowd.

At first, the scene appeared normal. A small outcropping of rocks was visible in the center, and five or six people were either sitting or laying atop. To the side, a few large signs and cardboard cutouts were face down in the dirt. Several were crushed and splintered, with tears crisscrossing their sunbaked edges. Surrounding the group, a dozen or so men and women held glinting objects similar to oversized candy bars. Kane couldn't determine what they were but saw they were pointed at those prostrated atop the rocks.

"What the hell is going on here?" he said to himself and stepped a little farther forward. Suddenly, a few of the men with the glinting objects charged forward, grabbed several signs on the ground and swung them around with gusto. Simultaneously, their compatriots pointed the glinting objects into the air.

"Oh shit," He realized they weren't holding gigantic three musketeer bars, but menacing-looking handguns.

Kane recoiled as a few of them fired into the sky, screaming at the crowd to stay away. The cat whipped back and forth, spooked by the loud bangs, and Kane struggled to keep hold of the cage.

"We're gonna execute these worthless heathens!" One of the berserkers with a sign had reached the rocks and was beating a cowering man with such intensity that he may as well have been full of candy. Kane had no intention of staying. Crazy people and their victims weren't any concern of his.

Surprisingly, not a single person in the crowd backed off. They stared forward at this spectacle like it was a rodeo, or a bullfight, and the man with the sign was *el Matador*. With a final swing, the wooden stick affixed to the cardboard snapped off, and Kane watched with increasing horror as the assailant whipped it around and held it in the air like a stake. Kane pressed himself backwards but found the crowd too tightly woven to move through. A few people behind him hooped and hollered, cheering for blood as the man slowly worked his way forward—bringing the stake high to strike.

Kane winced and held his hands before his eyes. No way in hell did he want to see this. He had enough trauma as it was. All at once, the crowd went completely silent, save for a loud hissing from Muffins(z). The pistol stopped firing, and

Kane heard the man on the rock groaning in agony. Why didn't anyone act? Kane pressed himself more tightly against those behind him. What the hell was wrong with these people?

Kane already knew the answer. They were the same as him: numb cowards shirking from the flame while their humanity grew cold.

It would only be a second. The stake-man had bent over and was preparing for a coup-de-grace. His hand raised higher, and Kane felt the blood race from his face towards his toes.

"Hey!" a woman's voice screeched from the side. The stake-man turned his head slightly, but not in time to avoid an uppercut to the jaw which sent his head kareeming upward. The man's teeth cracked violently as he gurgled and collapsed onto the rocks.

A deep, thick silence settled over the crowd. No one moved a muscle, not those who were attacking nor the masses surrounding them. No one besides Kane.

"Sue!" he cried out, dropping the metal cage and bolting towards his sister. To hell with cowardice, to hell with the cats! In a split second, he knew he had to stand beside her. Although, as he passed by one of the cardboard signs that read *Tim's Edge of Hell* and saw the fury in the mob's eyes, his resolve swayed a bit. They're not cowards, they're complicit. However, Kane had made his split second choice, one based on love and sacrifice, and knew it was too late to turn around. Even though it was only for a moment, letting his fear go was delicious.

"Sue, what the hell are you doing?" Kane whisper-yelled, putting his hand on her shoulder and pulling her away from the other assailants.

It took a moment for his sister to comprehend who he was, but as she did her face lit up. Was that a smile? "Welcome to the party, Kane," she said. "I didn't think they'd let you into a place like this."

What the hell did that mean?

"I'm assuming you don't have a plan," he retorted softly.

"Nope. Do you?"

"Nope."

"We could run," Kane suggested.

"Shoot you in the back."

"We could duck and hide."

"Shoot you in the head."

"What about charging?"

At this, his sister buried her finger in her gut and wiggled her hand around.

One of the men took a few steps forward. Although vicious looking, Kane could see a clear confusion in his eyes. He must feel like a rock star whose concert had been interrupted by someone from the audience leaping on stage.

The dazed look rapidly vanished, however, and the other men and women cocked their pistols in a wholly unnecessary act. They had already been firing into the air and besides, one gun was more than enough. How ridiculous; Kane repressed a gallows-humor grin.

"Oh shit, Sue, are we going to die?" he sputtered out, feeling his legs weaken.

"We sure are in a pickle. Guess we're gonna have to *dill* with it," she responded dryly.

Kane turned to his sister, mouth agape. Was that a joke? Sue's face wasn't jovial or haughty, however. Her features were taut and placid. Humor may be her defense mechanism, but dad jokes weren't going to save them.

"Best bet, we tell them who we are," his sister said softly.

"Tell them who we are?" Kane was confused. "We're not celeb—"

Before he had a chance to continue, Sue stepped forward.

"Attacking unbelievers isn't what Tim would have wanted!" Sue yelled at the group.

The approaching man retorted, "Oh yeah, and how the hell do you know that, little girl?" His voice was gruff, raw, the voice of a lifelong smoker.

"Because this little girl is Tim's sister."

SEVENTEEN

"BECAUSE THIS LITTLE GIRL IS TIM'S SISTER." SUE SQUARED HER shoulders and leaned forward to project her voice.

The dazed look returned to the man's face, and this time, it didn't vanish. With wide eyes, the man stopped moving forward and opened his mouth before shutting it with a gulp. Saying she was Tim's sister was so brazen a bluff, the entire scene ground to a halt. The man's eyes worked their way across her face, and Kane could tell he was scouring his memory to assess her claim. Gods help them if he had accidentally threatened the great Tim's sister. Eventually, he placed his hands in the air and stepped backwards, clearly unsure how to proceed.

Sue saw her opening. Turning away from the man, she addressed the masses. "And you!" She pointed and wagged a scolding finger. "Shame on all of you! Tim's warnings were meant to save people, not hurt them." At this, she walked over and knelt next to one of the injured protesters. With an arrogant, foreboding expression, Sue stared at the assailant.

"Even if they are unbelievers. Especially if they are unbelievers." And in that moment, to Kane's utter shock, Sue leapt upwards and punched him once again square in the face.

The scraping of his shoes deafened amidst the growing silence. One or two of the others raised their pistols, but the man, blood pouring from his nose, gave the signal to stand down. Even with the palpable danger, Kane smiled at the thought of his sister scrapping with a man twice her size. He was involuntarily reminded of the time Molly had saved him from a mugger by kicking his crotch the second she saw a knife. Of course, Kane had been cowering behind her. That was right before they separated. Coincidence?

The bleeding man lowered his hand and stepped forward with violent intent. Sue was in no position for another surprise attack, and her petite size became more apparent the closer he got. Like David and Goliath, except there was no stone or sling in sight. Was this it? Kane wobbled anxiously forward, determined to stand by his sister in their final hour.

A few feet away, the man looked over at Kane and instead of attacking with unbridled, animalistic rage, recoiled in horror. For a moment, Kane thought the black swirling mass had become visible. Those thoughts were doused, however, as the would-be assailant blurted out, "You're Kane. Which means that—"

Once again, the man gawked at his sister, his eyes bulging. "Which means you're Sue." Kane watched him shrink into himself, deflate and hunch forward. "For the love of Tim, I'm so—" in place of a complete sentence, he dropped to his knees and flung his hands out in a bow. The rest of the group promptly followed suit as well as dozens of people from the crowd.

For Kane, this moment was so surreal he felt paralyzed. Who were these people? How did they know him? Why were they bowing? Why did the man look so afraid? These questions remained unanswered, each shoved aside to make room for the next.

Unlike Kane, the man's sudden repentance didn't faze his sister at all. Instead of submitting, she glared silently at the crowd around her.

The would-be-attacker was in such a panic, Kane wondered if he was fearing for his image, his life or his soul. Did Tim's siblings truly mean so much to these people? If Kane had been thinking straight, he would have exploited the situation. Why walk to their car when they could be carried? Why buy groceries or stay in their dumpy hotel when any one of these people would be willing to sacrifice life and limb to treat them as royalty?

Without realizing the full implications of their position, or how to abuse it, one idea did strike him. Would it be okay to suggest it? How would the man, whom his sister had sucker punched a few moments ago, react? Perhaps he'd be laughed at. Or worse.

Sue had stopped her aggressive shame-on-you look and was helping one of the protesters stand. Their eyes locked for a moment, and although quick, the intensity in his sister's face was enough to spur him to action.

"If you're really sorry," he said as the crowd held its breath, "you'll help us get inside."

For a moment, no one moved. Even Sue froze as she reached for the hand of another protester.

Shit, had he spoken too soon?

The large man stood up, holding his nose to halt the streams of blood, and took a step forward. His eyes were unsure, and Kane tensed as he waited for a flash of anger.

The hand with the pistol swung abruptly into the air and a few drops of pee freed themselves from Kane's bladder.

"Shit!" he gasped.

But the gun didn't go off. It wasn't even pointed at him. Instead, it was motioning for them to follow.

"My pleasure."

Following Kane's brazen request, the man leapt up, hastily gathered his things and led them to the front gate with a cordial, "please" and "this way". Kane felt a little prophet-esk as the crowd peeled away from their path. To their backs, whispers became murmurs and a long line formed in their wake. Thank the gods there was no water to baptize. He hoped they didn't expect to be fed—he was plumb out of bread and fish.

Twenty minutes later, they were standing in front of the large central gate, staring at what must have been an entire contingent of well-armed mercenaries, each donning *TL Foundation* badges and riot gear. The security troops were positioned behind two-inch thick metal bars wrapped in razor wire and placarded with dozens of signs which read *Danger: Electrocution* and *Trespassers Will Be Shot*. A few metal turrets and mounted assault rifles made sure the crowd knew the sign wasn't exaggerating.

"So much for Tim's healing message," Kane mumbled to Muffins(z), whom he stroked through the bars in a calming fashion. It had taken the better part of ten minutes to get the cats to stop growling and Sue had more than a few scratches on her forearm as a testament to how much panic the ordeal had caused their feline companions.

Behind the guards, a Jeep approached. The path beyond the gate wasn't paved and so the vehicle blasted dirt and dust violently into the air. The closer it came, the more a sickly feeling spread across Kane's gut. At first, it was a prickle like the wings of a butterfly flapping near his belly button. As the two passengers came into view, the nausea had morphed into a dizziness and cold sweat.

"Hey, Kane," his sister whispered, "are you ok?"

"Huh!?" Startled, he nearly toppled over. "What do you mean?"

"I mean, you look like shit. Here, let me hold Muffins for a bit." His sister reached towards the carrier in his hand but Kane retreated a step.

"No, I'm fine. I think I'm just a little dehydrated." This statement wasn't the least bit true. Although it was so hot Kane felt like he was having cuddle time with the sun, he had been drinking water regularly and didn't feel thirsty in the slightest.

Kane turned away from the approaching vehicle, but he still felt the vibration of its tires, the shine of the headlights, the stare of the passengers. The scene was wrong, but he felt too ill to focus on the specifics.

The butterfly in his stomach had started to flap around again; Kane felt the wings flicker against his insides. Where did it intend on going? Did it want to escape? Its tiny crooked feet attached itself to his esophagus, and its wings slid across the opening while rowing itself upwards. After it neared his tonsils, the tingling in his throat roared into focus—a throbbing turned prickling massage as he felt the flesh behind his nasal cavity peel off and birth...a wriggling object? Kane wanted to vomit but couldn't. Instead, he stared at his sister in horror, but she was completely oblivious to his distress.

"Sue," Kane mouthed breathlessly, but she turned to face the Jeep which had parked directly beyond the gate.

Oh shit. Was he having an episode? At this moment? Kane secretly wished this odd sensation was a symptom of withdrawal, but he knew that wasn't the case. It hadn't been long enough since his last hit.

The thought of collapsing into a pool of his own blood in front of these zealots was terrifying, but it paled in comparison to his fear of blacking out again. What if he awoke to find lifeless bodies strewn around him? Or he came to as the light faded from his sister's eyes, his steely grip wrapped around her neck?

Kane frantically scratched the flesh of his throat with his tongue. He had to get this to stop somehow. Whatever had birthed itself from behind his tonsils didn't give any indication it was interested in his worries. Instead of retreating, it slithered upwards into his sinus and gnawed gently on the delicate flesh directly above his nasal canal. This sensation was too much for Kane as he violently sneezed and watched blood and mucus spray outward into the dry air.

"Bless you," Sue said absentmindedly, her back turned towards him.

Was that in his imagination? The blood? Not a single face in the crowd looked the least bit concerned, and his sister hadn't even given him a second thought.

But the bleeding didn't stop, and the thing was now burrowed half way into whatever hole it had made. Kane was ready to ram his finger into his nose and claw the nasty little bugger out when the butterfly sensation reappeared. His nausea turned to horror as its butt wriggled and throbbed, depositing a slimy thing into the hole left by the entity in his throat.

As soon as the egg (was it an egg?) had been laid, Kane felt a wave of exhaustion crash over the winged-creature. With its last bit of strength, it worked its way upwards and burst from his mouth. Whatever retched out and flew into the sun wasn't even a butterfly. It was the deer from earlier, miniature and with a gnarled face, half melted by his stomach acid and dripping swaths of rotten flesh. Wings weren't carrying it; rather, the ashen flower petals whose thorns were wrapped in and throughout the carcasses like a twisted gordian knot. The stitching of the flower loosened with each flap, and soon the skin from the deer's body peeled away and sent it kareeming to the earth.

Not a single person in the crowd, including his sister, reacted as Kane watched it drop and twitch on the ground. Was this in his head? Definitely not withdrawal symptoms. Kane coughed into his hand, praying he wouldn't find splatters of blood. His hand was empty. Was he safe; was it over?

Before he could assess, he felt whatever had burrowed itself into his head dissipate.

"What?" he started but was interrupted by an approaching shadow. Looking up, he found himself face to face with a man he hadn't seen before. Or at least he didn't think he had as the man's face was covered with the same spinning black pool of midnight as his own.

"It's nice to see you again, Suzannah." A pair of lips moved from beyond the edges of the cloud. "And you must be Kane."

His sister gave the man a long, intimate hug, oblivious to the entire scene Kane had experienced. He wanted to speak up, but his mouth was so dry his tongue stuck to the roof of his mouth and tore and ached when he moved it. Rather than wait for an answer, the man stepped forward—his foot missing the head of the deer by half an inch. "Gabriyel Stver." His hand rushed forward to meet Kane's.

CHAPTER
EIGHTEEN

"You could have called!" Mr. Stver cocked his head towards them and yelled from the front passenger seat of the Jeep. Although Kane watched him strain, his voice hardly overcame the rumble and jostling of the vehicle speeding over dirt.

"Sorry!" Kane heard him screech "WE FINISHED GRATING THIS MORNING," his voice crackled and bounced. A desperate glance in Sue's direction followed before he shook his head in resignation and turned around.

Did Sue know this guy? Kane recalled the hug and shifted around in his seat. The thought made him uncomfortable. Extremely uncomfortable. To his knowledge, she wasn't affiliated with the Timothy Lamm Foundation. At least, that's how it had been prior to his disappearance. Although, the way Stver had spoken to her, the way they had embraced each other, was like long lost comrades or nostalgic lovers. Disconcerting was an understatement.

Clearly, much had changed over the past year, and Kane felt queasy at yet another personal topic to broach with his sister. Although, if she knew Stver so intimately why hadn't she simply hitched a ride in one of the dozens of private jets at the organization's disposal? Personally, he would have appreciated avoiding a three-day long road trip.

Kane gave a side glance to Sue and felt a trickle of sweat form on his brow. When Little Tim was alive, he wouldn't allow Kane or Sue to exploit his position and use the organization's resources for their personal gain or comfort. "Wood outside the fire doesn't help it grow," he would often say. Every penny was reinvested in expansion efforts with the goal of becoming so powerful, the foundation could intervene anywhere in the world and stop another Kabul from happening. If only that had been true.

Because of this separation of his private and public lives, the details of Tim's family were kept quiet. Who cared about normies like them anyway? They couldn't see the future, weren't particularly business savvy or pious. In all honesty, both he and Sue were more than happy to stay away from the limelight—Kane due to his stubborn sense of pride and Sue from loyalty.

"Having siblings in positions within the organization would only serve to muck things up. Like mixing spit and water," Sue would say. "You can't see it, but that doesn't mean you wanna take a drink."

And as time wore on, and as Tim became more and more irritable, avoiding him and his full gambit of cultish beliefs became the easiest choice in the world. At least for Kane. Had Sue changed?

Kane shifted his focus to the backside of Stver's head. The swirling black mass wasn't visible from this angle, but Kane knew it was there.

Kane recalled the surreal details of their recent introduction.

"And this is our lead structural engineer Jonah Irrer." Stver had stepped aside to introduce a short, balding man behind him—once again narrowly missing the deer with his foot.

With a sense of vertigo, Kane nodded. Jonah, Dr. Irrer, was grasping Kane's hand in the same way that Stver had: forceful, unapologetic but limp and fleeting as though checking a social norm off a list. The handshake wasn't the only thing they had in common. Kane had stared in amazement as he realized Dr. Irrer's face was also covered in the same swirling black mass. What the hell was going on here?

After the handshake had dissolved, Kane rubbed his eyes and peered around. To his disbelief, it wasn't only the two men with these abnormalities. Several of the guards and multiple people in the crowd also had them. Were they not seeing this? For a moment, Kane had wished he was crazy. Anything was better than the darkening implications of whatever was happening here.

Were they currently in danger? Would it be Kane's responsibility to save them? Kane was thrust into the present and felt around his face with a slight tremor.

How could he do that—save them? They couldn't simply stand up and leave. If he informed his sister of the lost time, the swirling black clouds, how would she react? Maybe she would get freaked out and bolt. Worst case, she would want to investigate further—even if that meant putting herself in danger.

The old Sue was high-octane but also highly pragmatic. Kane doubted she'd even entertain such an insane idea. However, with her newfound religiosity, he had his doubts. Although, truth be told, he wasn't overly competent at predicting how his sister would react to sensitive information. One thing was for sure though—no matter how she responded, it would mean dragging him along for the ride. Come hell or high water.

Kane bit his lip tighter. It was obvious he couldn't divulge anything to her until he'd made sense of a few more things. Or at least until he knew how to rescue them from this mess.

That sentiment didn't last long.

The rumbling from the Jeep receded to a gentle purr and Kane strained his eyes to catch glimpses of the entrance amidst the pockets of heavy machinery. It was smaller than he had imagined, reinforced with steel bars, and placarded with warning signs. It was barely big enough to allow the largest piece of excavating equipment through. At first, he imagined the hole as a blemish on the mountain side, although the shadows around the cave were so pronounced, it soon morphed into a gaping mouth.

A mouth covered with a large door, curtain or gate, Kane thought. The closer the Jeep got, however, the more he came to realize he wasn't staring at some dense screen but a thick, palpable darkness that bubbled and throbbed from the entrance. Bubbled wasn't the right word. The empty void radiated a mist that was carried away by the wind. Were his eyes playing tricks on him? Heat and light cause so many illusions in the desert, it wouldn't be any wonder if its shenanigans claimed yet another victim. Unfortunately, as they rounded the last large outcropping of dump trucks and tractors, Kane saw the fuming abyss was beyond the boundaries of his imagination.

Wisps of obsidian were wriggling outwards. The dark threads were so thick, so overt, Kane recognized they weren't shadows or smoke at all. The darkness was creeping, spiraling into hot desert air—detaching itself before being blown away.

And the Jeep was headed right for it.

"Uh, Sue?" Kane started, peering over at his sister with the most desperate look he could muster.

To his chagrin, Stver was speaking again, and Sue was completely engrossed.

"Really, Suzannah, we would have come to pick you up." Stver gave a weak frown in simulated offense. "If we had known you were coming, we could have—"

The Jeep was only a hundred meters away from the entrance at this point, and Kane contemplated if he should shove Sue out of the door or assault the driver. Whatever he was going to do, he better make it quick.

"Uhh, Sue!?" he said again with more emphasis. His sister responded by waving her hand towards his face in a quieting gesture.

"I haven't seen my brother much as you know. I thought it would be a good opportunity to visit with him." Kane took in a sharp breath. In spite of his situation, Sue's words hit him hard. She had gone on this stupid road trip with him to reconnect? That was sweet and made the weight of his previous lie weigh on him all the more.

But he honestly didn't have time to dwell on her words. Fifty meters left. Should he leap from the Jeep and cause them to stop? But how would he explain his behavior afterwards? If he acted so insane, the jig would be up. At that point, he would *have* to confess the past few days' worth of bullshit to his sister. Confess and live with the consequences. Wasn't that better than driving straight into the mouth of the mountain?

Forty meters. No time to think. He had to act.

"Oh, I can understand that. We could have at least arranged for more appropriate accommodations, though."

"I see you already found out where we're staying."

Thirty meters. Kane reached for the door handle but found it locked. *Shit.*

"Found out? Suzannah, the whole world knows where

you're staying. Not to worry—we'll post guards if you insist on remaining at that—"

"Crack den," Sue snarled.

Twenty meters. Kane frantically searched for the unbuckle button to his seatbelt. If only he could grab the wheel.

"I was going to say a local gem in the rough." Stver smiled. "But you have by far the more apt description."

Ten meters. They were nearly in the hole. The mouth. Kane was furiously yanking on his hair with one hand and pulling down the skin of his cheeks with the other. He couldn't find the button to unlock his seat belt. His head swirled around, his hands dropping to the cushion as he shoved them in between each nook and crack in sight. The button remained elusive. What would he do if he found it? Grab the wheel? Jump through the window? Kane pressed his feet into the floor and arched his back against the seat with a frustrated grunt. He had stopped his search and was breathing deeply. They were headed inside, and he was powerless to stop it.

Kane's back-seat tantrum caught Sue's attention. She abruptly stopped her conversation and glanced over at him. "What the hell are you doing?" she asked with a tinge of concern and more than a hint of annoyance.

"Sue, the cave." Right before he pointed at the encroaching darkness, the driver jerked the steering wheel to the left and the Jeep pulled next to a trailer positioned twenty feet from the entrance.

"I hope you don't mind"—Stver turned to them with a mischievous grin stretched ear to ear—"but we have some safety measures we're undertaking today, so we won't be able to enter the mine."

Kane nearly leapt from his seat with joy. "Mind, oh, no, we don't mind at all," he said with a little too much enthusiasm.

His own smile was stretching ear to ear as well, the edges buoyed by relief.

A healthy dose of suspicion was added to Sue's puzzled look. "We were hoping to see Tim's Edge today," she said hesitantly towards Stver. "Oh, I thought as much. Unfortunately, we can't let anyone inside until we've completed things. Safety things." With a quick nod to the driver, the Jeep shut off. "But don't worry; I'm sure tomorrow will be a new day."

"Gabriyel," Sue growled. "What's going on here?"

Stver's face oscillated between ignorance and denial as he struggled to disclose whatever had occurred. Did it have anything to do with the onyx tentacles which, even now, were wrenching themselves ever forward into the desert sun?

Stver spoke slowly. "Well, Sue, there's been an incident."

"What kind of incident?" At this Gabriyel shook his head slightly, puckering his lips.

"The type we should discuss inside."

Kane found his seatbelt button the moment they parked. It wasn't on the seat at all, but at the top of the band near the roof. "You have got to be kidding me." He sighed, watching it smoothly detach and fling itself rapidly backwards.

Stever and Dr. Irrer hopped out and opened the doors for Kane and Sue.

"Please, this way." Stver pointed towards a small white single-wide trailer.

"And my cats?"

"Why, they'll stay here of course. No need to bring them inside."

"Stver," Sue's voice was low, threatening, "they'll suffocate. It's too hot."

"Nonsense!" he responded, closing the Jeep's door with a smile.

His sister only needed a single step forward, fists balled, before Stver hastily added, "I'll have a worker stop by and grab them. We'll deposit your cats in the main office, and you can fetch them once we work out our next steps."

Sue remarked, "You'd better" and "there will be blood" before making her way inside the trailer.

Kane followed suit and was shuffled over to a plastic card table in the middle of what used to be the dining room. Kane had seen rundown trailers before. Hell, he'd slept in his fair share. Considering the organization's wealth, he was amazed at the level of shabbiness. Sun bleached, crumbling shades around walls of peeling 1970s wallpaper. The linoleum on the floor chafed and crackled with eons of spilled liquid and foot traffic. Even the cabinetry had large chunks of faux-wood veneer detached, revealing yellow stained, crusted plywood directly beneath. This room was more akin to a Stasi interrogation chamber than a waiting room of a multi-billion dollar organization. Had Little Tim's avarice and frugality permeated the culture that much?

"Emphasis cult," Kane whispered and sat in a small, slightly off-kilter metal chair.

After Stver had seated them, he poured the group several cups of coffee. It was appreciated, although the smell was so terrible Kane wondered if they hadn't lit the Folgers on fire before letting it sit for a week in stale water. Kane had tasted better coffee in crack houses. Where did this organization's money go?

"Is there anything else I can get you?" Stver asked with a sickeningly sweet politeness that made Kane's stomach wretch.

"Why, yes, there is," his sister countered with a devious smile. "The answer to why we can't get into the mine today."

Stver audibly sighed. After taking a fleeting sip from his own cup, he grabbed a chair and sat as well. "Suzannah—"

"Sue."

"Sue." Stver looked confused at the idea that a person named Suzannah wanted their name shortened to such a coarse abbreviation. Kane could plainly see this wasn't the first time she had had to correct him. "I can appreciate your request, and I'm also well aware of your position within our foundation."

This caused Kane to squint and lean in closer. So she *was* a part of the organization.

"But believe me when I say we have to deal with a few"— he chewed on his words a bit before deciding to swallow— "safety things before we can admit anyone else into the mine."

"Stver"—Sue narrowed her eyes and spoke from behind gritted teeth—"you know I could tell anyone of these people to maul you to death and they wouldn't even hesitate. Why don't you cut the bullshit and tell me what's going on?"

Oh boy. That was rough, even for Sue. Of course, she wouldn't go through with it—at least, that's what he hoped. Although, considering how the people outside the gate had reacted to her presence, it wasn't a hollow threat. Stver reclined in his seat with a smile, unfazed by his sister's sudden violent provocation.

"You haven't changed at all, have you?" He placed his hands behind his head in a sit-up fashion. "Well, I'm sure you've met my little group of vigilantes outside."

"Your vigilantes?" Sue was in complete shock. "That group of assholes belongs to you?"

"Why, yes. Of course. How do you think they were able to

get you inside so fast? What, you think that people outside the gates have my personal phone number?" He chuckled.

Both Kane and Sue stood up at once. "Dammit, Stver!" Sue slammed her fist into the card table so hard, the cups of coffee went toppling to the floor.

"Those pricks were gonna kill those people! What the hell is wrong with you!?"

In response, Stver lethargically bent over and grabbed his coffee cup. He stared around at both siblings and suppressed a yawn before drawing the cup to his lips and sucking out the last few drops with a disgusting *slurp*. After placing the cup on the table, he glanced at a fuming Sue.

"*Those people,* as you describe them, are actually a dangerous religious group dead set on undermining what we're working towards."

"But that doesn't give you the right to threaten them!" Sue punched the table again, but there was no coffee left to fling off.

Without blinking, Stver responded, "It does when they murdered three of our engineers yesterday."

CHAPTER
NINETEEN

"Earlier today," Stver began, "a few of those so-called protesters snuck in and stole a large dump truck."

"And what, they ran over three people?" Sue snarked.

"Why, yes, how'd you know?" At this, both Kane and his sister took a step backwards.

"Well, not directly *ran* over. More like locked several people in a small trailer in the mine and drove a dump truck into it." Stver looked at his fingernails as though seeing them for the first time. "Although, technically, driving into someone isn't the same as running them over, I believe both terms can be used interchangeably."

A deep silence fell upon the room. Although Kane couldn't see Stver's face, he imagined it blank, emotionless, completely void of empathy. At least, that's how his voice sounded.

"But why?" his sister stuttered, collapsing into the chair so abruptly, it creaked with the threat of collapse.

"Why?" Stver asked rhetorically. "Why, Suzannah? Because we're doing the devil's work, haven't you heard?"

"The devil's work." Sue parroted him with a blank stare.

"Oh, yes. Have you been avoiding the news? Haven't you heard the world is splitting? Half of it thinks we've found God, or something like God, and the other half believe we're the antichrist." At this, his hand glided over to his coffee cup but stopped after realizing it remained empty. "Or at least the devil, if you will. Whatever evil, shadowy figure suits whichever religion."

"Well"—Sue was exasperated—"call the police on them or post more guards."

Stver laughed loudly, heartily, without a hint of mockery. "Call the police on who? The police? Didn't you hear what I said, Suzannah? The world has split. Loudly. It's cracked right through the middle. You see the people beyond the gates, yes? Who do you think they are? Police, of course. Firemen. Pilots, priests, factory workers and accountants. Software engineers, forklift drivers and life coaches. Name the occupation, and a person in that crowd or on the way here does, or rather did, that thing." Stver stood up and sped towards the coffee pot. "And it's the same for our adherents across the globe. Airlines are booked so far out, people are renting cargo ships, entire cargo ships, to transport people from distant countries so they can come and see Tim's Edge."

Stver poured himself a cup of coffee and oddly enough, the air of apathy had waned. Kane noticed a subtle shake of his hand but couldn't tell if it was due to anxiety or excitement. Clearly, this disturbed him more than his stoic demeanor let on. Should that be cause for concern or relief?

"In a few short days, we've demolished entire economies, Suzannah," he continued. "People have abandoned jobs, children, spouses, their entire lives to make the pilgrimage here. And what, you think we can simply dial 911? You think I'm able to keep thousands, hundreds of thousands, millions of people from storming this place without draconian measures?" He raised the cup to his mouth again but lowered it before taking a sip. "No, we're on our own, Sue, and every day is only going to get worse."

"Campfire in a powder keg," Sue whispered, placing her face into her hands and rubbing slowly.

Stver took a deep breath and morphed once again into the soft-spoken, mild-mannered scientist-persona from before. "And so that's why you simply can't go into the mine today. We're establishing strict safety measures to ensure our workers stay out of harm's way."

The entire time Kane listened, his only thought was, *I've gotta get out of here.*

He repeated it over and over in his head like a mantra. He had no idea what was happening to the world, no idea what was happening outside. None of this mattered as it was hardly his concern, right? His only goal should be to leave and find the one thing that would make everything ok: drugs, or more specifically, meth. Until a few moments ago, the pull of addiction had been a gentle tug. The excitement, events and newness over the past couple of days had placed his worldly desires on the back burner. However, it now felt like the gas had been cranked to ten and his whole body was aflame.

A shiver worked its way up his spine and spread to his fingertips. He'd walk to the motel if he had to. Or he could use his newly minted celebrity status and hitch a ride. Stver and Sue seemed distracted with their thoughts and so Kane took a cautious step towards the door.

Whether Stver saw it or not, he couldn't tell. After tiptoeing backwards, the swirling black mass turned in his direction and said, "And you, Kane. What have you *seen* on the topic?" At this, Sue shot Stver a wide-eyed glance and made a subtle dismissive gesture with her hand.

What a weird way to put that question. A sense of foreboding crept into his chest. "Well, not much actually," he mumbled-whispered, peering directly into the swirling mass on Stver's face. "There hasn't been much news since we left Chicago, so I'm not sure what to think."

The fact that he didn't have to avoid eye contact gave him a bit of courage. "You've found the most important artifact in human history," he continued. "What did you expect to happen? More donations?" This was a poor attempt at a joke and was met with a proportionate dose of silence. Sue stared at the ceiling, and Stver stood so still, he could have easily been a statue.

A few seconds passed until the awkward pause was too much for Kane. "And anyway," he spouted out, "I think the world splitting is a bit of an exaggeration, don't you? When we were driving here, the roads weren't too bad. Restaurants were normal, hotels were normal, gas stations and convenience stores were normal. Beyond a few thousand people gathered outside, it doesn't look like much has changed."

Kane expected his statement to stir up a debate. Either with Stver, who remained hunched over staring into the beyond, or with Sue, who shook her head in obvious disapproval. To his surprise, no one uttered a contradiction. It was as though they were the audience, silently judging the protagonist's actions on stage.

After a long pause, Stver finally spoke up. "Well, I'm not here to argue with you, Kane. Although, I think you'll find the situation in Lunar City has drastically altered in the few short hours since you left. When the time comes, please reconsider my offer to stay in the mine. If we lost you, well, it may ignite a war." Stver chortled a monotonous gargle.

"But in any case"—his chuckles trailed off—"that wasn't what I was asking about." Reclining, he took a deep breath.

What a shitty game of cat and mouse. Kane bit anyway. "So, what were you asking about?"

The swirling black mass looked over at Sue, who was shaking her head more furiously, panicked.

"What I was actually hoping to find out is if you had *seen* anything." The way he emphasized the *s* sounded was snake-like as it hissed through his teeth.

Kane was oblivious to the hidden meaning underlying Stver's words, although the prickling sense of foreboding had deepened.

"Seen, Kane—visions!" It was Stver's turn to get agitated. "I'm wondering if any of this has appeared in one of your episodes!"

The prickling feeling erupted into a twisted sense of confusion, shock and rage. "Wait, what!?" Kane looked at Sue in disbelief, who was suddenly bright red and staring at the floor. "You told him about those? That was our secret!"

His sister's fury be damned, he didn't care if she punched him in the face, got mad or made him live the rest of his life irradiated from her emotional fallout. This was their one secret to share as a family—the one thing he thought he could trust her with. Sue knew that, so how could she give it away!? Kane wretched forward. And to this prick of all people.

Wait, if he knows, who else has she told? Was that why those people outside the gates treated him like a prophet?

"Kane, listen, I didn't hear from you for almost a year." His sister turned to him, arms crossed. "When Stver found me, when he brought me into this." She hesitated as Kane's face reddened.

"Kane, this group has helped me understand that your visions are holy, sacred, beautiful things. They're nothing to be ashamed of. You don't have to hide them anymore." Sue stood up and dropped her arms to her sides. Kane couldn't tell if she was going to hug or hit him. To hers and to Stver's surprise, he didn't wait to find out. As soon as she was within arm's length, he shoved her violently away and bolted through the door.

I've got to get out of here. I've got to get out of here. I've got to get out of here. The mantra was in his head again, ricocheting off every cell. Without an ounce of rational thought, he hopped in the parked Jeep and found the keys jutting from the ignition. The dark twine of tentacles swayed in his direction, but he didn't care. He needed to leave—even if that meant racing straight into their dark grasp.

"How could she do that?" he mumbled, starting the Jeep. "Why did I even come back?" he added with an angry sob.

His sister and Stver were running towards him, but he had too much of a head start. Shifting the vehicle into gear, he sped off right as Sue's fist pounded on the passenger side glass. "Kane!" Her yells were muffled by the roar of the engine, the grating of the tires and his pounding heart.

"Kane, I'm so sorry!" That was the last thing he heard before she became a spec in the rearview mirror.

"Sorry!?" He cackled and snarled his lips with a spray of spittle. "I hope you never get out of this mine, Suzannah."

CHAPTER

TWENTY

"Hmm, you don't look very serious," the bone-thin woman at the front desk of his motel said with a lick of her lips.

Kane placed his hands on the counter, palms up, in an act of submission. Although he wanted it to appear as a joke, a harmless flirt, the reality was it was neither. He was incredibly desperate, but he had no intention of putting his misery on display. It was obvious this woman was the type of person who fed on weakness and devoured those in distress. In spite of his best efforts, she had smelled blood in the water.

"I am serious, but I'm starting to doubt if you are." He gave a coquet smile. "You told me before you could hook me up. Now, you good for it or what?"

At this, her grin grew wider. He had switched his mannerisms and speech to a sort of bougi-street-lingo, the same type he often employed when buying drugs. Most people found it harmless, and it was obvious she thought it was, at a minimum, cute.

"And how do I know you're not a cop?" she giggled.

"Cop?" Kane instinctively took a step towards the door. He

had nothing in common with cops. Acted nothing like a cop. The only thing he and a police officer had in common was an ingrained love of donuts.

"Now you're definitely joking," he squeaked through gritted teeth, struggling to not lose his cool. This had been dragging on for twenty minutes, and Kane's mind was consumed by thoughts of pounding a needle into his flesh or taking a whiff of something sweet. Did she really have some goods or had she been toying with him the whole time?

Desire torched his body. Without intervention, a complete burn out was inevitable. "I saw you smoking outside when I got dropped off here. What kinda cop does patrol on a shitty dirt bike?"

With a wink, she remarked, "The kind looking to pull the wool over the eyes of a sweet, innocent, sweet little girl."

Kane forced a laugh, wrestling down the last bit of his self-control.

"You saw me come in here with my sister, I mean wife."

"Could have been your partner."

"And our two cats."

"Spy cats."

"Would a cop dress this shabby?" Kane grabbed a hole in his t-shirt and yanked it upwards.

There was a slight pause before she replied, "Pigs like to wallow in their own filth."

Kane shut his eyes for a moment. He had reached his breaking point. Her sarcasm, combined with an obvious satisfaction at his misery, left his patience tottering on a steep ledge. Before he knew what was happening, he flung his eyes open and yelled, "Are you gonna sell me drugs or not!?"

Even with the sudden tension, the grin remained plastered on her face. The look in her eyes only said one thing: *Gotcha!*

"Of course, I am, Mr. Angry Hulk," she mused, looking at

her hands as if inspecting a defect. "But I only have one thing in supply."

Kane was short of breath from his outburst. No one ground his gears like this, even his sister. With some effort, he took a deep breath and forced a smile across his lips. "And how much?"

Snap. The trap was sprung. He regretted showing how desperate he actually was.

"How much you got?"

After forking over all his cash, Kane wasn't sure it was worth it. Three times the price of meth and half the weight, and for a drug he'd never heard of. For all he knew, he could get a better trip heading into the desert and picking some wild peyote or sacred datura. Although, who could say if they even grew here and honestly, a pilgrimage in the afternoon sun sounded as appetizing as eating food served off his motel room floor. Besides, he was jonesing hard. His entire body felt like a balloon filling with hot piss and needles. Walking to the motel room would be hard enough, let alone a hundred feet into the desert. Hopefully, this would scratch his itch; otherwise, it wouldn't be long before he was running through the town alleyways screaming, "Meth!"

Kane snatched the little vial from the woman and strode briskly towards the exit.

"Wait, don't you wanna know what it is?"

With a sharp turn, Kane gave her a snarl. He'd had it with her bullshit. Her worth had become a level directly below a bullet to the head. Or another cat. "Fuck off!" he said, motioning for the door.

"No, really!" she yelled after him. "Don't take more than a mil. Stuff grows from a flower on the mountain and will jack you up with an OD. I don't wanna find your body contorted in the bathtub or—"

The door shut. Kane was off to his motel room. The sooner, the better. What the hell did he care if it grew on the mountain, on the sun or was sprouting from someone's asshole. As long as it got the job done, death was the least of his worries. In truth, it may be a blessing.

Upon arriving in his room, Kane was hit with a string of bad news.

"Oh fuck!" He felt around for his pipe before remembering he'd already lost it. The stuff in the vial looked sticky, so was smoking it the only option? Thinking back, the lady hadn't said if he was supposed to toke it, drink it, shoot it or snort it and Kane regretted losing his cool and not asking.

"Hmm," he grunted. No way in hell was he returning. She'd probably demand a kidney for half an answer. Kane would inhale it first, and if that didn't work, he'd cut his gums a bit and rub some on the wound.

The next unfortunate piece of bad news meowed at him from the dimly lit room. Kane felt his heart nearly rip through his throat as he closed the door and was immediately brushed against by a feline tail. Apparently, his sister had had a worker send the cats for Kane to look after until she returned.

"So ballsy." Kane shook his head in disbelief. How could his sister think it was a good idea to ask him for a favor after how he'd stormed off? Or could this be a ploy to get him to stay until he'd cooled down? Sue must think he was incapable of endangering something she loved, no matter how upset he was.

That was almost touching.

"Kane," a note on one of the cages read, "I know you're pissed. You have every right to be. Hear me out, though. There are good reasons I did what I did. I hope you know that I didn't mean to hurt you." This didn't sound like Sue in the slightest. Had she asked Stver, or likely one

of his assistants, to help her write it?

"But honestly, I didn't even know you were alive until a few weeks ago, so can you blame me for wanting a shoulder to lean on? If so, you're being selfish and shame on you. See you tonight. Love you, big bro."

"Nope, definitely from Sue." He stared mouth agape at the last few lines. Selfish? Was she insane? A few hours ago, her brother had gotten so angry, he had stolen a vehicle, made a daring escape from a heavily guarded compound and hitch-hiked the entire way into town. With that in mind, she remained brazen enough to ask him for help while calling him selfish? Never mind the fact they had agreed, promised with the solemn oath of family, that after Tim's death they would never divulge what was happening to him. *Let the cat out of the bag*, he thought ironically, glancing over at one of the felines pawing at the curtain. Yet in her deranged head he was being the selfish one.

Kane's eyes drifted over to the vial. Escape had never seemed so sweet. He simply couldn't process what had happened to him. The episodes, his day, his sister, Stver, his face, the cats. Obviously, the only way to right the situation was to fly far, far away. Unscrewing the top, Kane silently prayed this would be a one-way trip.

"What does an old person and Satan have in common?" he recalled his father asking one night during dinner. "Once they've fallen, they can't get up!"

Haha, Dad. Very funny. How very, very clever you were. Kane sat at the small table near the front door, crafting a make-shift pipe from a toilet paper roll and some tin foil he had brought along for just this type of emergency. His hands shook, badly, but he kept them steady enough to wrap the edge of the roll gently with the foil and bend it upwards like the tail of a fish. He would have rather used duct-tape or super glue to bind his make-shift pipe together but managed well enough with a roll of dental floss. Kane had built more with far less—one learns to use what they can in dingy motel rooms or underneath bridges where the only respite from life is a few cc's of liquid vacation.

The cats watched him from a distance, interested enough to observe but not move and investigate. What did they care what he did—so long as they were fed, had water and a place to shit? Sue had made sure of that—with each little cage containing an H2O dispenser, a small bowl of partially consumed food and some potty pads.

Kane finished threading the final string as the irony of the situation struck him. He wasn't the responsible one anymore, hadn't been for over a year. Sue had taken his place. Kane ground his teeth and closed his eyes for a second. His sister was still far, far from perfect, so what did that say about him?

"How much did the lady recommend I take?" Kane asked aloud towards the cats, as if he could interpret their meows as a cracked-out Dr. Dolittle. "That's right, it was a teaspoon's worth. Like I have one of those!" He pulled the dental floss firmly together and tied it in a pretty bow. He wasn't sure if any additional flare would spruce up this turd, but it was worth a shot.

Carefully unscrewing the vial, Kane's mind was instinctively thrust into the worst memories of this life. He wasn't sure why this happened, although he often guessed it was some ingrained guilt mechanism working to compensate for the pleasure he was moments away from experiencing. At least, that's what his therapist had hinted at. If only that *ingrained guilt mechanism* saw how he lived—often like an animal and more often like refuse: discarded and tossed anywhere his slime would stick. He didn't need any more balance reminding him of sin or guilt or what a terrible son and brother he was. This rationalization didn't stop the incoming train of terrible memories and regrets, however.

There was his mother, dying on the couch, his father praying over her after refusing to let his children call an ambulance.

"God will provide. God made cancer and can take it away." There was his sister, begging Kane to run away with her before Dad could touch her again. Coward that he was, he refused.

"I'm so sorry, Sue," he said silently, pouring a few drops into the foil. Finally, images of his brother appeared. This was where his mental gauntlet frequently ended. Tim. Little Tim. He had told Kane how depressed he was; he had warned Kane that he didn't know if he could take any more visions, fame and hopelessness.

"Nothing changes. Ever. No matter how much power I have or how hard I try. Lately, even my visions end in emptiness." And how had Kane responded? Well, he hadn't. At least, not properly. He had told Little Tim they all had problems and at least *he* had money to balm the scars he was carrying.

"If Dad were alive, he would tell you that blaspheming the Holy Spirit is the only unforgivable sin. I guess you're going to hell, Tim."

Tim had mumbled incoherently about already having been there—which Kane didn't understand till much later. That night, upon returning from a stroll, he had found his brother's brains scattered over the wall. The worst part was: no goodbye. Hell, he hadn't even heard the farewell shot. Kane looked at the vial of liquid and added a few more drops. Then, a few more drops.

And what had the final portion of Tim's note said? What had his brother written specifically for him minutes before his departure? *But you, Kane, will know how much worse.* Kane shook his head frantically, dumped the entire vial in the tin foil and reached for his lighter. He couldn't do this right now. There was no way he was going to start a trip christened with Little Tim's last words. With a nervous frenzy, Kane clicked at his lighter and shoved the toilet paper roll as close to his lips as possible.

Let the smoke build before inhaling. Burning is temporary, pain is temporary. He hoped his lips wouldn't be too blistered the following morning. He didn't care if Sue returned, didn't care if the cats shit on him and scratched his face. There was only one important thing right now, and it was steaming towards him.

The viscous liquid evaporated much quicker than Kane had expected. Within seconds, he could see it rapidly cooking down, bubbling upwards as little charred bits of residue were left on the sides. One more second and then a big breath. The steam was surprisingly tame, perhaps because it had such a low boiling point. Kane pressed the cardboard more ferociously into his face and let the fumes tickle his lips. It felt as though there was a flower inside, gently caressing him with silken-winged petals. When his eyes saw the last of the liquid had all but disappeared, he opened his mouth as wide as it would go and sucked it inside him.

Kane didn't even remember coughing as he sped towards a darkness as deep as any he'd ever seen.

CHAPTER
TWENTY-ONE

KANE'S DREAMS WEREN'T NEARLY AS LUCID AS THE WAKING VISIONS—
rather, ink blotches on black paper or shadowed hands
pressing through the night. The only thing he knew for sure
was that he was spiraling endlessly downwards into the
depths of eternity.

Flashes came to him, jolts and thunders of light and vision
lashing from the darkness. They were confusing, akin to fever
dreams, and didn't alleviate the mesh of nothing surrounding
his body.

In some, his parents appeared, smiling at him from the
grave with their rotting flesh swelling and cracking. His
father's lips were forming words with jittery twitches, but
before Kane grasped their meaning, the flash of light sparked
and vanished, leaving an image of his sister. Was she crying or
laughing? Kane couldn't tell. Her hands clasped the detached
head of Muffins whose spine was whipping around like the tail
of a fish. Kane wanted to reach across the void and touch her,
pull himself into her reality, but she evaporated into smoke the
moment he lifted his hand.

Many more visions came and went: visions of himself, of his past friends and even of Molly. They flashed briefly, senseless and terrifying in their utter absurdity. Near the end, when his body raced towards the finality of oblivion, the monolith appeared: Tim's Edge. Kane had never seen it but knew instinctively what it was. It appeared without a crash of light to herald another vision. All at once, the thing lay before him: endlessly wide and tall, featureless, and smooth with an impenetrable aesthetic as though no atom could ever be parted from its surface.

Kane felt himself glide towards it, slowly swaying back and forth. He didn't know what would happen if he touched it. Would an infinite void lash outward and cause the world to grind to a halt? Would he die or be stretched so thin, nothing of himself would remain? Or he would simply land atop it and go insane considering what was on the other side.

Just like Tim.

Right before his body thumped against the surface, a hand reached from the darkness and pulled him upwards. This touch was more shocking to Kane than anything else in this dark labyrinth, and he whipped around and shoved forward in defense.

But the person holding him wasn't menacing, and his tugs weren't rough or threatening. Rather, the touch held a familiarity and was purposely gentle and soft. It was Tim, Little Tim, and he was smiling at Kane through cracked lips and bloodied teeth.

"Kane"—the voice came from everywhere at once—"I told you to get out." His words were like coarse stones grinding together, shrieking as they mulled themselves into dust and nothingness.

Although he should have been shocked, even saddened, by

this visage of his brother, Kane felt no surprise. His body expected it, and the appearance made him whole.

All at once, he realized this place, his brother, everything was the same as the episode in Sue's apartment. At the time, Tim had been a grotesque shadow ticking beyond the door, waiting for him to open the endless darkness so he could impart the same words.

"Get out," the lips hissed, air squealing outwards. It was the same message as in the letter, always the same message: *Get out.*

He couldn't take it anymore. The letter, the vision, and now this drug-fueled psychotic breakdown. Even in death, his brother was toying with him. He had to be. This constant hold Tim had on his life enraged Kane.

"Get out!?" he whisper-responded through gritted teeth, feeling as though he was swinging blindly at a piñata. "Get out of what? From where?"

He expected his brother to parrot his rage, but his provocation went unanswered.

"But you, Kane, will know how much worse the future stops." Kane took a frightful gasp. *Oh no.* "You'll know the only true emptiness," the shade continued, "as you race towards the lie you've told yourself since the beginning."

Kane recognized these words at once, his mind dizzily jostling and shaking. Shit, it was the last part of Tim's letter. Although he wanted to reach out and halt Tim from speaking, he was only able to mouth the word: *no.* It was a feeble attempt and doomed to failure.

"The monolith, the end, the nothingness and the unknown. Kane, you too can get out; it's the only way to save yourself from what's to come. Follow me, and together we can get past it, together we can see the other side. Together we can know. First, Kane, you have to get out."

The lie Kane had told himself. Getting to the other side. *Get out.*

It felt like a hand was creeping into his throat, wrapping its fingers around his vocal cords and grasping what made him human: his groans, shrieks and cackles. His words. None of this made any sense, but then it did make sense. His parents, his sister, his brother—there was no way to reconcile with them. His life was shit, ruined by his childhood, his father, Molly and worst of all, himself. The encroaching monolith of nothingness was coming, and there was no way to get past it. And the lie? Even as he read the letter for the first time, he knew what it was: that he was born to live. No, he wasn't. He was born dead. From the beginning, this Earth was empty for him. He was powerless and a danger to those around him. His brother had made that known, but it was the monolith that put it into focus.

There was no way past the nothingness he was speeding towards. Soon, the whole of humanity would realize this same fate—for themselves and those they thought they knew and loved.

"So, what's the point of suffering anymore? Of all this?" As Kane sputtered the words, choking on the contraction in his throat, his brother vanished. It was as if he hadn't existed in the first place; his memory fluttered into oblivion. In his place, Kane's hand grasped a pistol, white knuckled.

Kane glanced at the monolith before looking at his hand. The choice was obvious. He could feel the drugs coursing through his veins, wrapping around his heart and pulling it into collapse. What did it matter? Kane held the barrel of the gun to his temple. His life was ruined anyway. His sister had abandoned him. Had changed. He was more homeless than not, dependent on the distraction of meth and whatever else the dingy, fluid splattered walls of the dens he frequented offered. Even Mollie had left him. That was the most ridiculous part.

In life, his brother had so much more, but even he found himself helplessly floating down the stream leading to the inevitable falls. Still, Tim had found his way out and not only gifted Kane with his visions, but the way to make them stop as well. He had shown Kane how to get out.

And that way was clutched in his hand, he was sure of it. It glinted in a light that didn't exist. Would never exist.

Kane pulled the trigger, his last thought being, *God, I hope at least my death has some meaning.*

CHAPTER
TWENTY-TWO

A DENSE DARKNESS ENSHROUDED KANE. IT PERMEATED THROUGHOUT his synapses, binding the neurons together while thoughts and memories jostled into a black sludge. He had pulled the trigger and felt the bullet slowly make its way into his brain. He was drifting into an eternal quietus, free and yet caged. There were no more visions, no more sensations, no more visits from memories. It was perfect nothing, and even Kane's relief dissolved into numbness.

However, to his dismay, a prodding tone kept darting into the sphere of emptiness and provoking flashes and tingling bursts of light. It was a voice, it was hysterical, and it was violently wrenching him from the end he so desperately craved.

"Kane!" For a moment, his name was clear before warbling into muffled incoherencies.

Just let me die, Kane thought as the act of plying up words from his cemented brain caused extreme disgust and discomfort.

But the voice didn't abate. Instead, other words streaked

past. "Kane! Where the hell—outside—what happened?" The tone had become torrents of energy and sound which threatened to collapse the beautiful ball of emptiness he had surrounded himself with. A prickle let Kane know sensations were returning to his limbs. He groaned, desperately searching his mind for the pistol he held a few moments, or an eternity, ago. *Don't save me. I'm begging you.*

"Kane!" This word came crashing through the drug-fueled haze, and his eyes fluttered open to find his sister perched atop him, grabbing his shirt and throttling him violently. At first, it was hard to speak, but the effects of the drugs wore off with an engineered precision. Before he knew what was happening, the haze and dizziness dissolved, and he found himself face to face with his sister, her bright red cheeks marked with tears.

"Kane!" She grabbed him harshly and gave him a deep hug.

For a moment, he wondered at her utter ineptitude at judging his condition, but those thoughts soon vanished as he found himself hugging her as well. If he had to go on living a little longer, at least Sue would be there.

Unfortunately, those good feelings didn't last. Once Sue realized her brother was okay, she abruptly released him, stood up and looked poised to unleash a killer rage.

"And what the fuck happened here?" she asked, looking around. Kane followed her eyes and was shocked to discover the remnants of their hotel room. Most of the wallpaper had disintegrated along with chunks of the underlying drywall. Where boards were exposed, they were bleached in sickly white, aged and tattered. The floor around Kane was burnt in the shape of his body, which lent the air of a crime scene. However, the strangest part were the beds. Somehow, through some unknown, terrible force, they had flipped on top of each other and melted together. Kane wasn't sure how that was possible, but the mattress, the sheets and the wood were fused within themselves, like a mirror had been placed in the center and one was staring at its opposing image.

Kane could feel the crackling of the charred carpet before a large, awkward object pressed into his spine. Without thinking, he rolled over.

Oh no, he thought.

"And what the fuck is that?" His sister leaned forward, her hand plunging behind Kane's back.

"Shit." Kane closed his eyes. Why had he moved? If he had just stayed calm, he could have easily blamed the entire scene on another episode. Sue would be pissed about the hotel room. She'd force Kane to apologize to Stver so he could pay for the damages, but now?

"Are you serious, Kane?!" Sue's hand emerged grasping his makeshift pipe and the little vial. Her face contorted as she smelled the contents and then furiously tossed them across the room.

"Sue, wait, before you say anything..." He racked his brain for a lie.

"Say what, Kane? That you're a drug addict? That you triggered an episode and wrecked this whole fucking place to get a fix?"

"Hey, now, you don't know that."

His sister snorted, shaking her head in disbelief. "This whole time, I should have known. Those long bathroom breaks, those times you looked so dazed you struggled to form words. Ha!" she mumbled to herself, turning around once again to inspect that damage.

"And what, I'm supposed to feel sorry for you? I thought you'd died!" She snarled, although with the amount of tears streaming down her face, Kane could tell she was anything but unconcerned.

"This is the same thing that killed Tim, you fucking asshole!" She whipped her hand forward to throw the vial and pipe but realized she'd already tossed them away.

"Killed Tim?" Kane was unfazed by her outburst. "Killed Tim!?" he said louder. "Are you insane? Drugs didn't kill Tim—a bullet did! For fuck-sakes, Suzannah, I was there!"

Sue's face softened, and Kane rapidly continued, "And why the hell do you think I'm so fucked up anyway? Tim took drugs for the same reason I do. This life is unbearable. You think you have it bad, try finding your brother dead directly before inheriting his waking nightmares. You have no idea, Suzannah. None at all of what my life has been like. What, you think you can judge me for wanting to alleviate the pain a little bit?"

His sister wasn't looking at him. Her empty eyes stared at the floor to the left of his feet. After a deep breath, the red in her face drained out and left a pale green.

"I see," she said quietly. "I thought you'd lost your job, lost Mollie, and avoided me because of the episodes. That had nothing to do with it, did it?" She looked at Kane, and her face was completely atonic. "*You* ruined your life. With drugs and who knows what other bad decisions."

"No, Sue, you don't understand how awful it's been." Kane stammered out, his confidence and furor dissolving rapidly. "Our parents, Little Tim's success, the episodes, the—"

"I had the same parents, Kane. And you never had Father like I did." At this, Kane went silent. Years of excuses fell apart, the tapestry of lies and arrogance unweaving thread by thread until the entire mosaic became tattered strands. "We all suffer, but it's what we do with that suffering that matters."

That phrase was ripped right from Little Tim's biography —the coined phrase he would say during interviews or right before some grand prediction. It was straight out of the mouth of a dead man—a corpse who had killed himself because he couldn't deal with his world anymore. Yet Sue believed it. And although Kane hated himself for it, he did as well.

"I'm sorry, Sue—"

His sister cut him short. "Save it, Kane." Tears formed in her eyes again. "I can't believe I came back for you. I can't believe you would do this."

"Sue." Kane stood up and looked around the hotel room. His words sounded hollow, and he knew it: "Look, I'm sorry. I'll explain what happened to Stver. I'll go into rehab. You'll have your brother back. I promise."

"No, Kane. You can't fix this. It's all your fault, and you can't fix this." Sue was pointing over to the cages where Muffinz and Muffins should have been. Should have, but weren't. The room was too small and the front door was off its hinges. Not only that, but each cage was torn and twisted, their metal bars crumpled together and dissolved. It was obvious what had happened. They had either both escaped, which wasn't likely, or succumbed to the same surreal power that had aged this room a century. Either way, they were dead.

"All my fault." He breathed out, frozen in place. This was all his fault. If only he had the strength to avoid the drugs. If only he had stayed dead. It would have been easier for those around him.

But why did he turn out like this? Why did he isolate himself, hide his pain and blame the world for things when he had his sister who cared and was willing to help? *Was* willing to help.

Could he honestly blame this on his parents? On his brother, the episodes or on Mollie? Or was it him and him alone? If only he had stayed dead. Although, if he had died, what was the reason for his suffering? The episodes, his brother's death, his childhood. Wasn't there some greater meaning to this? There had to be, because if not, then dying here wasn't merely the saddest option, but the best one as well.

If that was the case, Tim's Edge truly was the finish line. For everyone.

"You're not my brother, Kane. You've changed." Her voice was frigid and held its own darkness. "I'm going to the mine until this is over. I don't want to see or speak with you for the rest of my life. Ever."

The Monolith creates another end.

But that wasn't true, and he knew it. Through his own doing, he had single-handedly wrecked the two most important things in his sister's life: her cats and himself. Even worse, in losing Muffinz, he had stripped away her opportunity at redemption and growth. Sue must think his episodes were self-induced through addiction. That he'd somehow chosen to do this, to become this.

Kane sighed. She might not be wrong.

There was no reason to ask her to stay; no apology would suffice. His only option was to stare at her through tears, wishing he'd never been born.

CHAPTER
TWENTY-THREE

BROKE AS THE SHATTERED HALF OF A HOMELESS TOY. THE THOUGHT limped around Kane's mind, abstract and yet oppressively detailed.

After his sister left, he lay on the floor for a long time, eyes open, hands crossed like he was in a casket. For hours, he neither slept nor moved; he stared upwards towards an ashen ceiling in thoughtless abandon.

His father's words repeated in his head: broken as the shattered half of a homeless toy. True in every sense, even the figurative ones. Kane could hardly feel his limbs, the tips of his fingers and toes numb and tingling. His neck was crooked, and his lower back throbbed and ached. It was par for the course: broken, shattered, discarded—a toy without a chest, a plaything without purpose.

Kane wanted to lie on the stained carpet forever. Hell, this was as good a final resting place as any. Then, after what seemed like hours, a feeling deep in his body prodded him to stand. It started as a twitch in his nose before transforming into a throb in his throat. Seconds later, the throb morphed into a pinch of the same soft flesh the fingers had wrapped around in his dream. Kane flung himself upwards with a heavy fit of coughing. The pinch wasn't a pinch at all. It was a tug towards the front door. It was obvious the urge to leave wasn't his own, but he didn't care. The tug, the itch, only lessened as he weighed leaving the room.

Kane groaned at the pops and snaps, and forced himself upwards. After emerging from his stupor, his eyes felt so dry he wondered if he had even blinked.

"Ah, dammit!" Another groan. The itch was awful, but he had no intention of fighting it. Even if he had the energy to resist, he didn't have the will. He was shit at leading his own life, so why not let something else take charge for a while?

But why did the sensation in his throat feel so desperate for him to go outside? As Kane stood up and walked into the night, he realized the *why* didn't matter. Asking was as meaningful as asking the heart *why* after each beat.

Although he wasn't sure what time it was, the flaming opal glow in the sky told him it was nearing dawn. How long had it been since he'd eaten? Since he'd drank anything? The real question was: Did any of that matter? He had no idea what he was doing out here. None at all. When Kane searched himself for purpose, the response from his body was simple: *Press on.* To what? Maybe nothing. Maybe everything. Kane could only follow its pull and feel delicious relief that he was no longer in control.

The streets of Lunar City were bustling. In the short time since his dirt-bike ride into town, the population must have grown twenty times. The roads were crammed like multi-colored sardines stuffed into an oblong can and a shanty town had built its way up for miles in each direction. If Kane had mustered more awareness of his surroundings, he would have wondered at signs which read "Two hundred dollars for ten gallons of water OR ten pounds of food," "Balancing on Tim's Edge: Psychic Readings" and "Private Security." But as it stood, he was too engrossed in his own thoughts to notice more than a few inches beyond his feet.

No part of Lunar City displayed anything less than a vivid, boisterous energy. A vibrancy was dancing around the multi-colored tents - sparks of human electricity spraying out and bouncing across the landscape. Loud music could be heard, drinking, reveling and a host of other sounds that lent depth and texture to the shifting festival mosaic.

Kane passed by them all, occasionally dodging a drunkard falling from atop a make-shift bar or observing a gathering of people praying in a large group hug. Chanting, cursing, moaning, screams, fireworks, gunshots, car engines, the smell of pot, fried food, burnt plastic, blood and piss. Kane felt as though his face was strapped to a carnival kaleidoscope as he luged down a rainbow into a dumpster full of partially digested skittles. It was overwhelming.

"End of the world party," Kane mumbled, stepping over a lifeless body who had either collapsed or died near an over-flowing plastic outhouse.

Eventually, he spotted a break in the sea of multi-colored lights and sounds. It was a small hill, and Kane realized it was the same one he'd seen entering Lunar City a few days ago. Although it used to be right on the outskirts of town, directly near the "Welcome to" sign, the shanty town now continued for hundreds of meters past this point.

The thing in Kane's throat, the muted tug, drove him atop the hill with a subtle tenacity.

"Oh good," he mumbled through gritted teeth, "another hike."

After an arduous trek upwards, he paused to catch his

breath. Why this oasis remained uninhabited was odd. The sides were steep, but it only took him a few minutes to ascend. Kane guessed the revelry below was too enticing to bother climbing up here.

After perching atop the highest point, he found himself completely alone, watching the distant sky as dawn approached. The sounds below were muffled by a cool breeze buzzing across the landscape, and Kane marveled at how muffled the rest of the world had become. It was so quiet, Kane could hear his own heartbeat.

Suddenly, the horizon went ablaze with rays of light from the encroaching sun. Kane was taken aback as he found himself facing Moon Mountain, its jagged silhouette obvious amongst the smooth shadowed backdrop.

The tug in his throat intensified: a feeling of miniature spindles writhing and unwrapping deep in his flesh. He coughed once, but this only agitated and hastened its momentum. Kane reached up to touch his Adam's apple but paused as he became aware of a stark change in the dark outline of Moon Mountain. Was it his eyes or did the silhouette look sharper, spikier, as though it had grown more teeth? Kane strained forward to see, but the dim light cloaked the landscape in a thick shadow.

"They have to be trees," Kane whispered to no one in particular, tilting forward and squinting to bring their gentle sway into focus. "Must be the breeze." But as light crept over the crest, the true horror of the scene flared into focus: the entire mountain and miles of the surrounding desert were teeming with black tentacles—gigantic and wriggling like newly born maggots sprouting from flesh. Each of the large ones were dotted with several small feelers, spiny, thin and lashing about the air chaotically. Those on the mountain enlaced the rock whereas the smaller ones were popping up from the ground for miles in each direction.

Over the course of a few seconds, Kane saw dozens of new tentacles thrust upwards from the earth, contorting and writhing. Their spinning and graceful flailing gave Kane the impression they were searching for something, but he had no idea for what.

With each passing moment, the larger appendages gained in mass until they threatened the size of the entire landscape itself. It was a ballet, and Kane could hardly breathe, let alone look away. "Am I having another episode?" he mumbled, glancing at the surrounding town before focusing once again on Moon Mountain. The hustle and bustle hadn't eased. In fact, the morning sun only imbued new energy to the carousing as if it were nearing the climax of a ritual.

It wasn't an episode. It was real. Gods, it was real. The mountain was somehow infested with an ethereal parasite.

Without thinking, he charged down the hill, skating dangerously across steep dirt before tenuously catching his footing on a few outcroppings of rocks. He was sweating; his racing heart pumped adrenaline into cramping guts as his vision blurred. The mountain was infested. The entire thing.

Kane leapt off a ledge a few meters above the bottom of the hill, landing on the roof of a car which had parked itself beside the sign to the town. A horn blared and a voice cursed at him from a nearby tent, but Kane didn't stop running. The important things in his life, in his pitiful existence, suddenly came into focus. "Sue!" he gasped.

The right chord was struck and the entity guided him through the alleyways and tumult of the encampment. Kane could feel they had the same purpose: they had to get to Moon Mountain as soon as possible. He had no idea why their goal was the same, nor did he care if he was heading into a dangerous trap. None of that mattered. His worthless life had found a reason to live, a purpose which made the bullshit he'd gone through worth it. He would save his sister, even if it took his last breath.

CHAPTER
TWENTY-FOUR

KANE DIDN'T KNOW IF IT WAS FATE OR LUCK, BUT SHORTLY AFTER diving headfirst into the make-shift alleyways of Lunar City, he stumbled upon the same motorcycle he had ridden earlier. Its driver was pouring gas in the tank from a small plastic canister, clearly a few moments away from departing.

Kane sprinted towards the vehicle breathlessly, ready to plead and beg for a ride. However, as soon as he approached, the man grinned, patted the seat and said, "Hop on."

A familiar rumble emerged and Kane nearly tumbled off as the small, yet surprisingly fast dirt bike sped off with a roar.

"Hang on!" the man yelled, his voice nearly inaudible amidst the drone and gurgle of the engine. No warning was needed. He was already clutching the man's jacket and squeezing his thighs together until his abs hurt.

The driver avoided the packed main roads, instead choosing dirt paths which cut across the desert arbitrarily. Unfortunately, these roads hadn't been maintained in decades, and the constant washouts and poor grating jostled Kane into a sickened state. Through sheer will, he kept from throwing up and only asked the driver to stop once for a quick breather after nearly plummeting into a ravine.

Originally, Kane had hoped to get as close to the gate as possible but found the encampment in front of the mine had ballooned so dramatically, it stretched hundreds of meters from the entrance. Upon seeing this, and without a "thank you" or "goodbye", he ripped his helmet off, leapt from the motorbike and plunged into the crowd.

He felt as though he were swimming through an ocean filled with wreckage, desperately flinging his arms this way and that, pushing and pulling to move a few meters forward. Some of the crowd grunted, others swung at him, but Kane was relentless, imbued by a mortal fear for his sister and the horror surrounding him.

For Kane, *horror* wasn't a word that could aptly describe the entirety of the scene. People weren't the only things he had to dodge. The sprouting tentacles were far more plentiful and thick than he had initially believed. Some areas were so over-grown, they outnumbered the unsuspecting crowd and formed a small onyx-colored forest.

Whatever infested the mountain sprouted farther and farther from its base. Although dense, none of those in front of him gave any hint they'd noticed the danger. Kane' stomach bunched into knots as he worked his way forward, watching those same obsidian tentacles wrap around unsuspecting victims' legs, stomachs and necks. After forcing their way into the throats of a few in the crowd, they threaded outwards through gaping holes in their chests.

"Oh," Kane gasped. How could he be the only one seeing this? Even those who had been stuffed and gutted moved about inconspicuously. After the tentacle rammed through the face of the victims, their features faded, darkened and had the color of their skin drained into monochromatic hues charred by utter blackness. A few seconds later, the same swirling black mass of midnight appeared, swiveling around an unseen focal point

At least it was happening slowly, Kane failed to console himself while stepping over a tentacle writhing up from the earth. Until now, only a few dozen people had entirely succumbed to the transformation. *Concentrate, Kane!* Whatever was going on here, he would have to deal with it later. Sue came first.

Oddly enough, the tentacles didn't give any indication they'd noticed him. Was it because he already had the black mass on his face? Or was his safety contingent on playing a part in some unknown force's machinations? The latter was so terrifying, Kane shook the idea from his mind.

It had only been a day since his tantrum-fueled departure from the mine, yet the area surrounding the front gate had drastically changed. The guards and employees had withdrawn from view, leaving large cement blocks and barbed wire in their place. Where previous signs had once stood, new handwritten ones had been posted: "Warning, high voltage electrical fence", "Warning, area beyond this point landmined" and "Warning, snipers will fire on trespassers."

As Kane stepped beyond the packed crowd, the unfurled scene caused him to drop to his knees. Before him lay a war zone: dismembered bodies flung in small craters behind the fence, graffiti sprayed slurs and blessings covering the walls and dozens of charred remains leaning against the electric wire. These people had called the foundations bluff and lost.

The crowd at the gate were viciously screaming, even those stuffed with tentacles. Kane shakily stood up and took another step forward. This wasn't a battlefield. This wasn't a fight; the people here were agitated prisoners in an internment camp. A death camp. Kane flinched and turned with a wince as a sparking and flash to his right caused a man who had ventured too close to the fence to start smoking. They were in a gigantic bug zapper, and even his violent encounter with yesterday's crowd was a paradise compared to this madness. Holy hell, this conflict had escalated quickly.

Kane worked his way closer to the gate, holding back a growing nausea, and was surprised to step into a small clearing at its front. Although, on second thought, why was this unexpected? The entrance was on complete lockdown—chains, barbed wire and cement blocks were strategically placed to stop anyone from climbing over. With landmines, snipers and who knows what else waiting directly beyond the reinforced steel plates, breaking into the facility from this point, or even loitering here too long, was flat-out suicide.

"Suicide," Kane whispered. A luxury he didn't have.

The tug in his throat pulled him forward and so, with a deep breath, he walked to the front and rattled the bars. He half-expected a deadly shock to blast through his body and trembled with relief when it didn't happen. How ludicrous would it have been for the sensation guiding him to suddenly want him dead. Right?

"Sue!" he called out, sidestepping a tentacle that squirmed upwards near his right foot. "Let me in, you bastards!" He grasped the bars tighter and throttled them without effect. Like the mine, they were tightly locked and hardly squeaked at his violent pounding.

"It's me, Kane!" he yelled again. "Let me in!"

He desperately hoped that a worker watching from the inside would recognize and come out to get him. Hopefully, Sue hadn't already mandated they bar his entry—which was harsh, even for her. If that was the case, he wasn't sure what his next move would be. He hadn't expected the circumstances at the mine to have changed so drastically, and he hadn't considered he would have issues getting inside. Ethereal help notwithstanding.

"Stver was right," he mumbled to himself, looking around for options.

If he couldn't get in this way, what else could he do? Once again, Kane looked over to his right and left. Both sides had the same electric fence running across them. Should he hike around to see if it was any different? There could be a break in the fence somewhere with less people. Of course, less people meant less sprung traps. And honestly, he knew that with hundreds of people gathered in the surrounding area, the back door had already been tried.

"Sue!" he yelled again, unable to think of anything else. "Sue, dammit!" Kane bashed the bars with the flat of his hand and screeched an inhuman cry. To come this far only to fail. His chest bunched together as panic nearly caused him to freeze. He couldn't stop here. His sole purpose was to save his sister. If he lost that? Kane recalled the gun he shot himself with and shook his head violently. That could wait until after Sue was safe. Right now, he had to save her. Save her or die trying.

But how? This place was like Fort Knox. From the count of bodies both within and outside the fence, dozens of people had already attempted to get inside. Was he actually smarter than any one of them?

Kane grunted and bashed the bars again, waiting for the tug in his throat to lead him on. Silence. Was it stumped as well or was it waiting for something? He had no idea, no plans. He had nothing.

"Nothing?" he heard his father say as a memory burst into his head. "Don't you know the best part of having nothing?" Pops had that stupid grin on his face, smirking at his depressed son who'd struck out and lost his little league team the game.

"When you have nothing, there's always someone you can ask for help."

Is that what Kane should do in this moment? Get on his knees and beg God to carry him straight to his sister? This was the same God Kane didn't believe in and to Whom he and his brother must be blasphemous abominations. The reality was, Kane wasn't even sure his father had meant God, the Holy Spirit or Jesus. More likely, his father had meant himself.

"When you have nothing, there's always someone you can ask for help." The line raced around his head. Who could he ask for help if God was removed from the picture? The people here were as weak as he was. Just as frail and wanting. Suddenly, it hit him. He knew who he could ask.

The idea rammed into his brain and Kane wished God were real for the first time in his life.

·

CHAPTER
TWENTY-FIVE

HE HAD NOTHING. IN FACT, LESS. IN MAKING HIS LIFE'S GOAL TO SAVE his sister, he was staring into the abyss—one step away from crumbling to the bottom.

"When you have nothing, there's always someone you can ask for help," his father had advised.

Regardless of the originally intended patron, Kane knew his last remaining option was not what Dad would have wanted. Taking a deep breath, he closed his eyes and let the morning sun caress his face. He had stumbled too far down this rabbit hole to claw his way out. *Since God can't help me, I may as well look below.*

Kane gulped and focused on his throat and the entity he felt dwelling within. It was obvious they had the same purpose: get inside the mine. At least, that's what he hoped. The thing had already helped steer him towards the man with the motorcycle. It had also led him atop the hill right before dawn. Without those urges, he wouldn't have known Sue was in danger, nor would he have been able to arrive here so rapidly.

But now, although their combined journey was far from over, Kane had lost the feeling of guidance. Whatever was in his throat had slithered into its hovel the moment he'd arrived at the fence. Even as Kane stood in front of the gate, the thing remained aloof. Was it waiting for something? That such a dominant, pervasive force would lie in wait was ridiculous. Ridiculous and terrifying.

Kane placed his forehead on the bars and felt the cool of the metal spread throughout his face. He was missing a key detail and didn't have time to sort through what it was. His back muscles tensed as the jittery feeling of impatience rippled through his quaking limbs. He didn't have time for this shit. He needed help, and pronto. Regardless of where it came from and what it took.

"You there?" Kane centered his mind's eye on his throat. No movement or response.

"Hey, thing. Ethereal thing. I said, 'Are you there?'" In spite of his mental yell, he didn't feel a reaction. No presence, no movement, no voices or demonic gargling in his head. Was it sleeping? Or was its MO to only appear in the most inopportune times?

"Look, I'm begging you. We need to talk, if that's even possible. I need your help. My sister—I need to get her out of there. I'll do anything. I know you have the power."

Kane took a deep breath and concentrated on the last spot he remembered feeling it. "I have no idea what's going on. Please. I don't know what else to do."

Sweat formed tiny sparkling beads on his brow as the silence continued. Tears welled up in his eyes.

"Listen, you little asshole—I said I'd do anything! Anything—do you hear me? I know you want to get inside too. I felt it. Why aren't you working together with me on this!?"

The entity remained wholly dormant or wholly ignoring him.

"Why!? Why!?" Kane let his anger loose, the words slipping from mind to mouth. "Why won't you help me!? This doesn't make any sense!" His imagination generated images of his sister, an onyx tentacle wrapped around her neck as she became infested by the surreal disease infecting this place.

Kane panicked and slid into a reckless abandon. For the first time in his entire life, he made a promise he had no intention of breaking. "I'll do anything!" he shouted into his hands. "Anything!"

At that moment, it was true. He would do anything: lie, steal, cheat, kill or kill himself. All of it was on the table. At any scale.

Losing control was terrifying but oddly freeing as well. It was like jumping from a cliff and realizing you only have to fall. What other option did he have than to enjoy his last moments before splattering on the ground? And as he gave himself up, once he truly meant it, the freedom of being controlled was intoxicating. For once in his life, events weren't born from his own incompetence, from his childhood trauma or ingrained character faults. He had no personal responsibility, and that was a beautiful thing.

This feeling of submission grew, and with it, a sense of belonging. Kane felt a prickle dislodge itself from his tonsils and spread throughout his body with miniscule spindly roots. It was innocuous and electrifying. He realized that success or failure didn't rely on his own virtues. This was the new Kane. Another color in the sea of black. And yet, even as he was torn apart and sewn together atom by atom, a piece of his old self remained. He had to save his sister. If he did that, whatever cosmic force was commanding him could do as it pleased.

As the tingle of tiny threads of darkness spiraled outwards

to his fingertips and toes, the stark sensation of belonging and control melted away. He was the water and the entity was the salt. Unified yet imperceptible. Kane took a step backwards and opened his eyes, squinting at the bright, washed out landscape. He felt the irresistible urge to walk right and although the why was a mystery, his covenant demanded obedience. Kane didn't doubt the path for a moment.

After a few hundred meters, he found a large outcropping of rocks similar to where he had faced off with the anti-protesters the day before. In fact, this was the exact same place. What a coincidence.

Atop the highest rock, a man shouted into the crowd, most of whom nodded in approval while raising their fists and shouting in response. Strangely, no tentacles had sprouted in this area, and those which made their home nearby were smaller and deflated. Was there some power here, some unknown force, driving the darkness away? Possibly, but what did it matter?

As for the entity, Kane didn't sense a reaction after passing into the clearing. Did the other tentacles not want to be there? Another piece in a puzzle he had no interest in solving.

"If we go in together, there's no way they'll be able to stop us!" Kane heard the man on the rock cry out. "We'll topple the fence and storm inside, overwhelming them with our numbers!"

"What about the landmines?" a voice from the crowd yelled.

"Don't worry, they only placed them in front." The man smiled confidently.

As Kane approached, he wasn't surprised to find the man had the black mass swirling around his face—albeit detached from any tentacles. This sort of fervent lunacy had to be driven by an energy beyond human comprehension. Right?

"It's true!" Another voice emerged from the crowd and a woman stepped forward. Her face had the same dark shroud as the man. "We watched them last night. They didn't have enough to cover everywhere, so they only put a few dozen near the main entrance."

"Landmines, snipers—even if those things were fully in place, they can't stop us." The man hopped from the rock and walked around the crowd, putting a verbal coup de grâce on any resistance.

"God is on our side, brothers and sisters. Through His help, we'll stop this unholy abomination and free the world from the grasp it has on the minds of its zealots. For we do not wrestle against flesh and blood, but against the rulers, against the authorities, against the cosmic powers over this present darkness, against the spiritual forces of evil in the heavenly places. But the work of God is this: to believe in the one he has sent. And I wasn't just sent, brothers and sisters— you were sent as well. Sent to wage war against Satan and his vassals."

The crowd was wholly raptured, enlightened and drawn in simultaneously. Kane understood how they felt: a part of a grand story arc, warriors in a noble battle, freedom at the loss of control. They were capable of anything now, killing and being killed. They didn't even need tentacles; words were their strings and attached themselves much faster than any ethereal darkness ever could.

Suddenly, there was a flash and the sound of bulbs shattering one after another. Kane watched as rows of lights dotting the fence burst into pieces and went dark. Soon afterwards, the gentle hum which marked the entire electric fence went silent.

Cheers from the crowd—loud, fervent, intoxicating. The preacher gestured softly, and two men ran towards the fence and began cutting. Within seconds, a large piece fell to the ground. More cheers.

Somehow, Kane knew it had to be this way. He would have to remain behind a while, but this was exactly where he needed to be. Most of what the preacher had said was a lie, or at least how he had employed it, but Kane felt no responsibility to stop him. This was a part of some grand plan, and he was merely a piece of a puzzle waiting to be played. Kane had already made his decision to give himself over to a greater cause. Anything to save Sue.

But as the crowd stormed the facility and the first land-mine went off, Kane flinched.

CHAPTER
TWENTY-SIX

"EACH MAN'S WORK WILL BECOME EVIDENT; FOR THE DAY WILL SHOW it because it is to be revealed with fire, and the fire itself will test the quality of each man's work." Kane's father used to employ this verse whenever he caught his children acting out in a way which didn't merit the belt.

"The belt," he would say, "tempers and molds. But fire, well, fire destroys and consumes that which can't be saved."

In general, this had meant material objects like a dirty magazine he found in Tim's room or a picture of Sue and her boyfriend. In those cases, beatings simply wouldn't do. Only fire could cleanse and purge.

Kane recalled his father shoving unwanted objects into a metal trash can before over-dousing them with lighter fluid. Sometimes, before setting them aflame, he would kick the can over for dramatic effect, watching with his family as it rolled away and scattered ashes of sin into the night air.

"But the chaff he will burn up with unquenchable fire," his father would mumble at the end.

As dozens of people moved through the hole in the electric

fence, onward towards the mine's entrance with a lemming-like zeal, Kane briefly wondered if they were the chaff or the fire.

The answer came quicker than expected.

While watching the carnage unfold, he wondered what led these people here. What left another person so willing to put their life on the line? Did they also have a sibling to save? Whatever the reason, whatever spiritual battle of good and evil they found themselves embroiled in, they currently stood on the front lines. As thousands charged forward, spurred on by the preacher, some blog, meme or divine revelation, only one truth was evident in their eyes: they wouldn't stop. Not even at the bitter end.

And the end was bitter.

Within seconds, a few hundred people breached the gate. After a lengthy sprint, they traversed half the gap between the fence and the mine's entrance. Kane watched the crowd swarm the mountain. They had been enraptured and fed the lie of invincibility.

They were omnipotent.

Is this what children feel like as they storm off to war? Kane wondered.

Then, a rumble heralded the coming carnage.

Kane watched as a puff of dust flung itself into the air and spiraled upwards. Seconds later, another explosion rocked him so hard, he nearly toppled backwards. Amidst the crackling of rocks falling to the ground and a hot buzz of air, another menacing sound erupted from the hillside.

Directly after the first explosion, those unaffected by the detonations collapsed. Kane watched as flashes of light twinkled from the barrels of snipers dotting the mountainside. Beyond them, mortars had been positioned atop a plateau, although they only fired canisters of gas into the encroaching horde.

Smoke, burned flesh, whirls of dust and ash were cut by gun fire and screams. To say it was reminiscent of a battlefield would be trite. This wasn't a war; it wasn't even a slaughter. It was a culling on a scale he could hardly imagine. Kane's legs trembled as the entity in his throat asked him to walk straight into it.

He peered around at the cheering crowd. There was no way those surrounding him weren't seeing the exact same thing as he was: death, fear, a hopeless march into oblivion. However, as he looked into their eyes, those unaffected by the tentacles, he saw a sight which scared him most of all: resolve, fearlessness, self-proclaimed virtue. Either they thought the battle would end after only a few moments or they believed the fighting beyond the gate would be over before they went through. Or they thought death only happened to other people, particularly if God was on their side. Kane watched them march, charge and die, racing carelessly towards snipers, towards landmines and gas. Towards nothing. Their own personal monolith.

After the third wave breached the fence, tearing through and birthing from the other side, Kane felt the entity in his throat give an undeniable tug forward. In spite of the carnage, his accusations and misgivings, he couldn't resist. Hell, he didn't want to. Although, unlike this fodder, he knew there truly was a plan. That gave him some assurance, even as another explosion forced him to stumble backwards.

Kane slipped as he reached the opening and caught himself on an elderly gentleman who was limping towards the gate. Was tripping part of the plan as well? Hopefully, he hadn't botched the timing. Although, with the hillside snipers relentlessly firing and each second heralding a new blast from a landmine, this moment was as good as any. He forced himself against the fence, spread open the spiny metal of the flayed wire, and dashed towards Lunar Mountain.

Every few dozen meters, another explosion echoed around him. Kane coughed dust from his lungs and frantically squinted to avoid watching the bloodbath unfold. It wasn't only dirt being flung around, but body parts as well. Each explosion brought another fountain of death as organs and blood sprayed across the ground. Often, the geyser was so dense, puddles of human liquid had formed in the craters.

How many people had already died? How many had already been sacrificed? How many more would die before he reached the entrance? Kane wasn't sure how long this could last. Were so many people willing to sacrifice themselves?

And yet, Kane felt secure. Even after a blast near the middle of the field blew him to the ground and caused a stark ringing in his ears, he felt confident he'd make it inside. What would the point of his entire struggle be if he died here? The possibility was beyond comprehension.

Shivering, Kane forced himself upwards and patted his body down to ensure it was intact. His clothes were a bit singed, but his limbs were affixed to their rightful places. Kane heard a groan to his right and found a mangled woman had taken the brunt of the blow. She lay face down in a puddle of charred earth and was jerking uncontrollably. Should he go over and see if she still had a pulse? Was that the humane thing to do?

A small puff of dirt flung up near his left foot and Kane heard a bullet ricochet behind him. Instinctively, he sprinted forward once again without giving the woman another thought.

How long had he been running? Thirty seconds, a minute? Ten hours? Only a few stragglers had made it this far, a hundred meters or so from the entrance. Kane read the desperation in their eyes, although he doubted it had anything to do with their own safety. No, these fanatics were desperate to get inside and wreak whatever havoc they could. They were runners in a gauntlet, although the finish line could be more dangerous than the race. Who knew what awaited them beyond the darkness hulled entryway? A firing squad? More landmines and snipers? Whatever lay before them, death was assured. However, none of this tempered the determination of his temporary compatriots.

As Kane glanced over to those running alongside him, he noticed an odd detail: each of the five remaining people, none of whom had the swirling black mass, were running in unison with a shaggy man in their middle. A heavy-looking briefcase was dangling from his right hand, swaying violently off-beat to his gait.

Another sound caused Kane to flinch, although it wasn't a blast or impact. It was a crackling coming from the entryway to the mine. Even though he was beginning to understand the timing of his charge through the gate—the landmines detonated, the snipers distracted, so many sacrifices to ensure he made it through—he still saw failure kareeming towards him.

"Those bastards are sealing the front," he gasped.

With wide-eyed horror, Kane watched as thick metal sheets protruded one after another from the side walls of the entryway before slowly creeping together.

"Shit!" He wouldn't make it through before they shut.

If he had been hyped up on meth, he could have pushed through tearing muscles and a ballooning heart. But sober, exhausted and desperate, even his adrenaline rush would easily put him short by a few seconds.

Buzzzzzz. The crackling transformed into an electric whirl. Hidden wheels squeaked and ground while thick metal plates jutted farther and farther from the rock. The process wasn't quick; it was sluggish, yet steady, and Kane had no idea how to stop it.

Was getting stuck beyond the doors part of the plan? That hardly made any sense, and Kane questioned how he'd failed. Was it when he'd tripped? Worse, had he not listened intently enough to the urges he'd been handed? But that couldn't be true. Kane had obeyed each command hastily and without hesitation. Why was this happening?

Kane heard a scream and turned to find two of the six people lying in thickening pools of blood. One sprayed liquid from their neck while the other quietly spilled out with a slight jitter.

The shaggy man barked unintelligible orders, and two of the remaining three people sprinted past Kane with a fury he didn't believe possible. Were they Olympic runners or was he just that out of shape? Within seconds, they had traversed dozens of meters and closed in on the metal doors. *Oh shit, they're going to make it!* Kane felt a sense of relief.

But wait, even if they get inside, what's the plan? Did they intend on finding the control mechanism and opening them again? That was quite the gamble. By that time, Kane and the shaggy man could be dead—shot or maimed. That was assuming the two runners encountered no resistance while blindly searching for a way to open the doors.

"Oh man, are they serious?" Kane mouthed breathlessly as their plan suddenly unfolded.

They had no intention of making it inside. They had no intention of finding a mechanism to open the door. Their plan, their entire plan, was to stop the doors from closing in the first place. Without anything to block them, there was only one option: sacrifice their bodies.

A gag worked its way up his throat as the surreal horror of

their martyrdom became evident. Whoever this man was, or whatever he carried, had to be worth more than the lives of a dozen people.

Kane, the man and his companion reached the entrance as the first crack and gurgle popped out of the two bodies lying horizontally between the large plated doors. It was obvious the wheels were struggling to regain momentum but wouldn't be impeded for long. The sprinters' sacrifice had bought the group a handful of seconds, but Kane wasn't sure it would be enough.

A menacing squeal burst from one of the plates as the doors jammed the bodies together like two fingers pinching through Playdough. The group was only a few dozen feet away now, staring into a crack wide enough for a human body to fit through.

It was now or never.

Suddenly, Kane heard another scream behind him. In full sprint, he turned to find the man's final companion dead on the ground with the man himself wincing and stumbling forward in pain.

Before he could react, a feeling screeched inside his head. "GET INSIDE!" it hissed loudly. "LEAVE HIM!"

Kane froze. The volume was so deafening he nearly blacked out. Another crunch from the doors told him the wheels were moving again. If he was going to get inside, he only had a few seconds left.

Wasn't this why he was there—to save Sue? Damn everything else. He didn't know this guy, didn't know what his intentions were or if he was even worth saving. All that mattered was his sister. It was so obvious. He had even made a covenant.

These people were sacrificing their lives without meaning anyway, some misguided belief system where mysteries they didn't understand were the devil. Why should he stop them? Why should he help them? He was different; his goal was tangible. Kane turned around to face the doors.

As this feeling of apathy struck him, an odd thought tore itself from the darkest recesses of his mind: *If I don't turn around, if I don't revert into the brother she knew, she'll never allow me to save her.*

The shaggy man gave a grunt as Kane grabbed and pushed him inside the mine.

CHAPTER
TWENTY-SEVEN

THE MINE WAS DARK, BUT WHAT DID IT MATTER? DARKNESS WAS better than walking into a shooting gallery or spotting dangling tentacles swaying from the ceiling.

After a boom heralded the large doors slamming shut, the cavern became eerily devoid of noise. Kane strained his head forward but only perceived a gentle hum from dim lights and distant machinery. Surprisingly, he didn't spot a single soul. Although, who knew what was lurking unseen?

Kane glanced right and found heavy equipment jumbled together in carelessly scattered pockets. On his left, a mobile trailer had been parked near a few small tunnels which shot off into different directions. Pipes were zig-zagging this way and that, and Kane saw enough barrels and crates to fill a small warehouse. Who could say what prowled behind the mobile home or any one of these objects, but Kane reckoned the chances of immediate danger were slim. Why hide and stalk them from the shadows? Only two of them had made it inside, and neither were armed.

Kane gritted his teeth and silently hoped Stver and Co.

hadn't left the room unguarded because it was booby-trapped. Although, he far preferred that over the possibility the monolith had murdered everyone in the mine, including his sister, and left behind an empty tomb. In that case, it was likely he and the other man had been lured into an ethereal feeding ground and only a few seconds remained before they became lunch.

If that were true, however, the room wouldn't be as immaculate and peaceful as it appeared. He didn't see bodies, signs of a struggle, or tentacles. If the monolith had enough control, malice and hunger to begin devouring people, why had it let the doors shut? None of this made sense.

"Sue, where are you?" His teeth clenched tighter.

Kane heard rustling and turned to find the shaggy man tottering upwards with a grunt. Was that a thank you? The man stumbled, and Kane reached forward to steady him but was thrust away.

"Hey, are you ok?" Kane's question went unanswered as he watched the shaggy man limp towards a smaller tunnel without a single glance behind him. "Jeeze, what an asshole."

All at once, the booming voice from earlier roared in his head. "STOP HIM!"

What!? Kane dropped to his knees and clutched his face. His head throbbed and felt thick. The shaggy man was oblivious and stoically continued his frenetic hobble forward.

"STOP HIM!" the voice came again, blasting upwards.

All at once, Kane felt a thudding in his throat. A split-second later, frantic images danced through his mind: piecemeal scenes cobbled together in jumbled, low-resolution flashes. He spewed dark liquid as his sister roared into view, her face melting as she screamed in agony. "Sue!" He opened his mouth but the air felt stuck in his lungs.

The image of Sue evaporated. In its place, Kane watched his

own body turn to ash and crumble into infinitesimal pieces so small their existence ceased to matter. As the last burnt remnant fluttered into a pool of darkness, the scene abruptly morphed into the face of the shaggy man. His features were magnified a hundred times until Kane could see the pores on his pocky cheeks. The man was poised in front of the monolith and laughed so intensely, his grinning jaw had split open. Was he laughing at Sue? At Kane?

As quickly as the vision took hold, it vanished. The only lingering sensation was a throbbing nausea and the air of urgency he felt towards the shaggy man. "Stop him!" the voice cried out distantly. Kane listened to the words warble into oblivion.

Kane got on his hands and knees and spit blood. Below him, dark red stains had formed on his pant legs. "Oh man," he moaned. "An episode?"

The shaggy man remained in the main chamber, and if Kane hurried, he could catch him. But why would he do that? Why did he feel such urgency to stop this stranger? Not just urgency, but unbridled disgust. And something else.

Fear.

The more Kane stared at the shaggy man, the more he found him utterly detestable and suspicious.

"Stop him," the voice whispered; this time it was so quiet, it could have been overcome by a soft breeze.

Kane stood up and looked around for a heavy object. A large stone lay a few feet to his left.

"Too thick," Kane muttered. He could hardly lift such a heavy thing, let alone charge and attack with it. If he missed, what then?

A few feet beyond the stone, Kane saw a large crowbar propped next to a crate. Directly behind the crowbar, Kane spotted a hammer.

"That'll do," he whispered while imagining the metal tip bashing into the man's skull. The image was disgusting, but in the end, it wasn't him doing it. He didn't have a choice, after all. *Stop him!* the words echoed in his head.

He would have to make it quick or the other may simply disappear into a side tunnel. Although the shaggy man didn't appear muscular, Kane had no idea how strong he actually was.

"A quick blow to the head," he whispered again, swinging the hammer around a few times.

But as he watched the tip glide back and forth, the odd memory of a piñata surfaced. It was during his sixth birthday, and Kane had heard whimpering from behind the bandana covering his eyes. Who the hell cried right before getting candy? Of course, mystery sobs hadn't dissuaded him from lumbering forward and batting the magical candy-filled doll.

After Kane had swung, he heard such a scream of agony, he'd pissed himself from fear. As the screams continued, Kane had ripped the cloth from his eyes. With a gasp, he found he hadn't slugged a piñata at all, but his sister, whom he later learned his father had placed in front of him as a punishment for stealing candy. But Kane had been her accomplice, eagerly devouring the tasty bits until both their stomachs churned and ached. Was injuring Sue his punishment and another side of the discipline-coin his father so eagerly spent?

"When our Lord walked the earth, thieves would have their hands cut off. How lucky you are to have a merciful father like me."

The hammer was swinging slower in Kane's hand. He didn't want to strike the man the same as he didn't want to hit Sue. What was he thinking? His head felt thick and taut, his thoughts blurred. He swayed his chin left and right to dislodge himself from the stupor. Did the entity actually want the man in front of him dead? If so, why was it Kane's task specifically? Couldn't the thing do it on its own?

He glanced at the hammer and his fingers loosened. The handle slipped beyond his grip and as it struck dirt, Kane felt a rift cleave between himself and his covenant. The threads of darkness unwound, and he no longer felt a tug on the flesh of his throat. Its presence had been replaced by an eerie isolation. Any sense he was being guided evaporated, and Kane was left wondering at the newfound emptiness. It was like losing a limb. He hadn't realized the depth of need until after it had vanished.

But even as Kane struggled with the weight of loneliness and the cold feeling of exile, he recognized separation was the right path—the only path. If the universe willed it, the entity would be merciful. Remembering his sister's screams had undone his erstwhile devotion and Kane hoped the thing could understand and accept the erratic side of human behavior. He had made a covenant, sure, and if the entity reappeared, he would honor what he could. However, Kane recognized his limits, and that gave him hope he was slowly changing from the monster Sue thought he was. That Kane thought he was.

Hopefully the sentiment lasts. With clenched fists, he watched the man stand hesitantly in front of one of the tunnels, peering forward as if discerning shadowed directions. After a time, the man's head drifted to the ceiling of the cavern. If he was praying, Kane had no idea to whom. A moment later, he vanished into darkness.

The shaggy man was long gone when Kane finally gathered the wherewithal to press on. For a moment, he considered traversing the same tunnel. But then, what would happen if they met again? Would he be rocked with an uncorked, uncontrollable bloodlust? Kane shivered at the thought of the hammer and felt his confidence waver.

With a deep breath, he walked into a different tunnel on the right. If memory served, this was the same one Stver and the reporter had entered during their interview. Or had it been on the opposite end of the cavern? The tunnel was unlit, as the others were, and the sheer depth of darkness caused a rippling contortion in his gut.

"For Sue," he mumbled, closing his eyes and stepping forward.

Walking through any tunnel was unnerving, but one so endless and utterly void of light was unbearable. Where was he headed? Could he find the exit without the entity's guidance? The absence of light was so dense, it was palpable. Light licked the entrance walls, but only droplets spilled inches across its borders before being devoured.

Kane shuffled forward, hoping his eyes would adjust and allow a glimpse of a dim exit. He placed his hand on the tunnel wall and scraped his feet along. As the drops of light from the entrance evaporated, Kane felt less and less confident in his choice.

"What if there are a few side paths?" he asked aloud, hoping to repel some of the fear with the sound of his own voice. "Or a sudden plunge where a vertical shaft was built into the ground?" he continued, the echoes of his words bringing him growing discomfort. Hadn't he heard that somewhere: miners love digging vertical shafts in the middle of horizontal ones? Or had he made that up?

"Oh fuck," Kane moaned loudly, taking slow deep breaths. Why hadn't he stopped and looked around for a flashlight? Didn't miners wear those little hats with the lights built in? He had more than likely passed by tons of them lying around in the last chamber. Earlier, Kane hadn't considered this aspect in the slightest. He was piss-poor at practical matters like planning and, as his father used to say, it may actually kill him one day.

"Today's the day." He glanced over his shoulder to judge how far he'd walked. To his surprise, the light from the entrance had completely vanished. Kane wasn't sure if he had unknowingly rounded a corner or the lights had been cut. He desperately hoped it was the former because darkened lights usually meant intent. The additional thought of a person or creature stalking behind him provoked an anxiety his mind struggled to contain.

Kane froze and listened, but the only sounds emanating in the darkness were echoes from his breath. It was so unbearably quiet. It was as if he'd been swallowed by the tunnel and was careening through its bowels. He wasn't sure what was worse: hearing nothing or hearing something. On one hand, the sounds of dripping water or rushing wind would be a godsend. On the other, any crunching or squishing noises, and he might wet himself before blacking out.

After a few moments of silence, a prickly, creeping feeling worked its way from his fingertips to his shoulders. It was as though his body had noticed a subtle detail he hadn't.

Kane peered around and strained his ear against the darkness. Nothing. It was all in his head.

"All in my head," he whispered as the tingle transformed into goosebumps which blistered over his entire neck.

"All in my head," he muttered again, placing his hand on the smooth, cold rock to avoid tipping over from the anxiety-induced vertigo.

He pursed his lips and pulled his hand back when a miniscule vibration discharged from the surface. Kane froze. That couldn't be right. The vibration had been so tiny, so utterly devoid of strength, he was confident it was a fabrication of his nerves.

Kane bent towards the ground and placed his ear firmly against the rock. The stone was as silent as ever. "Thank goodness." He sighed deeply.

Then, without warning, the vibration returned, increased and contorted into a gentle hum. Kane gasped. Whatever provoked this sound was still desperately faint, but indisputably increasing. Clenching every muscle in his body, Kane pressed his ear harder against the wall. Less than a second later, the slight vibration morphed into a steady throb.

Kane ripped his ear from the rock and strained his eyes into the darkness. The sound vanished. Wiping the sweat from his brow and mumbling a silent plea, he once again bent over to listen. *Hhuuummmbbb.*

"It's not in my head." His breathing turned sharp. It was getting louder.

"Shit." Should he keep walking or sprint back to the entrance? Before him lay the unknown. Behind him, the absurd. Kane imagined a monster had shut the lights off for an easy kill. Should he ask the entity in his throat for help? Beg and plead until it awoke and led him to safety? Kane seriously weighed this option, but upon recalling how it felt to be so deeply controlled, decided against it.

After a momentary hesitation, Kane decided to continue forward—albeit at a light jog.

"How long could this damn tunnel be?" Kane's hand caught a sharp rock. "Ouch!" He forced a laugh at the notion he'd touched teeth. The stone had been sharp, but Kane didn't feel any blood on his hand. "That would be the cherry on top, wouldn't it?"

"Hopefully, no sharks live in this tunnel."

As if waiting for a cue, the sound simultaneously erupted

from the walls, the floor and air. It was like he found himself trapped inside a plucked guitar string. Although initially tranquil, the intensity rocketed to deafening decibels.

"Shit." Kane kept his language in step with the magnitude of the sound. This was crazy; he had to get out of here. He peered behind himself but found only darkness. He should call 911.

"911!" His hands fumbled through his jean pockets. "Why the hell didn't I think of this earlier?" Within seconds, Kane triumphantly grasped his phone. "Twenty percent. Not good but better than 19 percent."

With a quick thumb press, the screen unlocked with a radiating glow. Wiping his brow, Kane hit the flashlight icon and watched a beam of light flare out.

"Oh no," he moaned, swinging it around. The angle was meaningless as the sharp illumination remained powerless to penetrate the onyx curtain surrounding him. No matter which way he whipped his hand, how close he held it to his own body or the wall, the drops of light were absorbed into the eternal ether of nothing.

Kane took a step back, and the humming noise morphed into a cacophony of unrelenting volume. Had the light revealed his location? The odd screeches sounded like a thousand voices being distilled through a melting accordion. Kane shoved his palms against his ears as the volume intensified to maddening heights. Worse, it was right behind him.

"Fuck!"

CHAPTER
TWENTY-EIGHT

Over the past twenty-four hours, Kane had run more than he had in his entire life. His body ached and his muscles screamed in agony. Kane pleaded with them to endure a little longer. Whatever stalked him didn't mimic his exhausted stumbles through the darkness.

Stumbling was the wrong word. Kane felt like he was driving a go-kart blindfolded at max speed. Every few feet, he would bounce off a different wall and wobble forward in a desperate attempt to catch his balance. The chaotic symphony didn't slow or waver, not even as Kane chucked his phone behind himself with a myriad of curses.

He wasn't even sure what *it* was. The magnitude of the sound was the only indication of proximity and currently, it was deafening. If he wasn't devoured first, his head would burst open from the sheer vibration.

Kane whisper-shouted, "No!" at the option of involving the throat-entity. Only monsters demand everything or nothing and dealing with one cosmic horror was bad enough. Kane's nostrils flared at the idea that the throat-dweller was the soul of his father who had returned to teach him one final lesson on religious piety.

Is that you, Dad? Come to lay in your open tomb? Kane called inside himself, slamming into yet another wall.

His supply of adrenaline waned and a cold nausea trickled into his appendages. At this point, the origin of the violent sounds couldn't be more than a few dozen meters behind him.

Kane seriously considered ending it all by halting his run, sitting on the cold earth, and stoically observing as his existence was snuffed out. Why continue to struggle? Acceptance would at least provide a few seconds of peace. After he was ripped to shreds, would he see his brother again, his mom? Would he see Sue?

"Sorry I couldn't save you," he wheezed out.

His sister would have to fend for herself once again, alone. It wouldn't be any different than the time drugs and his own personal salvation had caused him to leave her high and dry. Kane had never considered how much this had cost both of them, and for the first time in his life felt deep regret. Not for his own loss, but for Sue's. She'd already lost him once, and now she would lose him again. What a terrible feeling that must be, knowing that even those close to you are light years apart and those you love are separated by a wall of their own creation.

Coming to a stop, Kane clutched his knees and panted. What was the point of this? He couldn't go on and this was as good a spot as any. It wouldn't be long until he was caught and...and what? Devoured? Shredded limb from limb? Hopefully, it would be quick and painless, and he'd finally have some peace. "Or I'll burn in hell like my father said I would." He laughed hoarsely.

Kane meant to lean against the tunnel but yelped as he toppled backwards and crashed onto the ground.

"Oww! What the hell?" Where was the wall? Flailing back and forth like an overturned beetle, Kane flipped over and felt around. The wall had vanished.

At first, he thought he'd already been overtaken by the monster and thrust his limbs forward in defense. However, as his fingers brushed a beveled, L-shaped column he realized what had happened. Whether by luck or divine intervention, he'd found a side tunnel.

All at once, his entire perspective changed. "I am not dying here!" he screeched amidst the deafening cacophony of sounds. Leaping up, he charged forward with the fury of a madman. Was that light ahead?

"Shiiiiiit!" Kane struggled to slam a heavy metal door shut, its hinges creaking and squealed. A few seconds earlier, he had felt thousands of tiny tentacles wrapping around his skin, prodding in and out in a stitching fashion. If he had run a bit slower? Kane shuttered.

Did he seriously think a small metal shell would resist whatever had chased him? Kane looked around for escape routes and found himself in a cavern half the size of the main chamber. Dangling LED lights were flickering above and showered the room with enough light to illuminate a few ragged pieces of equipment and another small trailer home. At the opposite end of the cave, several more tunnels darted outward, each with their own metal door. He was stuck in a subterranean beehive, and the queen bee was his pursuer.

What a stupid thought.

Kane faced the tunnel in a Western-style stand-off, rigid, tense and ready to blow away anything that moved. The only problem was, he didn't have a weapon to draw.

"Not much of a fair fight," he huffed out, stepping backwards.

Although childish, Kane hoped the creature's sounds would evaporate after he shut the door. Taking a step back, he fell to his knees and gasped for air. The strange grinding and screeching continued, unabated. No matter how many steps he took in reverse nor how deeply he pressed his hands into his ears, that awful sound of gnashing, swishing and high-pitched shrieking wouldn't lessen. At least, the door was holding. For how long?

Kane inspected his surroundings and discovered two options. Either hide in the trailer or continue into another tunnel. Or should he stand his ground? He quickly shooed the idea away. The memory of the otherworldly tentacles pressing in and out of his flesh was too fresh.

Abruptly, the horrendous sounds vanished. Kane was so startled, he whipped sharply around, making sure the creature hadn't snuck up on him.

Water dripped in a dark corner of the room. Beyond that, the cavern was as silent as a tomb.

Had the thing grown tired and left? Was a thin metal door really able to keep it at bay? Or was it toying with him, letting him believe he'd won before pouncing down for the kill?

"Just like a damn cat." Kane tensed his fists and looked towards the ceiling. The stone walls rose to meet a dense patchwork of darkness that made it impossible to tell if a nefarious eldritch monstrosity crept about. The silence was so thick, sound's existence could have been snuffed out. He felt around his face. No blood. Definitely not an episode.

Kane was tempted to crack open the metal door and peek into the darkness like some idiotic horror movie extra. The moment he pressed his ear against the door to listen, the creature would burst into the cavern with slimy tentacles and pull him into endless doom.

Kane shook his head. He'd have to be a moron to get closer. With a huff, he backstepped briskly to the center of the room. Should he take refuge inside the trailer? The thought of more tight spaces caused feelings of claustrophobia. He'd be damned if he was going to put himself in a more confined spot.

If luck was with him, he'd find a flashlight or lantern and make another suicidal journey into the tunnels. "Anything for Sue." His head whipped around as a small dislodged rock fell to the ground.

"I could get lucky and find a weapon. A gun would be nice, but I'd even be satisfied with a stapler. Maybe the creature hates office supp—"

A squishy, gnashing sound erupted in full force. It wasn't coming from behind him, however, but from one of the tunnels ahead.

"You have got to be kidding me!" Kane raced forward and begged his legs not to give in. If he didn't block the tunnel's entrance, he was screwed. He might be screwed anyway.

After a quick sprint, he slammed the metal door shut. The sound died away instantly.

"Oh shit!" Kane clutched his side and forced a clot of vomit into his stomach. He went to lean against the door, but a tempest of noise once again rattled the cavern. Kane swung around and frantically searched for its origin. Had the creature finally used force to fling the thin metal open? Sweat poured into his eyes, and Kane wiped his face with a grunt. It wasn't coming from the tunnel he had recently closed, but from the next one over.

Kane dashed yet again, albeit slower. He was so exhausted. Would he make it in time? Right as the darkness flexed into the light, he reached the door and slammed it shut. Kane took a single deep breath before the noise shifted tunnels and filled the room from a different direction.

"Shit. Shit. Shit." He huffed as a stitch jabbed his innards.

Tunnel after tunnel, Kane ran around the room closing each off in turn. Only at the last one had he barely made it. As he ran towards it, his gait was so slow it mimicked a walk. This had given the creature enough time to shove the front portion of its body through the narrow entrance.

Kane was a few feet away when a sinewy glob thrust its way out. It was onyx-colored, shimmering and writhing with impossibly thin appendages which unfurled from the darkness. In that moment, a primordial instinct took control, and he dove head first into the metal. The door crashed against its frame, and a shriek erupted amidst the cacophony of sounds. He looked at the ground and found a few severed tentacles dissolving into ethereal ash. His body ached, but he'd won. At least, this round.

Kane was so exhausted, he collapsed onto the frigid earth. He didn't mind the fact that, in spite of his sweat and aching muscles, he was shivering. He had bigger things to worry about. He had to work through a way to get out of here and continue his search for Sue. If she wasn't in the main chamber, there was only one place she could be. The thought of her location was so anathema to Kane that he bunched his face together and made a loud spitting noise. If Sue was still alive, she would have to be near Tim's Edge. He knew her well enough to understand that was the only option. He couldn't imagine her sheltering anywhere else.

How the hell could he get there? Was there a map in the trailer? Kane spread his limbs out and winced at the thought of getting up. Even if his supposition was accurate, escaping whatever cosmic horror lurked in the tunnels was unfathomable.

Look for a map, try his luck finding Sue and be torn to shreds, or sit here and do nothing and be torn to shreds. How could his options get any better? At least, the cold floor felt great on his aching back.

Kane stared at the ceiling, mulling over his next move, when an odd commotion in the darkness above caught his eye. The ceiling was mixing? That couldn't be right. Kane strained to rub his eyes and peered into the crooked shadows once more. They were growing deeper somehow, swirling and weaving, churning placidly with the illusion of permanence.

"Of course, it's not over!" He slammed his fists into the dirt. In that moment, the darkness draped over the sides of the cave walls and spilled downwards. In parallel, an onyx-colored liquid flooded into the room from underneath the doors, spreading with petulant voracity.

"No. No. No!" Kane would have been in full tantrum mode if he had any energy left. He'd come so far only to be blocked yet again. If not for Sue, he would have abandoned hope and let the flood of dark water overtake him. No, he couldn't do that. He had to fight with every last breath. If not, was redemption even possible?

Forcing himself to stand, Kane stumbled over to the trailer. He had no other options.

Hopping over a dark stream, he charged up the stairs which led to the shabby front door. With a quick glance over his shoulder, he found the room rapidly filling with mysterious black liquid.

"Mother of—"

The dark water had reached the base of the metal stairs and was slowly climbing upwards. Kane turned to the dingy entryway and was overcome with memories of close-call-ODs in filthy crack dens.

"I've almost died in worse," he grumbled.

Kane wanted to be frantic. He wanted to be stubborn. He wanted to be more of a fighter—angry and tirelessly heroic to the bitter end. Oh, but he was so exhausted; his last stand was looking more like the Titanic than the Alamo. With a deep, bitter sigh, he twisted the rusted aluminum handle and flung the door open.

"What else could go wrong?" he groaned.

"Hello, Kane." Stver smiled from across the room.

CHAPTER
TWENTY-NINE

KANE BURST INTO THE TRAILER, CHARGED OVER TO STVER AND grabbed him by the neck, squeezing with both hands.

"Where's Sue!?" Kane spittle flung onto Stver's atonic, yet redding face. A flurry of questions followed.

"What the hell is going on here?"

"What's the fuck is lurking in the tunnels?"

"How do I get out of here!?"

With Kane's hands firmly locked around his neck, Stver's face grew purple before taking on a tinge of rotting blueberry as a quiet pale green snuck into his cheeks. The light in his eyes drifted into oblivion before Kane slammed his head against an adjacent wall and took a step back. With a tumble to the floor, Stver clutched his forehead and gurgled a cough.

"Coffee?" he croaked, putting his hand up in a conciliatory gesture.

Kane stared in disbelief. Coffee? Now? Stver spotted this slight hesitancy and gingerly forced himself upwards before limping over to a small pot near the kitchen. After a brief moment, he turned with a coy smile and held out a styrofoam cup towards Kane.

Why he had expected a better taste was beyond him. It was luke-warm and as miserable as before, although the stale burned character of this new batch lended it a depth earlier pots lacked. Kane sipped it while taking deep breaths. His eyes were locked on the trailer window and the dense black liquid quietly rising around them. All at once, the coffee he held was far less appetizing. Kane emptied the cup in one terminal gulp.

"Amazing, isn't it?" Stver had stationed himself next to him and whispered these words with a mixture of reverence and serenity.

Amazing wasn't Kane's word of choice. As the onyx waves lapped against the bottom rim of the trailer, the only word that came to his mind was: *revolting.*

"I am a cage, in search of a bird." Stver put his hand on the window and pressed his fingers against the glass. "Kafka said that once, although I hardly think there's been a more appropriate use of that aphorism until now."

Kane grunted in response.

"You sure have"—Stver rubbed his throat and hacked for a few seconds before recomposing himself—"your sister's penchant for brutish over-dramatism."

Kane wasn't sure why Stver's comment pissed him off so much. Was it because it insulted Sue? Or had he simply had enough of this kooky old engineer and anything he said was grounds to lay him flat? He turned to throttle him again, but Stver's hand shot up in defense.

"Wait! I'll answer your questions. No reason to get hasty." He gave a slight gurgle.

Kane watched as Stver rushed to pour two more cups of coffee and took a seat at the opposite end of the tiny card table.

"Stver, I have to get out of here and find Sue. Now." The chair creaked and moaned as he sat down as well.

The other didn't bother to look up, still rubbing his throat with one hand as he nursed his coffee with the other. "She is sorry, you know. She told me how much she regretted leaving you."

"Wait, you saw her!? Is she okay? Where is she?" Kane reached over the table and thumped his hand down.

"Close"—Stver clutched his shaking coffee and leaned back—"and yet impossibly far."

At this, he glanced over his shoulder and stared outside. The pools of dark liquid covered the entire cave floor and rose with a relentless, albeit languid, velocity.

"What the hell does that mean!?" Kane arose and threw his coffee to the side. "I don't have time for these cliche riddles! Tell me where my sister is, or I'll throw you face-first into that nightmare tarpit!"

"Hmph," Stver snorted, pausing for a moment to meet Kane's glare. "Last I saw her, she was heading for Tim's Edge. Farthest tunnel to the right, next room. A few hundred feet or so."

A few hundred feet. He closed his eyes and felt his whole body tense.

"And how the hell do I get there?"

"You'll have to walk. That's the only way."

"Walk?" Kane collapsed back onto the chair. "Through that?" He nodded in the direction of the window.

There had to be another option. Perhaps he could tear off some siding from the trailer to use as a boat or force Stver to carry him on his shoulders.

But as Kane weighed the various alternatives, walking emerged as his only choice. Jerry-rigging a makeshift raft was absurd, and if the darkness was poisonous or filled with monstrosities, being carried would only get him so far.

Kane balled his fists and considered finishing Stver off for good. That would teach him to dish out hope and despair on the same plate. He may be behind this entire situation anyway. Even if he wasn't, as the leader of the dig, he deserved to be punished for unleashing this madness onto the world. Right?

Kane stared at Stver and relaxed his fists. Killing him was pointless. Worse than pointless, taking his life would truly mean the end of his relationship with Sue. Besides, he recognized Stver was being honest. His sister was in the next room, and his only option was facing the darkness.

"But that's suicide," he heard himself say.

"Tim's death was suicide." Stver shrugged. "People constantly walk through darkness and emerge alive. Some would call it courage."

Kane recalled the squirming, hair-like tentacles that had caressed and penetrated his body. Anyone who had experienced that would think twice before employing a grotesquely deformed word like *courage*.

Kane stood up and stepped towards the window with a long sigh. How the hell was he going to get out of here? He let out an exasperated mental groan. Should he be praying? Begging God or the throat-entity to throw him salvation in his time of need? Kane shook his head. This was exactly why he didn't believe. Begging wasn't his style, particularly when it came to asking for mercy from his captor. There was no hope in asking for the impossible, only insurmountable disappointment.

"When your sister first joined our group," Stver said to Kane's back, clearly unconcerned if he was listening or not, "she had barely come out of her own shadow. She told me she had recently lost a brother. We thought she meant Tim."

Kane rolled his eyes, half listening while he calculated a way to escape. Why the hell did Sue let her emotional baggage loose on Stver of all people?

"At first, even as Tim's sister, I didn't think we had a place for her in our group. Tim made her famous, yes, but her proclivity for violent outbursts and stubborn tantrums was a liability. She couldn't be designated a leader who gave interviews, did tours, or led the flock."

"Stver, why the hell are you telling me this?!" Kane lost control, walked over and grabbed him by the collar again, placing his face so close he could feel the warmth of the other's skin.

Oddly, Stver was wholly unfazed. Instead of struggling to free himself, he simply continued talking. "She told me watching her brother vanish like smoke wasn't the hardest part. It was watching him burn beforehand." Stver smiled gently and the violent anger faded from Kane's arms.

"What do you mean?" Kane released him.

"Exactly what I said, Kane. You may be too thick to understand, but your sister loved you. Watching you suffer in silence before disappearing traumatized her to the core."

Sue meaning he was the one she'd lost and not Tim took his breath away. For each time he'd spent playing the victim, he couldn't remember ever contemplating how his sister felt. He hadn't even considered her response to his disappearance. They had avoided discussing it in earnest, and Kane was not the type to unpack the emotional baggage Sue was prone to carry for the remainder of their lives.

"And what, your little cult saved her?" He had meant for the words to sound sarcastic, aggressive, but instead they carried a vague admission of guilt.

"I'd hardly call it little. Over a billion people ascribe. Presidents and generals from across the world to plumbers and cashiers. And yes, your sister—who came to us not only to deal with her past, but to determine why she was powerless to stop the bad things happening around her."

"Just like Tim," Kane muttered, wondering what *bad* she was powerless to stop.

Stver's chuckle bordered light panting. "Tim had visions of grandeur that he simply couldn't cope with. Why have a power to see the future and a desire to save people if the events can't be altered? In the end, he thought he was a sick cosmic joke. A divine prank where he was as cursed as Cassandra after rejecting Apollo. But Sue's pain was more localized."

Kane scoffed. "What do you mean, localized? What, she regretted being incapable of saving Tim or me?"

"Save you? How, Kane? Even someone as pigheaded as your sister recognized there was no way she could change her brothers' morose dispositions."

Kane shook his head. He didn't understand. If Sue didn't regret not intervening in Tim's suicide or his own leap into the abyss, what was she so sorry for?

"I can see you're not getting this," Stver said coldly. "You have to understand, Kane. Sue wanted to be there with you on your journey, regardless of the destination. But you never let her in. How could you? Hot-tempered Sue, atomic Sue, bulldozer—those were the things you and Tim used to call her, correct?"

Kane nodded, but his entire head felt numb. Ever since they were children, his brother and he would never dream of divulging anything more than necessary to their sister. If they did, she would be relentless—chiding them, problem-solving, fixing the situation against their will. Kane recalled her nearly beating another kid to death because he had pushed Kane to the pavement in a school parking lot. Leaving Sue out of things was just a part of their relationship. He had often hoped she would understand, or better yet, not notice. Although, in hind-sight, both of those ideas were utterly childish. Had she wanted to be a deeper part of their lives the whole time? But there was no way she could, unless—

"Sue came to us to change, Kane. After you left without a word, after she realized how much the hints of your suffering pointed to a rotting core, her entire world went dark. Why hadn't you spoken with her? Why hadn't you let her into your life? You and Tim were stubborn, but there had to be more. There had to be something wrong with her as well."

"And this place gave her that ability. To change, I mean, so she joined us in suffering?"

Kane had expected a lengthy answer, but to his surprise Stver responded with a simple, "Yes."

"So, is that what happens here? Tim's Edge changes people?"

Stver snickered, peering through the window into the darkness. "We don't know what Tim's Edge does, but it surely doesn't have that kind of power or significance."

"What do you mean?" Kane stared through the window as well. How in the world could Stver make such a claim in plain view of what was happening around them?

"We didn't begin to dig to find power, Kane. We dug to understand. This morning, most of the miners found, for them at least, a conclusive perspective in the light of the monolith. After this epiphany, they chose to kill themselves in a mass suicide. They said they finally understood, and seeing the nothingness of Tim's Edge was like watching their souls drift into an empty void. There was no more point in the world. They'd seen the end."

Kane nearly tumbled over. "Wait, what!?"

Stver was once again unfazed and continued as though chatting about the weather. "But it wasn't Tim's Edge that made them do it, Kane. Those people, they gave it power when they made their choice. The same as Sue gave this place power when she decided to change."

"Don't you see the black pooling water?" Kane responded. "Are you nuts? Something clearly wants to kill us. At the very least, it wants to stop me from getting to my sister."

"Power without meaning. Power without significance. The same as Tim's ability."

Kane hesitated a moment to process. "If that's true, why don't you get out of here? Run away and save yourself?"

At this, Stver smiled a limp, tired smile.

"I can't run away for the same reason you won't wade through the dark waters to see your sister."

"What, we're both afraid?"

"No, Kane. Obviously not. There are a million people directly outside the walls who see me as a savior and another million who think I'm the devil. Both of them have put meaning into what we're doing the same as you have decided that what's going on outside is the work of some creature who wants to disembowel you. Because of that, there's no way I'll leave here alive, so what's the point in moving?"

Kane didn't care if Stver lived or died. Whether he was torn to shreds by the crowd or quartered as a heretic didn't bother him in the slightest. Whatever happened after he left this trailer, he knew this would be the last he ever saw of him. Kane was happier for it.

The pooling liquid had crested the bottom step and showed no signs of abating. If Kane intended on wading over to one of the other tunnels, it would have to be soon.

But his head throbbed from exhaustion, from imagining Sue joining this cult to change for him, from the realization that everyone in the mine was dead and the possibility this swirling darkness had no part in it. Kane laughed a dark, cold laugh as he thought of Tim's Edge like a metaphor for the vale of death. Incomprehensible, and yet the driving force behind the actions of the world. Many people had worked to discover its secrets and, in the end, they had found nothing. The same end that even the great Tim, Little Tim, couldn't get past. But being content with nothing was impossible. No other recourse existed than for the world to ascribe it a variety of meaning and significance. To give it power.

Kane shook his head. That couldn't be right. Clearly, the thing was out for blood. It was a deranged, tangible Hollywood monster and nothing more. It had forced his brother to kill himself, paralyzed and caused decay in his own life, irreparably injured him during each episode, lodged itself in his throat and even convinced him to kill a man and ignore the suffering of others. It attacked him in the tunnels, and even now, it was planning on drowning him in a vile pool of dark liquid. If it wasn't evil, what else could it be?

Kane held his breath as an uncomfortable, inconvenient thought struck him. *Had it done those things?* In spite of both the horror and hatred Kane felt, he must have overlooked a critical detail. He stared into a patchwork of darkness, where each thread was merely another shade of black. What was the pattern?

Rubbing his temples, he turned to Stver, who stared into his cup without blinking. Would he lie to him? Why would he lie to him? If Sue was out there, the only option he had was to trust.

"It's easy to make a decision when there's only one option," he mumbled, remembering how his father would follow it with, "And at least you know you're right."

Stver gave a grunt before ambling next to Kane to peer through the window.

"Amazing, isn't it?" he whispered.

Kane's hands were trembling with thoughts of leaving the trailer and facing whatever horror lay within the liquid abyss. His decision was made, however.

"I am a cage in search of a bird." Stver put one hand on the sill and pressed the fingers of the other firmly against the glass.

Kane grunted in response and made his way outside.

CHAPTER
THIRTY

As Kane placed his first foot into the liquid, he recalled when he and Tim had snuck out as teenagers to go swimming with some girls from school. It was pitch black, and a cool, delicate breeze wafted through the grass with a curious guidance towards a pond near their house. Kane had watched as the headlights of a car approached, and the brothers had hidden in the grass, expecting it to be their parents. They would get beaten for this later, that was as sure as the rapture, but the spoken and unspoken promises from the girls far outweighed any punishment their father could concoct.

Kane watched insects dart by, their buzzing the acoustic blaze of a shooting star streaking across the canvas of rustling leaves and light breaths. As the headlights slowly faded, whispered excitement mixed into a palette of sounds, and Kane and Tim nearly hugged as they imagined having escaped.

They could hear the girls giggling in the distance, their coquettish chuckles carried by wind and wanting ears. Kane and Tim had arranged to meet them in the middle of the pond, on a small outcropping of rock which jutted gently from the water as though experiencing the same excitement as the brothers.

Slowly, not shaking from the cold, they placed one foot in front of the other and waded into water which resembled cosmic gems glinting in the deep of space. The moon, expansive and taut, succumbed to the caress of the approaching clouds. Kane and Tim didn't care about temperature or lighting. Intoxicating desire was driving them onward.

Water splashed on their waists as they took a deep step forward. Kane was moments away from swimming when a voice croaked out from behind them, shattering the scene.

"Mom and Dad know you're gone. They're on their way here right now."

Both Tim and Kane shot around, unsure if they were more terrified of the sudden intrusion into the lustful quiet or the message. For a moment, Kane couldn't even recognize where the voice had come from or who was talking. Then, it hit him.

"Sue, you little bitch. Did you rat on us?" The expectant giggles and eager whispers from the center of the pond were cut off like the drop of a gallows.

Kane charged from the water, ready for a fight. His sister could hold her own, he knew that. Regardless, his hormonal bubble had burst, and this made him flush with rage.

"Two boys missing. Only pond for twenty miles, and they took their swim trunks?" Sue responded coldly. "A half-wit monkey could have realized where you two left for."

Kane was trembling. He didn't believe a word of it. Even if they had left clues, there was no way his parents would have noticed their departure without being ratted out.

"You're lying." He stood as tall as he could and made a beeline for his sister. However, as he approached, he saw a sight he wouldn't see again until their mother died: Sue's cheeks were glistening with a soft moisture. Kane had thought it was guilt but later realized she had been telling the truth the whole time.

"I could have covered for you," she had responded while he and his brother snatched their clothes off the sandy earth and scouted for the quickest way home. "All you had to do was tell me, and I would have told Mom and Dad you went downtown to sneak a film."

Kane was so furious, his vision blurred. His entire night was up in flames. The promises, the whispered words of desire and a rapidly closing youth were ashes scattered into the darkening sky. He shook his head, collected his shoes and walked in the direction of their house. "You'd just ruin it, Sue. You always have, and you always will."

This was the memory that flashed before Kane's eyes as the liquid lapped around his waist. Only at this moment did he doubt that Sue had tattled on them. Only now did he regret not involving her in their plan. What had he and Tim punished her for? Being too loyal? Being overly protective? No, they had punished her because they couldn't control her. The same as Tim punished himself for being unable to alter the events of the future and Kane punished himself for being unable to manage his episodes.

And Kane liked being in control, even if that meant being the conductor of a derailing train.

"Ah damn, I'm sorry, Sue," he said aloud and felt the dark liquid reach his ribs. There wouldn't be anyone to call him back at this point. His sister was ahead, not behind. He felt a strong desire to be with her, even if that meant they were both doomed to be eaten by the darkness. If he made it through this, they could conduct this crazy train together.

He was tormented by the realization she had been so lonely, so isolated. It was as though she were swimming in a dark pond her whole life. Karma.

Kane's feet collided with an object he hoped was a tool or container.

Sue had even given herself up to this place, this religion so she could change and reconnect with her brother. Not even reconnect, rather connect. Form a bond that hadn't existed and live life together, struggles included.

Kane had thought she was dense, strong and stubborn-willed. Now, however, he realized that may have been a show, a façade she created to deal with her evil father and the twins who were constantly pushing her away. Was the mischief, fights and bad decisions her attempt to join their group and drown out the terrible bullshit happening around her? To her?

The thought of Sue as a child emerged: desperately fighting for acceptance while staving off her malicious father and crying out silently for help while being unable to determine why she was being abandoned. Once she finally had overcome her childhood, worked through her pain and decided it was time for change, her brother vanished, and she was once again left alone.

Kane was unnerved, saddened and at a loss for how he could have missed it. Even after they had come together again, their second chance was ruined by him. What had her pain been for? All the effort? In that moment, he realized his sister wasn't upset about the cats in the hotel. No. Sue had become hopelessly enraged after finding him headed somewhere she could never follow. Even though she had worked so hard and even though she had spent so much love and energy, the result was the same as ever. Her change didn't matter. She didn't matter.

Sue was alone again.

The liquid sloshed against Kane's chest, and he struggled forward with fervor. He had a new reason to find Sue. He had to explain that he understood, that he didn't want her to be alone and that he was sorry. He had to explain that he was equally at fault and if given another chance, he would make things right. No more drugs. No more disappearing. No more suicide attempts and self-isolation. It was truly pathetic that it had taken the veritable end of the world and creeping, cosmic horror to drive him to that realization. If God did exist, he must be laughing at him. It was like winning the lottery and learning you have terminal cancer on the same day.

Or maybe God wasn't laughing because there was as little meaning to this as there was to whatever was pooling around him. *Just another day in the universe.*

"The rain falls on the good and the bad," he recalled his father saying. "So pack an umbrella."

But the liquid wasn't coming from the heavens, it was coming from his feet. Kane doubted any umbrella in the world could keep it from surging upwards and drowning him.

Kane worked his way across the room, wading slowly as he pondered his next move. How could he get to his sister? And after he found her, what would he say? The only silver lining to the rumination was how it distracted him from the squishing sounds and gentle caresses of thin whisker-esk appendages rubbing in and throughout his calves and thighs.

"It's easy to make a choice when there's only one option," he consoled himself, shivering as the same feelers worked their way around his chest.

Although he could feel their embrace, they hardly exerted a force on his body. Kane wanted to believe that Stver was right, but the sensation of being probed and groped by whatever horror was swimming around him simply didn't allow for that large of a leap of faith.

From time to time, Kane could feel the thing actually inside him, poking into his skin and bones. It was twisting itself around the fibers of his muscles, penetrating marrow and cell as it searched around. Kane exhaled with relief as the probing remained gentle, completely lacking violent intent. Even after the strange tentacles exited his body for another pass, there was no pain, no blood, no feeling that he'd been robbed of energy or life-force.

But none of that mattered. At least, that's what he told himself. He would keep trudging forward, avoiding the liquid touching his face and holding his breath when a few drops splashed around his lips. His only genuine concern was the creature may be toying with him and would rip him to shreds right after he found the exit. Purely due to spite.

Kane peered around and found himself a few dozen meters from the far right tunnel's door. Curiously, there were small dark vines shooting from the frame-like ventricles leading from the heart of a smoker. These were growing rapidly, and Kane saw the same flower he had seen the deer munching on earlier, budding and expanding as it spread across the wall.

Both the fully developed and recently sprung flora pulsated to an inaudible, mysterious beat. Although seemingly unaware of his presence, they writhed and shivered as he approached. Some of the larger ones had lost their petals, collapsed in on themselves and formed strange cocoons. Kane wondered what was lurking inside the fibrous, metallic-like outer veneer. Whatever was happening here, he had no intention of staying to find out.

The door was heavy and so with both feet planted firmly on the wall, he grasped the handle and pulled with all his might. He had no idea what the situation in the tunnel was going to be. Would it be flooded as well? Would opening the door cause water to rush in and suck him into oblivion? That would, of course, be the cherry on top of this entire experience:

to be so close to his sister only to drown them both by unleashing torrents of this surreal madness into the surrounding tunnels. But Kane was sure he had caught a glimpse of an upward slant to the tunnel after previously shutting the door. Hopefully, that was actually the case. Although, who could honestly say? He had only seen it for a split second and was in such a panic, he could be entirely wrong.

"Not that I have a choice," he groaned out, yanking so violently a loud pop from his shoulder shot out. The door didn't budge.

"Oh, come on!" he cried out, grasping the handle so hard he felt the skin of his palms flex and tear. No effect.

Panting, Kane let go and slid into the liquid once again. He had used most of his strength and the metal frame still remained locked in place. Was it jammed? Caught on a crooked rock or piece of jutting metal? Or was the force of the liquid around him so great, pulling it open was impossible? Damn that Stver; why hadn't he told him where to find his sister sooner! As this thought crossed his mind, he realized how petty it was. Kane had taken too much time ruminating after learning the truth. Too much time doubting. Stver wasn't at fault—he was. He had watched as the dark water rose around him and had waited until it was too late.

But was it really so hopeless? Kane's eyes followed the ventricles sprouting from behind the door and found a single, petalless flower wrapped tightly in their embrace. The small vines coming off it plunged into the water and, judging by their direction, were headed for the door frame. Although his body was screaming "no, don't touch it!", he took a deep breath and placed his finger on one of the vines, following it underwater.

"Dammit!" he moaned, realizing why the door was stuck. This flower had wedged itself firmly against it and was providing enough resistance to make opening it impossible. Before he could think things over, a violent rage rippled through him. In a fit of desperation, he peeled away the crumbling rocks surrounding the plant, tugged on the vines from time to time and throttled the bulb with his fist. Each time his hand made contact, a small glow emanated from beneath its outer casing. Kane didn't know if this meant the thing was scared, angry or excited. What did it matter? He had to peel it off, or there was no way he was moving forward.

With the vines almost entirely stripped away, he placed himself firmly against the wall and tugged on the flower with all his might. A loud hiss emerged, and both Kane and the flower tumbled into the liquid. There was a momentary feeling of being probed to a depth he hadn't believed possible. This was followed by an intense understanding, which instantly vanished as Kane emerged from the depths, holding it triumphantly in the air. "Ha! Take that, you fuckin' prick!" he cried out.

The hissing noise steadily made its way to the surrounding vines, spraying from the flower like he had torn a balloon. Within a second, the connecting tubes shriveled and withered. This act was followed by a loud click, a creak and an odd scraping sound.

He still held the flower bulb above himself, a towering trophy to his reckless abandon, when two strange occurrences happened at once. First, the creaking sounds became visible as the door gently swung open. Second, the thing he was raising into the air made a noise Kane wouldn't have expected in a thousand years.

"Meow."

THIRTY-ONE

"Meow."

Two cats peeled themselves from the sack as the casing dissolved into a puddle of viscous green liquid.

Kane had already entered the side tunnel and watched this process in horror. What else could this terrible cavern and creeping darkness throw at him? He placed the bulbish sack on the ground and readied himself to flee if necessary. Of course, he could have left then and there—flung the bulb into the darkness and dashed through the tunnel towards his sister. But the *meow* had sounded so familiar, he simply had to see what would emerge.

From the depths of the flower, two cats clawed upwards—both gray, both identical. They were wet, trembling, and purring so loudly, Kane nearly collapsed into the dark liquid with joy.

"Muff-twins!?" he exclaimed, reaching to stroke their fur in spite of his better judgment. "How the hell did you two get here?"

Snatching the cats, Kane took a few more steps into the side tunnel, peering into the dark liquid bubbling and frothing directly outside the door. Although exposed to the opening, it remained impossibly stationary. Both cats were nestled in his arms and gently purred and cooed as he cradled them against his chest.

The static liquid was strange, but the cat's appearance filled him with bewildered awe: gray clumps of hair emerging from the depths of the flower, pawing their way to freedom. They hadn't gnawed, however. They had clawed and scraped until the skin of the bulb had given way and was torn asunder. Why the hell hadn't he run?

"Meow," both cats continued to purr and rub against his arm, thrusting him from his thoughts. Kane shook his head and shut the metal door leading into the cavern. The squishing sound of flowing liquid abruptly cut off, and he was left alone with his two new feline companions.

How the hell could he explain the cats' sudden appearance? Were these even the same cats or more copies? And how could the darkness know his secret, urgent desire to find and offer them to his sister as a sort of penance? Of course, he already accepted that as impossible, yet he harbored a faint, childish hope that they had escaped the hotel room and traveled dozens of miles before somehow finding their way inside the mine.

"Childish, but not so impossible after all." Kane grinned and cautiously moved through the onyx veiled tunnel.

Over the past few days, he had experienced so much that went beyond the realm of his comprehension. He was at the precipice of his brain stalling and tumbling into a freefall. Yet another thing that would have to wait until after this was all over.

Kane closed his eyes, felt the warmth of the cats against his skin and continued his trek onwards. Whatever the cats were, he couldn't leave them. Hell, how could they be more dangerous than anything else he'd encountered thus far? Clearly, he'd been wrong about the black liquid, wrong about the things swimming within it. Who was to say he wasn't wrong about everything else? Wrong about everything. It was safe. He should make that his mantra.

And as for his new feline companions—they didn't hiss or whimper at being lugged around. Every once in a while, he even heard a gentle purr and quiet *meow*. In the darkness, the soft touch of fur wasn't merely comforting, but a reminder he existed.

Kane was close to his goal, so close he could feel it. A dim light encircled the edges of the distant onyx vale—rings of light wrapping around an eclipse. Goosebumps formed as he contemplated what lay ahead. Was his sister still alive? If so, what would her reaction be to seeing him? In her heart, she must know he'd find her, that their earlier discord was simply the prelude to a grand symphony.

But whatever lay beyond the pale light, it was better than staying in the dark.

The light expanded, and Kane found himself a few dozen feet from the next room. A tightly shut door was bolted to the walls and held an outline brimming with a radiance that leaked through its seams. *Tick, tick, tick*—a wrapping beyond the tunnel. Kane glanced at the cats and found them silently bobbing their heads in unison. Had they heard it as well?

The light percolated through the frame. The serene raps echoed from everywhere and nowhere at once, with the edges of deep black on his peripheries provoking a stark sensation of claustrophobia. This reminded him of a memory from a distant past, a distant life. Before his existence had unraveled. Kane blinked and realized this was the exact scene from the episode he'd had in his sister's apartment.

During the vision, Kane had watched the door swing open, exposing an abyss of darkness that transformed into searing light. Beyond that was his brother, his ghoulish form haunting the ethereal plane. Tim had come to him then, come to whisper two simple words: "Get out. Get out," he'd rasped behind cracked lips and peeling skin.

What the hell did that even mean? Get out of this tunnel? Get out of this mine? Maybe, just maybe, he had meant: *Get out of this life. Kill yourself before your existence becomes insurmountable suffering. Get out, Kane, as death is sweeter than life-long agony and torment of the soul. Get out of life. Die.* Little Tim's final lesson.

But Tim was the dead one, not Kane. Ingesting wisdom from a corpse whose brains had to be scraped off the walls was like drinking poison.

"Sorry, little bro." Kane reached for the door's handle. "But your death couldn't change anything either."

The door creaked, and the ticking abruptly stopped. Similar to his episode, searing light burned against his face and nearly caused him to drop the cats and cover his eyes. Unlike it however, Tim's shade wasn't floating on the other side. He hadn't opened a door into the great beyond, nor had he stumbled into a living nightmare.

Kane blinked rapidly as his eyes took a few seconds to acclimate to the light. He'd spoken too soon.

"Oh my g—," he gasped. This was a living nightmare.

Dead bodies filled the chamber. Brains, blood and fluid were flung and scattered across like the canvas of a modern art painting. Dozens of people were mangled, hanging from pipes, jutting from jagged bars hastily buried in the earth or sprouting haphazardly from large drill equipment in the center of the cavern. As Kane's eyes whipped back and forth, he spotted tattered jaws, ripped off from the blast of a gun, and gaping throats whose severed jugulars split open and fell apart.

Kane dropped the cats and vomited. He hadn't eaten anything in more than a day, but his stomach still found enough bile to hurl and scatter across his shoes. Was this the group of miners who'd killed themselves? Kane felt the cats skitter away and looked up. He was blurry-eyed and nauseous but focused on the bodies once again. If he found Sue lying amongst them, he didn't know what he would do. Join them?

Kane's eyes worked their way around the faces of the dead. It wasn't exclusively miners. The reporting team he'd seen on the TV were leaning against a wall, a frayed power cord wrapped around. The camera man had broken off and ground down a tripod leg and apparently rammed it into his stomach before turning on the electricity in a modified-seppuku fashion.

"Holy fuck!" Kane gasped again as a heave forced him to his knees.

He could have stayed there forever if distant voices hadn't sent a jolt of adrenaline and panic scurrying through his limbs.

"Look at what this fucking thing did!? What the hell is wrong with you people!?" an unrecognizable man yelled.

Straining to prop himself up, he peered around. Where had the voice come from? Not on his left. Not behind the barrels. Kane crouched down and began to tiptoe forward when a response echoed through the chamber.

"It hasn't done ANYTHING, you crazy asshole!"

"Sue!" Kane shot upwards. The room wasn't large, a fourth

the size of the one he'd met Stver in. *If she wasn't over there, and she's not over there—*

All at once, he spotted her. She stood in a far corner a few feet from another person. They were shrouded in darkness, but Kane recognized the shaggy man. He faced his sister and clenched a shining object tightly against his chest. Was that the briefcase? It was too dark to see.

Throwing away good judgment, he charged over the bodies, slipping in blood and nearly toppling over a stack of corpses.

"Sue!" he cried out.

He was close. Unbearably close. Both his sister and the man turned at the same time. Her mouth dropped, appearing to question if he was a hallucination or not.

Her lips quivered. "Kane?"

They were positioned in front of another tunnel, a large natural crevice that jutted upwards like the birth canal of the mountain. It was so dark, even the surrounding stone seemed to be perpetually falling inside as its color was torn away and born anew. Kane blinked. It was as though he were staring into an optical illusion, where nothing and the world melded together in wisps of a tenuous unifying dissonance which threatened to tear both sides asunder. He watched a desert plane flood, or the edges of space give way to the birth of a star. The ridges of Pandora's box, the crest of the fruit of knowledge, utter nothing colliding recklessly against the frame of the material world like waves spraying against a raft drifting in an empty ocean.

"Oh sweet hell," Kane sputtered and froze. "Tim's Edge."

His internal pause button was struck. The sounds of the room, the dim dangling light, even his own movements were absorbed by the visage of absolute nothing towering above. This brief silence was short-lived, however.

"Not for long." The man's voice was suddenly near and held a dark horror only the monolith could compete with. Dammit. How could he have been so careless?

One hard thump on his head and everything dissolved into black.

THIRTY-TWO

Kane awoke to find his hands bound and his head throbbing and wet. Blood, no doubt. Nauseous, his blurry eyes pried open. How long had he been unconscious?

Kane heard his sister's voice, her words churning and oscillating lethargically in his battered skull. "You know what, you shaggy prick? Jesus rebuked his disciples for wanting to call down fire. But you don't give a fuck. That must make you an asshole."

Repressing a bout of nausea, he turned to find her seated next to him, bound with similar ropes and a face flush with rage. His head thrummed, but in spite of his physical state, he released a groaning chuckle as she promptly followed her sarcastic comment with a ball of spit.

The shaggy man blinked rapidly but remained unfazed. Kane watched as one hand pressed and turned an unseen dial within his briefcase while the other kept the sights of a revolver planted firmly in their direction.

"I don't think a religious diatribe is going to resolve anything." Kane yanked on the rope around his wrists and was surprised as the jumbled knot slackened. Had their captor clumsily rushed to tie him up? Although, even if he managed to free his hands, what would he do next? The revolver lowered as the shaggy man focused on the briefcase and Kane tugged harder. One hand slipped out.

Sue shot Kane a glance, her face a mixture of hot rage and relief.

"Kane," she said softly, closing her eyes and smiling, "I thought he'd really hurt you."

"Can't hurt steel." He gritted his teeth in a half-grin fashion and rolled over to a seated position. "Side note: I'm pretty sure calling our captor an asshole isn't going to fix this."

Sue's eyes flung open and her face went instantly crimson. "And do you have a better plan for SAVING US FROM THIS RELIGIOUS NUT JOB!?" she yelled in the man's direction.

Although he gave the same effort to ignore them, Kane saw a slight cringe ripple across his brow. The man then pursed his lips so tightly, it looked as though his face would collapse in on itself.

"Sue, listen," Kane whispered, "I don't know if we're going to get out of here, and I don't think we have much time. I need to talk with you before it's too late."

"Too late?" Sue fiercely yanked on her own ropes. "This guy's ready to nuke this place and you want to chat before it's too late?"

"Nuke?" Kane shook the words from his head. He couldn't get distracted. "Do you have a better plan?"

"Yes!" his sister whisper yelled. "Getting free and rushing this schmuck before he kills thousands of people!"

Nice intention. Probably impossible. Both of their feet and hands were bound and the man working the large briefcase was holding a very real gun. Escape was impossible. Kane could tell Sue recognized this as well but her ingrained stubbornness didn't allow for surrender.

Destruction, death, endlessness nothing—no matter what happened in the next few minutes, he had to apologize to his sister. That was what mattered. He had to tell her how sorry he was for not protecting her from their father, for isolating her, for disappearing. If he died here without saying it, without her believing him, his soul may as well go straight to hell.

"Listen, Sue."

Kane was interrupted by the shaggy man. "I'm not a killer," he muttered, "or you'd already be dead."

"Oh really!?" Sue barked. "Then why arm a bomb, topple this mountain and kill everyone around it?"

"Because it's better than what's to come." The man's pistol lowered further to tap an unseen object with both hands. Sue saw this motion and thrust upwards before immediately crashing face first into the ground. The man gave a weak smile, obviously amused, and pointed the pistol at them once again.

Sue rolled over and sputtered dirt into the air. With a grunt, she flung herself upwards and rocked onto her knees. "And pray, Sir Asshole, why don't you tell us what that is?"

The man was clearly confused and his face darkened into a scowl.

"This," he said, giving a quick, sweeping glance to the carnage a few dozen feet from them. "The devil is at work here, but the Lord will stop it."

"By blowing it up?"

"By erasing it from people's hearts and minds."

"So, let me get this straight: the same God who chastised Peter for chopping that guy's ear off commanded you to kill people?"

"And out of his mouth goeth a sharp sword, that with it he should smite the nations," the man retorted with a smug grin.

"Incredible. You're exactly like my father!" Sue moaned, once again yanking on her binds.

"Sue, stop taunting him. Please. We need to talk."

Now it was Kane's turn to be on the receiving end of Sue's wrath. "Why the hell did you even come back here!"

"To save you!" he replied more sharply than intended.

"Oh yeah, and how the hell's that working out for you?"

Kane let loose a biting response although everything inside him screamed not to. They were minutes away from dying and still couldn't get along. How ridiculous. This guy really should put them out of their misery.

"This is exactly why Tim and I didn't want to be around you!" he lashed out. "You're too fucking pig-headed, utterly selfish and savage for any one of us to stand!" Oops, not quite the apology Kane had hoped to give. As soon as the words left his mouth, he felt overwhelming shame. Why had he come this far, why had he risked his life? Was his intent to chastise his sister for having a mini-meltdown a few minutes before their death?

What made things worse was that Sue immediately recoiled.

The man working the briefcase said, "I hope your plan isn't for this drama show to buy you some time."

Kane heard the words and ignored them. He stared at his sister, who had stopped thrashing and was slumped over.

"You're right. I'm sorry, Kane. This is hopeless."

"No, Sue, that's not what I meant." He groaned. Why the hell was he so bad at this? Not even his pending demise could make him any better at getting his feelings across. He merely wanted to say he was sorry, but now they were both likely to blink into oblivion depressed, angry and filled with regret.

"Why the hell can't I do this right!?" If Kane wasn't bound and exhausted, he would have thrown himself to the ground, had a tantrum and rolled around. As it were, he could only flip over and strain in place to release his frustration. After writhing a bit, enraged by his own incompetence, his other hand slipped loose. *Great. Perfect.* Step one—the only step in a plan that no longer existed—was complete. Not that it mattered. As soon as he stood up the man would shoot him dead. It was obvious there was no escape.

"Sue, listen," he said, flipping himself onto his knees. "I was with Tim when he killed himself. I mean, not in the same room, but I was visiting when it happened."

His sister cocked her head towards Kane and let her jaw drop. He hadn't told her this, fearing her questions, accusations and aggressive comments. *Why couldn't you save him? Why weren't you there for him? What did you say to make him do it?* Every utterance valid and impossible to answer like angry prayers shouted into the night.

"Afterwards," he continued, "I felt so much shame that the episodes became a sort of penance. Combined with my addiction, I laid a path towards the only end a monster like me could endure: death. Miserable, lonely death. The whole time, when I could have asked for help, I didn't. I couldn't involve you, Sue."

"Kane—" Sue began, but he cut her off.

"No, Sue. Listen," he said resolutely, "I've avoided telling you things my whole life. You were our rock as kids and the best of us as adults. Yet, I couldn't bring myself to open up. It wasn't until recently that I understood how much that must have hurt you. Still hurts you. For that, I'm so terribly sorry."

Sue bit her lip and lowered her gaze. "I didn't realize how forceful I was, how mean. You don't have to apologize, Kane. I didn't deserve your trust because I would have just bent it to fit me anyway."

"I didn't avoid you because of any of that!" Kane interrupted. "Although that's what I told myself for years."

The shaggy man finished what he was doing and sighed profoundly before leaning backwards. Kane ignored him and continued.

"Talking with you was like throwing an egg at cement. The whole time I had been telling myself there was gold inside, guarding it carefully so I could live my life content with that lie. But the moment you got involved, the moment it would strike the ground, I would have to confront my own deceit. Not only that, I would have to confront that I was wrong and deal with the changes born of that realization." Kane dropped his head, too embarrassed to look at his sister. "And I couldn't do that, Sue: be wrong. Because if I'm wrong, what does that mean for me, for my life and where I'm headed? What if everything I've done has been a mistake and I'm not in control? What if I've given my life power and trajectory, but no meaning, and my actions were destined for the same end: nothing?" Kane took a deep breath and looked at his sister directly in the eyes. "You're the cement, Sue, and I'm the egg. None of this is your fault."

His sister's mouth opened and closed. The soft outline of tears trickled across her cheeks as she joined him in quiet sobs. If he had one regret in this life, it was that they wouldn't go on to live in the shadow of this reconciliation—healing, loving and growing to face the future together. But their time was at an end.

The briefcase clicked close as the expression on the man's face relaxed into serenity "Won't be long now."

THIRTY-THREE

KANE RESTED HIS HEAD ATOP SUE'S AND TOOK A DEEP BREATH. HE'D said what he needed. This closure brought a certain peace, and as Sue leaned against his shoulder, the air of nostalgic remorse was abbreviated by brief sobs and sharp, sniffled breaths.

The shaggy man leaned against the wall, glaring at Tim's Edge with a mixture of disgust and appreciation. Every few seconds, he would sigh and glance at his watch as though casually waiting for the bus.

"You see what this thing's done, right?" he asked abruptly, motioning once again to the veritable mass grave of bodies scattered to their left. "And you think I'm the crazy one for wanting to destroy it?"

Kane and Sue remained silent. If this moment was to be their last, they may as well savor it.

"When those military guys hatched this plan, when they chose me, I don't think I've ever been so content in my entire life. I'm gonna ride this blast all the way to heaven." He crossed his arms and grinned. "And you, you're gonna get blown to hell."

Kane placed his hand on Sue's knee, forgetting he was supposed to be bound. In spite of his lax demeanor, the man noticed and whipped his pistol up.

"And how the hell did you get loose?" He laughed nervously, scratching his head as a tremor rattled his thin limbs. "Not that it matters. There's no way to disarm the thing anyway." Looking at his watch, he added, "Two minutes left. Why don't you take your sister and run? See how far you get."

At this, the shaggy man walked over and stood directly in front of Tim's Edge.

"That such a thing could wreak all this havoc," he mumbled. "Devil, today you've lost." He knelt, placed his hands together and prayed.

"Oh Lord, my shepherd."

How he could guarantee the blast would obliterate the monolith was beyond Kane's comprehension. If it failed, even if it evaporated the entire crowd outside, millions more devotees scattered across the globe would undertake a pilgrimage to dig it from the rubble. Perhaps the briefcase held a bomb so dirty, the area would transform into a toxic wasteland and prohibit anyone from venturing here for a thousand years. Or a team of top scientists had discovered the secret to Tim's Edge and built an advanced weapon to combat it.

Yeah, right. Kane gave a weak smile. *More than likely it's a run-of-the-mill nuke.*

Blowing things up was too frequent an answer, especially when the enemy was too complex to understand. Wasn't that why Tim had killed himself? Wasn't that why Kane had avoided Sue and why his sister constantly tromped over his feelings and mulled them into dust? Their pain was too complex to understand, so why not blow it up before it dissolved into nothing?

This epiphany was so amusing, Kane forgot himself and

chuckled. Sue gave him a brief look of concern before smiling. The same thought must have crossed her mind as well.

In that moment, Kane witnessed a scene so horrendous and absurd, it bordered comedy. Behind the man, the mufftwins darted by and skittered directly into Tim's Edge. As they made contact, their gray fur assumed the same bending hue as the surrounding rock—a color which threatened to pull away and collapse inward while expanding endlessly into its surroundings. Within a split second, Tim's Edge devoured them, leaving nothing but emptiness behind.

Kane chuckled. Why the hell would they return for the sole purpose of disappearing? What was the point? Or was the point simply nothing?

Again, Sue must have seen the same thing as she shook her head in disbelief and joined Kane in laughter. Together, they couldn't contain themselves. The sheer absurdity of the situation was causing their minds to crack. He started howling. There was probably a minute left anyway, so what did it matter?

Unfortunately, the shaggy man wasn't amused.

"And what's so funny, you dirty heathens? Is being cast into the outer darkness with your lesser god so damn amusing?"

"Kind of," Kane replied through tears, cackling louder.

"At least two is better than one," Sue added.

Both of them had stopped crying and were filling the tomb with giggles of the damned.

"Seriously, what the hell is so funny!?" The man was on his feet, waving the pistol at them angrily.

"Everything!" Kane shouted through tears. "This pain, your devotion, our deaths and the grand finale coming undone and being blown away. It's all based on nothing!" He was howling now, raptured by a light, dizzying feeling of insanity. The cats chose to abandon this madness. *They got out.*

Kane's eyes widened in realization.

The man and his sister gave a start backwards as Kane reached towards his feet and undid the binds holding them together. Jerking to the side, his sister went silent and shot him a wide-eyed, worried look.

"What the hell are you doing? Kane, stop—you'll die! Please don't let me watch you die!" It was Sue's turn to plead for patience.

Looks like the tables have turned again.

"There's less than a minute, Kane. Let's enjoy our final moments together. Please, don't do anything stupid!"

The shaggy man picked up where Sue's screams left off. "You can't be that dumb, right? Maybe if you stay seated and accept your fate, God will find it in his heart to forgive you." The man aimed the pistol in Kane's direction, rocking back and forth with shivers. "Not that it matters. Blast or gunshot, you'll be dead soon anyway."

"Thou shalt not kill, remember? And you're not a killer." Kane worked the final rope from his feet and stretched them a bit before standing. The entire time the man looked indecisive, anxious. This bolstered Kane's resolve.

After watching the cats vanish, he had been struck with an impossible plan. Even if he succeeded, he had no idea how it would end. Of course, the entire thing was literal suicide— although with far more meaning than Tim's. As he had watched the cats scamper into non-existence, he had seen a way to get out of this. Well, at least for his sister. If it didn't work? At least he would die knowing he truly did everything in his power.

"Kane, stop! What the hell are you doing!?" His sister was

frantic, her muscles rippling and bulging as she pulled and tugged on her own binds.

"Sue," Kane said calmly, turning his back towards the man, "you have to trust me."

He wanted to add a cliche about them always being together in her heart, but he was out of time. Besides, he wasn't sure if he believed that anyway. The reality was far more tenuous.

"No, Kane, no!" Her tears whipped around as she strained to free herself. "I just got you back! I don't want to be alone anymore!"

Kane gave her one last smile and said, "it's only for a little bit. We'll see each other again. I'm sure of it." The first unselfish lie of his life.

His sister whispered, "no, don't leave me," but had stopped tugging on her binds. Kane turned towards the man, who was trembling and dripping sweat. This was the face of a man who'd dropped from the gallows. Even with death as immediate and unavoidable as the dawn, he remained terrified of facing it.

Silently, Kane walked over and grabbed the briefcase. Simply throwing it in Tim's Edge wasn't an option. Who could say what was on the other side and what would happen to Sue after he left? He would have to go in with it, come what may.

At that moment, the first shot rang out. Kane glanced over and found the man shaking, clenching the pistol with sprung eyes and dilated pupils. Within a second, another shot erupted and Kane felt his gut clench together as his whole body trembled with searing pain. Being shot sure as hell wasn't as gentle as the tentacles, nor was it as subtle as the entity in his throat.

He heard Sue scream out. "Kane!"

Looking at his chest, he found he was bleeding badly. Blood

bubbled from beneath his shirt and pooled into a rapidly expanding red stain. Luckily, the pain was dulled by the adrenaline, and Kane was able to stumble forward towards the monolith. Another shot erupted, and then another. Kane felt a thump in his chest and wheezed as his lungs rapidly filled with blood.

A violent stabbing sensation jabbed his throat and Kane heaved forward, sputtering up chunks of flesh and mucus. A bullet whizzed by his head. The jabbing vanished and Kane turned to find the man had dropped the revolver and was charging at him with outstretched arms. One shot for the suicide of whomever he scavenged the weapon from, one to his feet, two misses and two direct impacts. The man still hadn't sunk his battleship. Kane was a broken toy, a cracked piñata spilling candy, but he would see this game to the end.

With a faux-heave, Kane made a motion to throw the briefcase into the endless void. As he did, time slowed to a crawl: the shaggy man leapt forward to tackle him, Sue screamed in the background and Kane, who's feet scraped on the dirt, leaned backwards into the monolith. Right before the man made contact, Kane turned to find Sue's eyes. They were shrieking "No!" but behind the veil of tears, he found unexpected comfort. Her weeping held strength. Strength and a goodbye.

Kane smiled.

In that moment, the shaggy man rammed him, sending both of them thundering backwards into the empty abyss. The briefcase made a *tick, tick, ti-* and then nothing.

CHAPTER
THIRTY-FOUR

"No!" Sue screeched as both men tumbled into the darkness, the palette of their skin mixing together into a violent gray hue before evaporating into emptiness. Writhing in pain, she scraped at her binds and shrieked out an animalistic cry.

How could the world be so cruel? She'd finally made peace with her brother and was allowed into his life. And for what? In the end, he'd asked her to trust him. She'd stopped struggling and watched him bleed to death as he tossed himself into Tim's Edge. The climax of their reconciliation was his death and now she was alone again. Is that what all this sadness was for, the pain and suffering they'd both experienced? Instead of culminating in joy and peace, unity and understanding, the conclusion was the same as the beginning: lifeless, cold, nothing.

Sue toppled onto the cool earth and wept bitter tears. Her only comfort was the goodbye her brother had read in her eyes. Seeing each other later? That was a lie.

Why had they wasted so much of their lives fighting? Why had they kept so far apart from one another? So much regret, so much loneliness, so much unnecessary hurt. This same pain had driven Tim to kill himself, loaded with emotional guilt with nowhere to dump it. It was the same pain that caused Kane to abandon his life and seek the comforts of addiction and descent as he strove for his only possible release: death. It was the same pain that caused Sue to distrust those around her and lash out at anyone who dared get too close. She called herself the protector when she couldn't even protect herself. *Ha!* It took her brother's suicide for her entire narrative to unravel.

"Tim, Kane, I'm so sorry." She sobbed gently. Her sorrow was only half the truth. Taking all the blame for their collective lives wasn't reality. Her parents weren't completely at fault, their childhood, Tim, Kane. The truth was that each carried a piece of the story, each a brush stroke on the canvas of their existence, and the grand reveal was yet to come.

The fact was, she remained alive. Thousands of people beyond the reach of her anguish remained alive. Kane had saved them, she had saved them. Even Tim, in his own way, had played a part. None of their actions, not even Kane's death, had been in vain. None of it was meaningless.

Sue looked at Tim's Edge through tears. As long as she carried on, as long as the past few day's occurrences weren't forgotten or twisted and spun, hopefully one day she could look back and see it as necessary. One day, it would be the discordant chords in a long, beautiful symphony. But not now. The pain was too raw—the events an open and bleeding wound.

Sue laid her head on the cold dirt, moist and soft from her tears. Thoughts of what happened to the bomb, escape, protecting or hiding Tim's Edge and what to do with the tens of thousands of people outside—those whose beliefs hung by a thread attached to this palpable nothing—they were simply too much. Her brain was frazzled, spinning and sparking with steadily regurgitated, truncated thoughts. In the end, her mind could only focus on Kane, on his smile while falling backwards, and on how much she regretted everything. Like when her mother died. Her brother had saved her, but in the end, she would have rather died together than face this alone.

Sue was sure she could have laid there forever if not for a sudden curling and sputtering from the void. With a weak glance upwards, she saw the nothing pulling apart and combining with the surrounding rocks in a colorful dance. Splashes of light and stone darkened into onyx hues before reemerging brighter as they streamed down the edges protruding from the center of the monolith. Darkness transformed into a flowing pool where contrast and material swirled around emptiness. Whatever was happening, it was clear Tim's Edge was slowly shrinking. Relief crept in, but Sue held it at bay. This solution wasn't comforting in the least. Deep in her heart, she desperately hoped this process would signal a collapse of the whole cave, or better yet, the whole mountain. If that happened, she would die buried in the rubble. Just like she wanted.

"Maybe Kane wasn't lying and I'll see him sooner than I thought." She chuckled amidst the light tremors swelling around her body.

With the same swift evaporation which swallowed the cats and her brother, stone appeared where Tim's Edge had been. At first, it was splotches of rock, but within seconds jagged edges jutted outwards like rapidly expanding stalagmites. This continued for a few moments until all that was left of the darkness was a pinprick on the outer right edge. Even that disappeared as a gentle pop shattered the final piece.

"Ow!" Sue yelled, rubbing her neck with her shoulder. A small, sharp object had painfully struck her. One of the stones must have shot from the mounting pressure of the unexpected formation of tangible material.

"Dammit!"

Rolling over, Sue forced herself onto her knees. A quick death by asphyxiation or crushing was one thing, but she had no intention of dying from tiny shards shooting from the newly formed rock.

To her surprise, rolling around the ground had loosened her binds to the point she could slip her hands through. Within seconds, she had completely undone herself and wobbled upwards.

As satisfying as her newfound freedom was, the scars of Tim's Edge towering over her—a monument to her lost brother—nearly sent her to her knees once again. However, a tremor and slight cracking sound from the ceiling caused a rush of clarity.

She would have time to mourn Kane, Tim and her entire existence later. If she was buried alive, wouldn't that make Kane's sacrifice meaningless? Their entire lives had culminated with her salvation. It was a gift she didn't want, but one she could hardly toss away.

Another rumble echoed from above as little droplets of dirt and stone rained down and scattered across the floor. She couldn't stay here.

Sue traversed the first tunnel without issue. Although the mine shook and jittered, the hanging lights didn't flicker or dim. Listening to the gentle creak and throb of rattling stone reminded her of blood pumping through a web of arteries. Sue realized she could have as easily been trapped in the heart of some gigantic beast. *Spit me up, whale,* she thought after stepping over a puddle of water.

After a few minutes of wandering around, she came across a tightly shut metal door. Did this lead to the main cavern? She bit her lip and wondered if Kane had passed through this same place. If so, had she been on his mind as well?

"No, Sue, focus!" she growled. A few deep breaths later, she rocked the handle loose and forced it upwards, wincing as it released a violent squeal. If she were blind, it would have sounded like she was gutting a large pig or stomping a giant insect to death.

The door was rusty from the odd moisture which permeated this underground labyrinth but finally budged after a few tugs. As it creaked open, Sue found herself in a smaller chamber with a single trailer parked to one side. She had left Stver there a few hours ago. Although she had wanted him to come with her, he remained immovable and refused vehemently.

"I can't stand the sight of death," he'd bemoaned. "If the gods are willing, the only corpse I'll ever have to see again will be my own."

Had he also killed himself? Sue imagined his body draped from a rafter and took a deep breath. Hopefully not. Stver had been the only person in this whole ordeal who had shown any sort of restraint and sense of reality. He was also the only one who had believed that the shaggy man she had seen on the security monitors was actually dangerous.

"Poor Stver," Sue whispered, glancing away from the trailer so she wouldn't see his dangling silhouette. "If I leave here alive, you all will get proper burials."

So much death, so much carnage caused by a thing that none of them truly understood. Would Tim have even mentioned this monolith of darkness if he had known what showing it to the world would cause? Probably not. Fame and glory had caused him to sink into self-righteousness, but his suicide showed that, above all else, his heart hung on saving people.

Or did it? Sue wanted to believe her brother was good, even in the end, but couldn't shake the whisper of an idea that was slowly taking hold of her. What if he killed himself *because* he saw the consequences of Tim's Edge? What if he had seen his death and knew that everything, even his choice to commit suicide, was immutable? Or had he believed he could stop it by ending his life? Then why leave the letter?

Sue once again forced open a rusted metal door and stepped into a tunnel leading to the main chamber. She wanted to believe Tim hadn't given up, that he had fought to the bitter end. If only she could have read the final part of his letter, perhaps that held the key to unlock all of this. Unfortunately, the only person who knew its contents was gone, vanished into vivid memories on the fringes of her reality.

She couldn't decide if Tim was good or evil, a wicked coward or one of the bravest souls she knew. Were his actions black or white? Could they even be removed from shades of gray, textured with nuance and a context outlined by an existence she could never fully grasp? Perhaps he was both good and evil. He and Kane were two sides of the same coin. That answer was difficult to accept, however. If true, could anything he'd done actually have the grand cosmic meaning she so desperately wanted to attribute?

Sue stepped into the main cavern and spotted the two bodies crammed at the bottom of the main doors. In that moment, she realized the world of Tim's Edge left no room left for gray. The world stood on nothing or everything, where in-betweens and middle ground were as distant as existence from death. But Tim's Edge was gone. It had vanished in sacrifice and love. Would seeking balance, harmony and compromise be what she spent the rest of her life striving towards? If so, she knew it would be as elusive as Kane, as fragile as Tim and as lonely as herself.

Beyond the bodies, the main chamber lay empty. It was no wonder—the mine personnel were laid to rest in a mausoleum of their own making. The shouts and cries from beyond the thick main doors had disappeared, and the only perceivable sounds were light trembles fading into the distance.

Sue sighed and found a button which opened a hidden side door. This path would hopefully allow her to exit the mine in safety. Of course, she could open the main doors, but she had no desire to deal with more death.

The tunnel was dusty, having seen little use. Regularly accessing a secret, emergency exit to the outside defeated its purpose, after all. A few dozen feet later, her throat ached where she'd been struck by the stray rock. She could feel a thick thread of mucus dangling directly beyond her tonsils and snorted loudly. It felt as though it were moving on its own, but Sue knew it was just her breathing. She inhaled sharply once again, performing a gross act and attempted to shoot it from her nose without success. The thing clung to her flesh as though its life depended on it.

"Oh no, and a cold to top it off!" she whisper-yelled. "How could this fucking day get any worse!?"

The door was only a few dozen feet from her, its outline ablaze with rays from the sun. If Sue were a poet, she would have described it as a ring of fire, hinting at the radiant source immediately beyond.

The closer she got, the more a light *tick* became audible. It was akin to a weak scratch from something to be let inside. *Tick, tick, tick.* The tunnel was so quiet, Sue imagined all sound had been forcefully stripped away and barred entry. *Tick, tick, tick.* Should she open it? What if it was someone dangerous; what if they were waiting for a chance to get in and she was assailed by an enraged psychopath? She wanted to turn around, but the prospect of venturing backwards was appalling. No, she had to get out of here. Come what may.

Tick, tick—Sue swung the door open and braced for impact. Her eyes were weak against the sun but still allowed her to watch a bird flutter into the blue of the sky. She must have startled it while it was eating.

"Just a bird." She nearly laughed aloud, scratching at her throat and relieved to feel a warm afternoon breeze waft against her face. "Just a bird," she said again, triumphantly, as her eyes followed the shadow gliding over the sun.

It joined a flock of thousands, tens of thousands, of similar onyx-colored birds whose acrobatic swooping and coordinated dives were tentacle-like as they extended and retracted against invisible gusts and drafts.

So many. Sue's mouth dropped. Had she ever seen so many birds in one place? Not even over the fields in southern Illinois where corn and wheat are as ample as honks and wind in Chicago. *What do they eat?* A small detachment broke off from the main group and slowly fluttered to the ground. There, Sue got her answer.

"Oh no," she coughed as the tickle stroked her throat once again. What had Kane died for? How could she ever find meaning in all of this death? She had to. Kane, she had to.

EPILOGUE

KANE RETCHED, HACKED AND WATCHED SHADOWED SPITTLE AND TEARS burst from his throat, mouth and right eye. They hardly spun an inch from his face before dissolving and swimming away as though belonging here.

The briefcase and the shaggy man had disappeared, fading into small threads of memory on the fringes of time and space. Where the hell was he? Was he dead? Placing one hand on his chest and the other on his throat, he found the bullet holes had vanished. In fact, all his clothes had been removed. Whatever this place was, it was patched together with pure nothing.

"Oh man," Kane moaned, although his voice sounded hollow and muted as though the air itself was straining to understand how to interact with his words. "Maybe my parents were right. I'm in hell."

It was at that moment he sensed a creeping around him, through him, over him and within him. The sensation was impossible. Each cell of his being was being torn asunder and recreated anew. As the odd feeling expanded and contracted inside his body, there was a sensation he didn't expect: under-standing.

Whatever was happening, his entire self being exposed and pried open. How could he be known so inti-mately, so perfectly. The idea was disgusting and he fought it —mentally throwing himself at the feeling in an attempt to confuse and frustrate whatever probed him. It was no use. Even the action of fighting was a part of the process, and soon no piece of him remained to lay bare. Whatever worked its way around him had seen and discovered tatters of his essence that not even he knew. Secret treasures of his subconscious that were the driving force behind his entire existence.

But Kane didn't stop wrenching, and through his frantic movements, a piece of something broke off within him. Was that a part of the process too? It was in his throat, right behind his tonsils and wedged so tightly it was now a part of himself. It didn't belong. Kane knew it. The entity knew it, and what-ever was probing him knew it.

At that moment, the understanding shifted into such reck-less violence, Kane felt as though he'd borne witness to the birth of a star.

It was hatred he felt. One so powerful that it woke him up from death itself.

www.ingramcontent.com/pod-product-compliance
Lightning Source LLC
Chambersburg PA
CBHW060900250626
47159CB00008B/2813